# MURDER
# IN PARADISE

## CARA KENT

*Murder in Paradise*
Copyright © 2023 by Cara Kent

# PROLOGUE

ONE RAINY THURSDAY, DAVID CARTER SAT ON THE sofa in his living room pleading for his life. He thought he had a lot to live for. While he had no immediate family of his own—he was never lucky enough to settle down—there were some nieces and nephews and cousins who liked him.

He was a savvy businessman and gave money to a lot of charities. These factors made him feel like his life was worth saving.

The man standing before him, or rather The Puzzler—he hadn't settled on a name yet—respectfully disagreed. He wasn't sure if he really needed one. All the greats had names or scary monikers: The Zodiac Killer, Toy Box Killer, Boston Strangler, The Mad Butcher. But he wasn't setting out to be like them. Serial killer wasn't on his list of dream occupations. But that was what he was, or at least what he would be by the end—when everything was said and done and his plan had come to fruition.

The day had started fairly normally. The Puzzler sat in a car a few houses down from David's. This was how he had started his day for the past couple of weeks. But today was different.

As he waited for David to leave for work, a thought flickered in his mind. The media would create a name for him. So he didn't have to worry about it. He just hoped that it wasn't something stupid or mundane. Not that it mattered.

David Carter exited his house and got into his black Lexus. A few seconds later, he drove off, going in the opposite direction from where *he* was watching.

The Puzzler waited for him to drive off and round the corner before he started his car. He knew where David was going. The same place he went every morning: work. Then he would go to a restaurant with a colleague for lunch, then back to the office, where he would stay until a little after six. He wouldn't get home until dark.

Instead of following him, The Puzzler went in the opposite direction and parked a few blocks away. While the car was his, the license plate was not. He had swiped one at a grocery store miles away from his home. Just in case someone had seen it in the neighborhood.

The Puzzler had taken great precautions. He wasn't a man who did things without thinking. Each step, each plan was crafted meticulously. Every contingency had been accounted for, and every backup had a backup. The Puzzler was ready for everything—right down to how it all would end.

Breaking into David's home was easier than he had expected. That was the thing about living in a safe neighborhood where nothing bad ever happened. David had the illusion of safety. But no one was ever really safe. No matter how things seemed.

David felt so safe that he didn't even bother locking his back door. All he had to do was wander through the backyard, walk up to the back door, and turn the knob. There was no security system either.

The house was clean. The cleaning lady, Mrs. Kāne, only came on Mondays, so he didn't have to worry about someone showing up while he was there.

David lived a remotely quiet life. He had friends he hung out with and had dinner with, but they never seemed to come to his house.

This gave The Puzzler time to breathe, search, relax in a home that wasn't his, and wait for the owner to return. It was a long wait, but he had known it would be. He wore two pairs of latex gloves on each hand as he perused around the house. Looking in drawers. In closets. Under beds. And anywhere else that looked like a good hiding place.

He wasn't sure what he was looking for or if he would ever find it. He walked around until he found the office. On one wall was a long bookcase filled with books. On the other side of the room was a wooden desk that looked too expensive to touch, let alone work on.

He sat at the desk and rummaged through the drawers. He moved the mouse, and the computer screen turned on.

"Password," he said. He sighed. He looked around the desk for a sticky note or something that could be used as a password. He found nothing. This didn't surprise him. David wasn't stupid, so of course it wouldn't be that easy.

No, he would have to wait for him to come home.

"I can give you money. An-anything you want." David's voice, trembling and hoarse, pulled The Puzzler out of his recollection. But it would do no good.

David was used to buying people. Everyone wanted money. Everyone needed money. Needed something. It's hard to say what he was thinking in that moment while he trembled on the sofa with his hands tied behind his back.

While he watched the man in front of him take a box cutter out of his back pocket.

While his body started to feel loose, his limbs heavy.

Maybe, he figured, the man with the knife wanted something. Needed something. And if he could just figure out what it was, he would be okay.

But The Puzzler didn't care about his family or his money. Nor his reason for living. His reason for dying was much more important.

"I'm sorry," whispered David. His voice was low, almost a whisper. The sorrow in his voice caused The Puzzler to take a step forward.

*Why would he be apologizing?*

He was sure David had no idea what was happening or why it was happening, and yet there he was, apologizing. A smile tugged at The Puzzler's lips. He wasn't wearing a mask. There was no point to it really. It didn't make a difference if David could ID him or not, as he would not survive the night.

"Why are you apologizing?"

David blinked. And then shrugged.

"You shouldn't apologize for things if you don—"

"What did I do? I must have done something to offend you." David shook his head. Tears and snot collected just under his nose, and he wiped it on his shoulder. "Nothing bad I've done is worth my life. Worth you going to prison. Think about your family. Think about how they will feel when they have to visit you behind bars. I can give you anything. And I… I won't tell. I won't tell anyone."

Despite the situation, David smiled. A small, hopeful smile. "I won't say anything, I promise. I'll act like I never saw your face." David averted his eyes. Tried to act like he didn't see him.

The Puzzler only returned the smile and then stepped into David's line of sight. David's eyes went wide, the realization finally taking hold that there was no way out of this.

"It doesn't matter if you see me. You won't be seeing anything else after tonight."

Maybe it was the way the man smiled at him when he said those words. Maybe it was the weight of the words finally settling on him. Maybe at that moment he finally realized the trouble he was in. Because then and only then did David think to scream.

The noise was short-lived. The Puzzler chucked an object at David's head. The scream died in his mouth. He slumped to the side. A patch of blood bloomed on the side of his head. Beads trickled down the side of his face.

The Puzzler sighed. "Maybe he needs a stronger dose. But I don't want to give him too much, and then he can't talk and tell me what I need to know." He eyed the body.

David's chest rose and fell rapidly, so he knew he was still alive.

"Maybe a little more. But that's going to have to be it until he tells me what I need to know. He gave David the shot and then stepped back while he regained his senses, only to have them dulled again.

"Please," David choked out. "Please don't do this." Tears streamed down his cheeks.

The Puzzler didn't say anything. He took David by the shoulder and pulled him until he sat upright on the sofa.

"What are you going to do to me?" His voice was soft and shaky.

"Well, in short, I am going to kill you. That I promise. But I need to know a few things first."

David's eyes went wide with shock. His bottom lip trembled as his eyes flicked toward the kitchen.

"Someone will be home—"

He waved his hand dismissively. "I know no one lives here but you, so don't start that. And other than your cleaning lady, you don't really like people in your home."

David's shoulders dropped a little.

"But first, let me tell you a story"—he sat in the cream-colored chair across from David—"a story about a guy who may or may not be a hacker. This *hacker* was hired by a company, but before he started working for the company, he had to do his research, you know. I mean, you just don't get into bed with anybody. Well, maybe *you* do, but this guy didn't do that. He preferred to work with the right kind of people. So while he was doing his due diligence, he came across some information. A client list. A group of people that have a certain proclivity for, shall we say, things they wouldn't want society to know."

David stiffened. He stared down at the floor.

"Now with that information, a guy could go to the police—"

"I will buy it from you. I'll pay you. No amount too high." The words tumbled out of David's mouth so fast he didn't have time to breathe between sentences.

The Puzzler smiled. "A guy could go to the police, but what would they do? They don't care. And just like you are trying to buy me, you can buy them. No, it's best that I deal with this myself. But first I need to know who's in charge."

David blinked. "What?"

"Come on now, David. There's a chain of command, and I want to know who is at the head."

"You think I know?"

The Puzzler cocked his head to the side.

"I swear I don't know anything! I just—"

Silence crept into the room, and he let it. He knew what David had been doing, so he didn't need him to admit it.

"David," he started slowly, "I know you are lying to me, and right now, that is not a good idea. No one is coming to save you. No one is coming to help you. It's just us. And I'm not leaving until I get my answers."

He eyed David; he didn't think it would take as long. He'd probably only have to hit him once, maybe twice. David didn't look like the type of guy who could endure a lot of pain. Or any really.

David was in his forties and had the creases on his face to prove it. His dark hair had started graying around his temples. He looked like a man that wasn't used to hard work or manual labor.

A man with smooth, silky hands.

A man not used to pain, physically or emotionally.

A man accustomed to inflicting pain and not receiving it.

The Puzzler smiled and held up the hammer. Tonight he would make sure that David would endure the most agonizing night of his life. He would make him wish he was dead.

Make him pay for all the people he had hurt. He wasn't sure how many, but tonight he would avenge them.

This was all part of it. The plan. The puzzle. He needed to leave the pieces, the clues just right, so that in the end, when he was done, someone could put it all together.

"Okay, David, let's start from the beginning."

# CHAPTER ONE

**Y**OU COULD HAVE CUT THE TENSION IN THE AIR WITH A knife. Silence hung in the air so thick I was amazed I could breathe. It wasn't that I thought graduating from the FBI Academy in Quantico was going to be relaxed. I mean, why would it be? The last twenty weeks had been grueling. And complicated. And anything but relaxed.

I guess I figured with that out of the way, the ceremony would be a little more… loose. A little more fun. Even though there had been no indication of that ever being the case.

The new agents sat in their seats, tense and hanging on the director's every word. She stood tall, her dark brown locs pulled into a high bun. Her ebony skin looked flawless even under the harsh lighting in the auditorium. Director Fletcher always looked flawless and stylish, and today was no different. Her white dress practically glowed.

"You should all be so proud of this accomplishment. And I mean that. Not everyone who walks through those doors makes it. And I must say for some of you… it was a little touch and go there."

A smattering of laughter passed through the room.

"I mean… I won't name any names, but"—she looked around—"we had some bets going."

There was another burst of laughter, mostly from the parents and families attending. The agents around me looked around. Each pair of eyes fell on another. Each person trying to figure out whom they had a bet on.

I could have been one of them. My first week at Quantico was a little rough. It took me longer to get my bearings, but once I did, everything worked out, and I ended up in the top five of my class. I had always wanted a career in law enforcement, and when the opportunity arose to join the FBI, I took it. Much to the disappointment of my parents.

"I know, or at least I hope, that as you all go out into the world, you will make me proud. You will serve your country by doing what is right and just—and help us all sleep better at night. Each of you has been entrusted with upholding the ideals of Fidelity, Bravery, and Integrity. This is the mission of the FBI, and it's the mission each of you have sworn to uphold."

After the ceremony, we received our service weapons. Amazing how holding a gun could make a person feel powerful. Feel like they could take on the whole world. Like nothing could stop them. That's how I felt when my fingers closed around the grip.

"Well, I guess congratulations are in order." My father pulled me into one of his big bear hugs. Although this one was a little lacking. Less of a bear hug and more of a church hug. The kind of hug you would give someone you know, but not well enough to wrap your arms around them. A safe hug. An "I should keep this person at a distance" hug.

My mother wrapped her arms around me and pressed her nose into my neck like she was trying to remember the way I smelled. Like she was trying to commit me to her memory just in case she never saw me again.

I wasn't leaving for another week, but they acted like I was already gone. Like they needed to get used to being without me.

"I guess there's no turning back now." My mother's voice wavered on the last word. Like she was asking a question instead of making a statement. Maybe she wanted me to say I changed my mind and wanted to stay.

The hopeful look in her eyes made me sad and a little angry. My family had a history of serving our country in some capacity. Mostly through the military. And all that was fine. No one had a problem with my brother enlisting in the Air Force.

We were all proud. But now that I want to serve my country, it's a problem. I smiled tightly. I didn't feel like having the same conversation with them over and over again. My mind flickered to the huge blowup we had when I signed up for the Academy.

"Why is it okay for Owen to enlist, but I get shit for wanting to join the FBI?"

My father had sat in his recliner reading the newspaper. He'd gripped the edges so tightly the paper wrinkled around his fingers.

"It's not the same thing, and you know it. Your brother enlisting in the military is different. It just is. You could be anything. You could be a lawyer or something. You could live a simple life. You don't have to put your life in harm's way," he'd said through gritted teeth.

"You've always been stubborn. A mind and will of your own. And we know that we can't talk you out of it, but we just wanted something different for you. That's all." My mother's voice had been soft. So soft and heartbroken.

What they were saying, without saying it, was that it was different because I was a girl. The only girl and they wanted to keep me safe. But there was no keeping me safe. Not now. Not in the world we lived in. Not when horrible things happened to people, to young women who looked just like me.

And I wanted to stop that. I wanted to help people. I wanted to snuff out the evil in the world, or at least try.

*And people kill their lawyers, so that isn't a safe job either.*

"What do you do now?" asked my mother.

I smiled. "Well, we all know our post, and they give us two weeks to get settled in our new position."

"I see. So you'll be here…"

"For a few more days. I'm already packed. And I want to get there early so I can get the lay of the land."

"That's understandable." She smiled at my father, who just nodded his head.

Kelsey waved her hand and caught my attention. Her parents were so against her joining the FBI that they didn't even show up to graduation. She stood next to Jackie and Ginger.

My mother looked behind her. "Go be with see your friends. We'll be here."

I hugged her again and ran over to meet them. I felt the tension melting away as I walked over to them. I loved my family. I loved my parents. I loved my brother, even though he couldn't come to my graduation but still made time to voice his objection. But I couldn't live my life for them. I couldn't be who they wanted me to be. I couldn't be miserable so they could be happy.

"You looked like you could use a reprieve." Jackie glanced over to where my parents stood.

I shrugged. "It is what it is."

"You going out with us tonight?" Jackie wiggled her eyebrows.

"Of course. It'll be our last night together."

I met Jackie, Kelsey, and Ginger my first day here. We became fast friends and each other's cheerleaders. There were quite a few days I didn't think I was going to make it—and I might not have if they weren't there for me.

"You want to meet us at Mike's around eight?" asked Kelsey.

"Sure." I glanced back at my parents. "Yeah, that would work." I figured, after spending the rest of the day with them, I would be ready for a drink.

"Right. See you guys then," said Jackie.

I walked back over to my parents.

"Friends of yours?" My mother's eyes looked behind me.

"Yeah. We're going out tonight to celebrate. Our last hurrah, sort of."

"Of course. Um… what do you want to do now?"

"Lunch would be nice," offered my father.

"Yeah, we could go have lunch," I said. "Just let me change, and I'll meet you guys outside."

Mom smiled. "Okay, love."

I left my parents in the auditorium while I ran to my dorm to get changed. After throwing on a pair of jeans and a white top, I headed back out only to be stopped inches away from the front door.

"Yo, Storm! Where you going?"

I spun around and my mood instantly dropped. Eli Wilson. Internally I rolled my eyes, but on the outside, I tried to keep my face as pleasant as possible. Sure, I didn't like him, but he didn't need to know that. He was smart but an asshole. A know-it-all.

*Why is he talking to me?*

"Where you running off to?"

I glanced behind me at the glass doors on the building front just as my parents' car pulled into view.

"Parents taking me to lunch."

"Oh. They must be proud."

"Not really. It's probably a last-ditch effort to talk me out of it. What about your parents?" I looked behind him for a face that looked like his, smug and disinterested.

He shrugged. "They didn't come. They wouldn't … they…" He cleared his throat. "Anyway, I hear you got the Hawaii post."

I decided not to probe any further. "Yeah, you?"

"Chicago." His jaw tensed for a second. An emotion passed over his face so fast I couldn't read it. It was there one moment and then gone the next. He wasn't happy about his post. "I guess you're the lucky one."

"I guess so." I glanced back at the car. "I should get going."

"Oh yeah. See you later." He turned around and walked away.

*I should have asked him to join us.* That would have been the polite thing to do. And if Eli hadn't been a smug ass for almost the whole twenty weeks, I would have. But he was. He thought he knew everything. Everything. And never missed a chance to rub it in our faces. He was smart. And passed all the exams with flying colors—especially with anything involving computers.

"Thought you had forgotten about us," said my mother once I climbed into the back seat.

"Nope. Just had to talk to someone. So where do you guys want to eat?"

We settled on a barbecue place not far from the Academy. The food was good. My father was surprised. I was too. My mother stared at me in between bites. It was like she was never going to see me again. Like she was taking every opportunity to commit my face to memory.

"I'll be okay. Geez, you guys are making more of this than you need to be. You didn't make this big a deal when Owen enlisted. And he was shipped off to a war zone."

"And you have entered into this too lightly," replied my father. "You didn't think it through. You could die, being in the FBI. You could get hurt. You could be killed. So don't act like we don't have a right to be afraid for our only daughter who decided she wanted to live dangerously."

My mother placed a hand on my father's arm. "Now, Bill, you said you weren't going to do that. We said we would just enjoy today. What's done is done."

I blinked. I didn't join on a whim. If it wasn't the Bureau, I would have become a police officer. I just wanted to help people. To make a difference. But no matter what I said, they just couldn't see that. Wouldn't see that. Couldn't accept that I was an adult and completely capable of making my own decisions.

I guess to my parents I would always be their baby, their only girl. And there was nothing wrong with that. I loved my parents. But I couldn't live my life for them. And changing their minds was not working. So I would do exactly what my mother said and enjoy today.

"Are you guys going to visit me in Hawaii?" I popped a spoonful of baked beans into my mouth and immediately moaned at how amazing they were. Sweet but not too sweet. A little spicy with pieces of ground beef in it.

"Of course," said my father. "If it's allowed."

"Of course it is. It's really not that different from a regular job, Dad. I'll have a salary. A normal place to live. I'll go to the office every morning and do paperwork and emails, and then if I'm not on an active case, I'll go home. I'll have PTO and weekends and days off just like any other job."

That seemed to placate him, and he finally relaxed a bit.

"I'll let you know once I get settled and find a place."

"How does that work?" asked my mother. "I mean, do they provide housing?"

"They give you two weeks to find housing before you have to start working full time."

"Just two weeks?" My father shook his head.

"Yeah. That's why I'm leaving a little early. I want to find a place before my official start date. I asked if it was okay, and they said yeah. I just don't want to get there, be working, and still be living in a hotel or something."

"Apartment or house?" My mother popped a piece of her smoked chicken breast in her mouth. Her eyes closed immediately as she tried to savor the bite.

"Honestly, I hadn't thought too much about it. I was going to see what's available once I get there. I could rent a house though. Something with enough bedrooms so you can come visit."

"Don't worry about us. Just make sure you're comfortable."

The rest of lunch went by pretty fast. We drove around talking in the car and then spent a few hours in their hotel room hanging out. I had to admit, it was actually pretty pleasant. My parents still weren't thrilled, but they opened up a little bit and started asking me some questions. Owen even FaceTimed in for a bit, and we compared some of the crazy stories between my experience in the Academy and his at boot camp. Eventually, my father even said something about visiting me as an excuse to lay out on the beach.

When they dropped me off in front of the building, it was almost eight. My mother hugged me so tight I couldn't breathe.

"Make sure you come see us before you leave."

"Of course. I'll call you, and we'll spend a couple of days together before I go."

"Good."

My father hugged me just as tight. My mother had to tap him on the shoulder several times for him to let go. We said our goodbyes, and then I rushed to my dorm. I had to hurry up and get ready so I could meet Jackie and the girls at the bar.

# CHAPTER TWO

A FTER A SHOWER, I THREW AN OUTFIT TOGETHER. Nothing fancy. Just a pair of black jeans, because who didn't look good in black jeans and a red sleeveless top? Usually, my hair always ended up in a bun. I liked it this way, even though Jackie always said it was boring. I liked that it was boring. It kept my hair off my neck and out of my way. But not tonight.

Tonight I let it down; the ends skimmed the middle of my back. I kept my makeup simple and put on a pair of comfortable—but stylish—booties. I tucked my wallet in one back pocket and my badge in the other. I had purses, but I didn't feel like dragging one around. When I arrived at Mike's, the girls were already there. It was almost nine.

Most of the graduating class were there, scattered around the room, branched off into their different cliques. Jackie and the girls sat at a booth in the middle of the room. I slid into the booth next to Ginger. Her red hair hid her face as she leaned forward to sip her drink through a neon straw.

"I was starting to worry—"

"Not about your safety," clarified Janet. "We know you can handle yourself. Just that you weren't coming. Second time you would have stood us up this month."

I sighed. They had asked me to come out with them last month, but I was so caught up in getting my work done that I had to turn them down. I thought I could have gotten it done in time but ended up falling asleep.

"I said I was sorry."

"We get it. It's the job." Jackie downed the last of her whiskey. She was never one for fruity, pretty drinks. She tucked a handful of her long brown braids behind her ear and smiled. "Come to think of it, I remember the last time we were out. You got so drunk you started dancing on the bar and made out with some guy—what was his name?" She looked at Kelsey and Ginger.

I scoffed. "I'm sure I have no idea what you are talking about. That doesn't sound like me."

Ginger laughed. "You're right. Not sober you." She waved the waitress over. "Let's remedy that, shall we?"

Ginger ordered a round of drinks—nothing bright or sweet, just four glasses of whiskey. I wanted to drink mine slowly. Savor the taste. I took a slow sip, and heat bloomed in my chest. By the time I opened my eyes, Jackie and the rest had finished theirs. Judging by the looks on their faces, drinking slowly was not on the menu for tonight.

After a few drinks, my whole body felt warm and fuzzy.

"Where are you going again?" asked Kelsey.

"I'm going to Honolulu," I announced, soaking in their envy with a smile. I had always wanted to go to Hawaii. I was so excited that I screamed when I found out. I knew it would all be much more than fun and games, but I would be lying if I said I wasn't excited for some fun in the sun.

Kelsey's mouth fell open. Jackie shook her head as Ginger downed the last of her drink.

"That's not fair," complained Jackie. "You get beautiful Hawaii, and I get boring Virginia."

"I got New York," said Kelsey. "Which also has rough winters. But at least it's, you know, New York." She waved at the waitress, who nodded her head.

"I got Chicago," said Ginger.

"Oh, you'll be there with Eli," I told her.

She dropped her head into her hands and groaned. "Seriously?"

"I guess I'll get the next round." I laughed as the waitress placed four more shots on the table.

"You sure will," groaned Jackie.

After another two rounds, my head felt light and my body loose. I felt good. Laughter and conversation were flowing, and we were all having a good time. Everyone was nervous and excited at the same time as we all stood at the horizon of what our lives would become. Even though we'd all be going our separate ways, I was grateful to have a group of girls like this in my life.

"That guy keeps staring at you," said Ginger out of nowhere.

We all stopped what we were doing and turned toward the bar, trying to follow her gaze.

"Who is he staring at exactly?" asked Jackie.

"I think he's staring at Mia," answered Ginger.

At the bar, there was a man with cobalt eyes and short blond hair slicked back. His forearms rested on the bar, toned and tattooed. He wasn't too muscular, but I could tell that he worked out on the regular.

"Go over there," said Ginger. She was definitely the most daring one of the group. She was always ready and willing to put herself out there. I, however, was not.

Maybe it was the whiskey coursing through my veins that made me stand up and walk over to the bar, but somehow I found myself sitting on the stool next to him. He smelled like cedar and amber.

I turned to say something. He smiled—less of a smile and more of a smirk—before glancing over my shoulder.

Maybe he recognized someone.

Or maybe he wasn't really staring at me.

"Hey, Jen ... ," he said to someone behind me before I could even open my mouth. I followed him as he got up and went to go hug some beautiful blond. The two chattered and laughed, and I suddenly realized he hadn't been looking at me at all.

My face went hot. But I stayed at the bar. I couldn't turn around. Couldn't look at my friends, not now. There was some scattered laughter behind me, but not directly behind me. Somewhere toward the back of the room. It's hard to say whether it was at me or something else. Turning around to check was not an option. So I kept my eyes on the bar, studying the smooth wood top intently.

It looked smooth, but when I let my fingers roam over the spot directly in front of me, I felt the groves etched into the wood. I ordered another drink. The bartender set a glass in front of me with two fingers' worth of whiskey.

Someone brushed against my shoulder, and then a body eased onto the stool to my right.

"Can I buy you another?"

I looked up to see a pair of amber eyes staring at me. He was tall and handsome, with dark-brown hair and a plethora of tattoos down each arm. He glanced at my glass and then back at me expectantly. I looked at my glass too. I barely had a sip of it before he came over, and I wasn't really in the mood to be picked up.

What was the point now? I was leaving for Hawaii in two weeks, and long-distance relationships didn't work. And I wasn't really in the mood to start another relationship. It had been so long since I had been in one; I probably wouldn't know where to start. Joining the FBI had been my main priority lately, and everything else just kind of fell by the wayside.

I put on my best "I'm not really that into you" smile and declined. I'd probably had enough drinks for the night anyway.

"Oh, come on. One more drink. A pretty girl like you shouldn't drink alone," he insisted. His hand grazed my thigh for a brief moment before settling just above my knee.

I smacked his hand away. "No, thank you. I just want to finish drinking my drink and go home. But thanks for the offer."

He grinned. "Come on. Don't leave me drinking all by myself."

*This creep!*

His hand found its way back on my thigh, only this time a little higher. I could feel my entire body turn hot. Blood boiled in my veins. Who did he think he was? Sure, he was cute, but I already told him no. Pestering me wasn't going to get him what he wanted.

I turned to face him. Now that I got a closer look at him, I saw that his eyes were red and seemed to have a hard time sitting up straight. He was obviously drunk. I smiled. This time it was a soft, sweet smile. The kind of smile that said I was down for anything.

He grinned, his eyes excited and eager.

"Why don't we go outside?" I asked.

He jumped off the stool before I could say anything else. I downed the last of my drink, threw some cash on the bar, and followed him out the back down into the side alley.

The night air was cool and crisp against my skin. It mingled with my sweat and sent a shiver down my spine.

And then he was on me. Pushing me up against the wall. His fingers roamed over my body. Down my arms, the curve of my waist, my hips. Tangled up in my hair.

His lips on my neck, my chest. Kissing me feverishly. Like he didn't want to give me a moment to think about it. To talk myself out of it. Like if he just kept going, I wouldn't have the chance to say no.

I tried to push him off. To tell him to stop. But every time I opened my mouth, his lips pressed against mine. Maybe it was his fervent panting. Maybe that was all he could hear. Or maybe his ears were so full of his own want that nothing else mattered.

So instead of using my voice, I used my knee. A swift, hard kick between his legs. He stumbled back. A groan escaped his lips, and he doubled over.

"You bi—"

"Now, now." I took a moment to smooth down my hair and adjust my top. "I told you to stop. But you didn't listen."

He lunged forward, but it was slow. Uncoordinated. I'd dealt with this a thousand times in training against guys much

18

bigger—and more sober—than this. Without even breaking a sweat, I sidestepped him, caught his arm, and twisted. He screamed.

I twisted it harder and then shoved him up against the wall.

"I'm going to call the police. This is assault!"

"That's ironic."

I pulled my badge out of my back pocket and shoved it in his face. He stopped talking.

"I... I..."

"Let's start with your name."

His mouth opened twice before any words came out. "T-T-Tyson."

"Well, Tyson, you know I could lock you up for sexual harassment? When a girl says no, she means no!" I snapped.

"I... I'm sorry. My... my friends bet me that I could—"

"Could what? Make out with me? Have sex with me?"

Tyson looked at the ground, his face as red as my shirt.

"Stop listening to your friends. They don't sound too smart, and listening to them will probably get you locked up."

"Yes, ma'am."

I blinked. I wanted to smack him for calling me ma'am. I was only a few years older than him, four at the most. I should have arrested him for that. Could I arrest him for that? What would be the charges? Talking while stupid? No, drinking while stupid. That was a crime. Well, it should have been a crime.

"How old are you?" I eyed him. Everyone looked different in bars. Maybe it was the smoky haze, the dim lights, or all the alcohol, but in the bar, he looked older. Outside in the cool night air, he looked like he was barely eighteen.

His bottom lip quivered a little. "Twenty-one."

"Go home!"

Without uttering another word, Tyson pushed himself off the wall and ran down the alley. He rounded the corner without even looking back. I shook my head. Maybe he learned a lesson tonight. Maybe he would treat girls better in the future. I was hopeful, but I wasn't holding my breath.

"Not saying we were worried about you or anything."

I looked up. Standing by the door to the bar were the girls. Jackie still had her drink in her hand while Kelsey and Ginger stood in the doorway behind her, craning their necks to see down the alley.

"But we wanted to make sure that you were okay," finished Jackie.

I grinned. "Worried? I'm an FBI agent, ladies. This is just a taste of the action."

"I know that's right!" whooped Kelsey. We all burst out laughing as we headed back into the bar.

"I'm gonna miss y'all so much," said Ginger as she raised her hand for another round.

I smiled. I was going to miss them too.

# CHAPTER THREE

T O SAY I WAS NERVOUS WOULD BE AN UNDERSTATEMENT.
It was a good word, but it just didn't fit the situation. I
had said goodbye to my friends and family and moved to
a completely new place that I had never been to before. I'd never
been more than a few hours' drive from my family, even in college and at the Academy, so to be on the literal opposite side of
the country and half an ocean away would be a new experience.
And while I was a little apprehensive, my excitement won out.

I landed at the Daniel K. Inouye International Airport a
little after one in the afternoon. It was a small airport, smaller
than any I had ever been to. But it was still nice and efficient.
And they didn't lose my luggage, which garnered them a lot
of points.

"Special Agent Mia Storm?"

My back straightened, and I turned around. "Yes?"

"Ahh, good."

Before me stood a woman that looked to be about my age with sandy-blond hair and warm brown eyes already reaching out to shake my hand.

"Aloha. Welcome to Hawaii." Her smile was warm and inviting. My shoulders relaxed a little at the sight of it. "I'm Special Agent Swift. Nice to meet you."

I couldn't help but chuckle at that. "Any relation to the singer?"

Swift's polite smile spread out into a much wider grin. "Unfortunately, no. No free tickets for me."

"I'm sorry. I'm sure you get that a lot. But I just had to ask," I said.

"It can have advantages. Sometimes people assume things," she winked.

She took two of my bags while I had my carry-on and another duffel bag, then ushered me to follow her, and we navigated the packed crowd of tourists together.

"Is this your first time in Hawaii?" she asked.

I nodded. "Yes. I always wanted to come though."

"Most people do, but never get the chance. You'll love it here."

"What about you?"

She smiled again before pointing the direction to the parking lot. "My family has always lived on the island. I've never lived anywhere else. Sometimes I think it would be nice to live somewhere with snowy winters."

"Well, I've done that, and this is better."

She laughed. "Come on. We'll get you settled in your hotel, and then I'll take you by the field office."

"Sounds like a plan."

We stepped out of the airport, and I immediately winced and held up my face to block my eyes from the sun. I don't think I was prepared for the heat either. Such a drastic change from Upstate New York. I had to take my jacket off before we got to her car. When she popped the trunk, she looked back at me and chuckled.

"Yes, the heat will take some getting used to."

We tossed my bags into the trunk and then got into the car. I took the opportunity to rummage through my bag and produce my sunglasses before we got started.

"So we'll let you take the day to relax and get settled. Then in the morning, I can come by and take you to the office. Officially you don't start for another two weeks, so you can take the time to look for permanent housing. I know a good realtor who can help you."

I nodded. "Cool."

Honestly, I didn't hear everything she was saying. I was too busy staring out the window. The airport gave way to a lush landscape filled with bright-green plants and beautifully colored flowers. Seagulls drifted lazily on big, puffy clouds, and the ocean sparkled like sapphires. There were so many places to look. So many new sights to see.

Swift looked over and chuckled. "You live here now. You don't have to see everything in one day."

I finally tore my eyes away from the window and smiled at her. "I know. Everything is just so beautiful." I think she took the scenic route just for my benefit.

"Here you are." She pulled in front of the building and popped the trunk as a bellhop jogged out of the building to unload my bags.

I immediately gawked. I don't know what I was expecting, but it wasn't this.

The Hibiscus Breeze Resort was by far the finest hotel I'd ever seen. Lush and beautiful flowers surrounded the doors, and I had to crane my neck just to see the top.

"Um. Are you sure this is the right place?" I asked.

"There's a little area of private beach out back too," she told me. "I'd make use of it while you can."

I didn't know what to say, other than, "Thank you so much, Agent Swift."

"Kasey," she insisted. "Here's my card. Text me if you need anything. But I'll be back at nine?"

"Sounds like a plan."

We waved goodbye, and I closed the car door and walked into the building, fanning Kasey's card back and forth to cool myself off. My heart pounded against my ribs. I wasn't scared. Nervous. I was nervous. New place. New job. New people.

I didn't know anyone in Hawaii. There was no one I could call or hang out with. Not yet anyway. Kasey seemed cool, but I couldn't ask her to keep me company all night. Mostly I was just tired. I was so excited about the move that I hadn't slept a wink. And I snored, so I was trying not to drift off on the plane. Didn't want to put the passengers through that.

Jackie told me once it sounded like I was trying to scrape paint off the walls when she and Kelsey fell asleep in my room after an all-nighter studying. I didn't think it was that loud. Although I had been known to wake myself up snoring.

The lobby was tall and grand and smelled like fresh flowers, and my footsteps echoed loudly on the marble tile. The walls were tastefully arranged with traditional Hawaiian art and decor, and bright, colorful floral arrangements inside gave the place an atmosphere that was something like paradise.

"Ma'am?"

I blinked. "Sorry," I told the bellhop, who was looking at me with concern. Apparently I had just stopped in my tracks. But I couldn't help it. I was overwhelmed by the whole thing.

I approached the desk, where a young Hawaiian woman smiled. "Aloha and welcome to the Hibiscus Breeze Resort," she said.

"Um. Aloha," I replied sheepishly.

I gave her my information, and her fingers moved fast over the keys. After a brief moment, she handed me my room key. Then she turned to the bellhop and told him which room to take my bags.

"Room 507."

He nodded and then disappeared with my luggage.

"Please enjoy your stay. I'm Lola, and if you need anything else, please don't hesitate to ask."

"Thank you so much."

The sweet, floral scent hung in the air no matter where you went. I smelled it in the elevator and all the way up to the fifth floor. The bellhop arrived with my bags two seconds after I got my door open.

He set them by the door, and I tipped him before he left. When the door closed behind him, I could no longer hide my excitement. Just like the lobby, the room was so nice I almost didn't know how to take it in.

Across from the door was a living room area with a plush sofa, a TV, and a large window. I ran over to the window and pulled back the curtains. Out the windows, I could see above the other buildings to a glorious view of the beach. The sky was a pale blue with gray edges.

"Is it going to rain?" It didn't matter. It could have rained all night. I was in Honolulu. This was where I lived now. And a storm wasn't going to change that. And I wasn't going anywhere tonight.

On the wall next to the TV, there was a doorway that led to the bedroom, which had a king-size bed and another large window. Another door led to the bathroom with the largest shower I had ever seen.

"This is amazing," I whispered. I went back into the living room and collapsed onto the sofa. My body was so tired. My arms felt heavy.

And there went my adrenaline. I had been so excited to come here. To finally start my life as a special agent. And now that I was here, all the excitement left my body. Now I was just tired. So tired that on the sofa in front of the large window, I could no longer keep my eyes open.

When my eyes did finally open, the room was dark. For a second, I forgot where I was. My body jumped off the sofa before my new surroundings had time to register. I fumbled along the wall for a light switch. I stumbled, walked into a table, and almost fell to the ground before I found one. It was on the wall by the door.

I checked my watch. It was well after midnight. I eyed the minibar. My stomach growled lightly as I picked up a bag of chips. *Hopefully, this will tie me over.* I tossed the chips onto the bed and jumped into the shower. Of course, the water pressure was amazing.

After my shower, I put on the big, fluffy white robe hanging on the back of the door and got in bed with my chips and the remote.

At three in the morning, I checked a chart on my phone. Syracuse was five hours ahead of Hawaii. They would certainly be awake now.

"You were supposed to call last night," said my mother.

I could tell from her tone she was irritated and that she and my father had talked about me not calling them last night.

"I know. But when I got in, I was so tired. I didn't sleep the night before, and I didn't want to sleep on the plane. I just woke up."

"Yeah. With the way you snore, you really shouldn't be sleeping in a public space. It's not fair to the innocent bystanders."

"Wow! It's not even that bad."

She laughed. "I keep telling you, you need to see someone about that."

"Thanks, Mom."

She laughed. "Your father is at work, but I'll let him know you finally called. Take care of yourself. Love you."

"Love you too."

"My snoring is not that bad," I grumbled when I hung up the phone. I glanced at the clock by the bed. I still had a few hours left before Kasey would come to get me around nine, so I drifted off again.

I woke up with the sun, finally feeling fully refreshed, ordered room service for breakfast, and got dressed. Sure, I wasn't officially starting yet, but I still wanted to make a good impression. In the field, I might be able to dress more casually depending on my assignment, but it would be business casual in the office: dark colors, slacks, dress shirts. I put on a pair of black slacks and a dark-blue blouse.

My food arrived right after I brushed my hair into a bun. The waiter wheeled the tray into the room.

"Good morning. I hope you are enjoying your stay, ma'am," he said. He was cute. Black hair, light-brown eyes, and when he smiled at me, he had a dimple on his right cheek.

"It's been amazing so far, and I just got in yesterday."

"That's good to hear."

I tipped him.

"Mahalo. Enjoy the rest of your day."

"You too," I said as I closed the door behind him.

I ate my eggs and bacon quickly. By the time I finished my coffee and got my shoes on, it was already eight forty-five. I double- and triple-checked that I had everything I needed and made my way down to the lobby.

The smell of hibiscus and other tropical flowers was somehow even fresher this morning. In the center of the lobby was a massive centerpiece of pineapples, berries, mango, and other fruits for the guests to take. I idly munched on some honeydew while waiting for Kasey to arrive.

She waved from her car as she pulled in, and I slipped quickly into the passenger seat, still wanting to avoid the crazy heat as much as possible. We chatted a little bit on the five-minute drive to the field office.

"Everyone's pretty nice… ish," she told me.

I raised an eyebrow. "Ish?"

"There's department politics, as I'm sure you can guess. But it's not so bad. We've got a pretty good team."

The day seemed to speed by. I got my key card assigned to me as soon as I walked in. It would need to be with me at all times to get in the building. I made a mental note to myself to put it on a clip on my belt or something so I'd never forget it.

The field office wasn't what I expected when they told me I was being assigned to Honolulu. I wasn't sure what I was expecting exactly. Maybe that it would be smaller. Four floors, not including the basement. Next to the check-in desk was a large door, and on the wall next to the door was a keypad. Kasey watched as I slid my key card through the keypad. Thankfully, the red light turned green, and the heavy door clicked.

"That settles it," she declared with a wry smile. "You're officially part of us now. No turning back, Agent Storm."

"I would never, Agent Swift."

The rest of the day consisted of me meeting so many new people. So many names were thrown at me that it would take me weeks to remember them all. I met three new special agents who arrived six months ago. Some senior agents who had been there for over five years. And even a few of the higher-ups who'd been in the Bureau practically as long as I'd been alive.

Kasey directed me to a woman maybe in her late thirties with short-cropped black hair who sat behind a desk covered in about a dozen different monitors, computers, tablets, screens, and mountains of paperwork. The whole thing seemed crazy chaotic, but closer inspection revealed that it was all organized pretty meticulously. The woman clearly had a method to her madness.

"Oh, is this the new Brandon?" asked the woman.

"One and the same," Kasey replied.

I frowned. "Who's Brandon?"

"I'll explain later. For now, this is Agent Baldwin. She's the case manager you'll be working with. When you are out in the field and some relevant information comes in about your case, it goes through her, and then she will send it to you."

Baldwin gave me a polite nod. "I try my best to make sure that as soon as I know, you know."

"That sounds like a hard job," I noted.

She shrugged. "It can be if a lot of information comes in at one time. I'm not the only person doing it though, I'm just the head. You'll see it in action once you get your first case."

I smiled. *What will my first case be?*

And just like that, she tapped something on her Bluetooth earpiece and spun around quickly. "Nice to meet you, Agent Storm," she called back as her fingers flew across one of the several keyboards on her desk.

"You too," I replied, but she was already juggling three more tasks at once.

Next up on the agenda was Special Agent Kai Richards. He was maybe twenty-eight or so, and very tall and lean. He gave me a crooked grin as I approached.

"Hey, new kid. Your graduating class must be jealous."

I laughed. "Yeah, they were a little upset."

"Good." He chuckled. His smile was infectious.

"Special Agent Kai Richards is our good-time agent," supplied Kasey. "If you are ever feeling down, this is the guy you talk to. He will cheer you up and make you laugh until you piss yourself."

I raised both eyebrows. "Is that a proven fact?"

Kasey and Richards gave each other a mischievous glance and looked back at me. Both nodded at the same time, which made me laugh. "I don't even want to know."

"Special Agent Richards is also an excellent shot. Marksman in the army. He also knows everyone too."

He rolled his eyes. "Just call me Kai. I don't know everyone. My mother knows everyone, so I—"

"Know everyone by default," I finished for him.

He pointed at me. "Exactly. She gets it."

"Sounds like my own mom back home," I said.

I chatted a little bit more with Kai before Kasey took my arm and we proceeded down the hallway. "Here's me," she pointed, then jerked her thumb to another cubicle just across the corner from it. "And there's you."

My eyes lit up as I looked at a pretty plain setup—a desk, a chair, and a filing cabinet. My computer hadn't even been set up by IT yet, but I didn't care. It was *mine*.

Before I knew it, it was lunchtime, and Kasey and Kai took me out to a pretty neat place just near the office. I tried out my very first Spam burger. I also learned more about the man I was sent here to replace: Special Agent Brandon Aolani.

"Wait, you never heard of Agent Aolani?" Kai sputtered as he popped a french fry into his mouth. "He's a legend!"

"I'm a rookie, remember?" I reminded him.

"He was one of, if not *the*, nicest special agents I ever worked with," said Kasey. "He was kind and helpful. Very empathetic. Whenever any of the younger agents were struggling, he was always there to lend an ear."

"And he kicked a lot of ass too," added Kai. "You know, they're talking about naming the field office after him."

"Guess I have my work cut out for me."

Kasey looked at me kindly. "No, no, you don't have to live up to him. Just be yourself."

It was hard replacing someone whom everyone liked. What if they didn't like me the same way? What if they felt like I wasn't good enough or couldn't do the job? And if something had happened to this legendary special agent, what could happen to me?

Maybe my parents were right. Maybe I shouldn't have taken this job.

"Um, what happened to him?" I asked nervously.

"Oh, he retired," Kasey said.

I let out a breath. What was I expecting—that he'd been shot in the line of duty or something?

"It was hard for him after his wife died. He kept saying that family was really important and he wanted to spend more time with his. He wasn't really there when his boys were growing up, so he wanted to be there for his grandchildren."

"That's a noble reason to retire," I said.

She nodded. "We are not expecting you to be him. Just be yourself. As long as you do good work and aren't an asshole, people here will like you."

I smiled. "I will keep that in mind."

# CHAPTER FOUR

IT DIDN'T TAKE ME AS LONG AS I'D THOUGHT IT WOULD TO find a place. I wanted something close to both the field office and the beach. Seeing the water was not mandatory, but it would have been nice. I couldn't find one *that* close to the water, but I found a nice three-bedroom house that was almost exactly halfway between them. I could run to the beach, and that was good enough for me.

I didn't really have any furniture, so it only took a couple days to move in. Lucky for me, the house came fully furnished. I arranged things where I wanted them and added a few final touches to make it my own.

Everything in the house was neutral, white, or tan. I would add some pops of color later, but for now, it was perfect.

I opened my eyes just as the alarm on my phone started to go off. Usually, I woke up before it. Especially when I was excited to start the day. And I was. Today was officially my first day.

But first I needed to run. I was trying to start a routine in Honolulu. One that resembled the one I had back home. I always started my day with a run.

It was important to me to get my body moving first thing in the morning, and Hawaii was far more beautiful than anywhere I had ever been.

I placed my feet on the cool, dark hardwood floor and sighed. After getting dressed and putting on my smartwatch and shoes, I headed out the door. The sun wasn't out yet. As I ran down the block, rounded the corner, and headed toward the beach, the sun started to rise. The sky went from dark blue to purple, orange, and pink.

The bright colors against the bright green of the trees looked like something I had seen in a painting. The further I ran, the more I could smell the ocean. I wanted to run to it. Take off my shoes and wiggle my toes in the sand.

There was something about being close to the ocean that was... humbling? Restorative? I was never sure how to explain it. Standing next to it, smelling it. The waves lapping at your feet. There was something about it that always made me feel better. Made me feel at peace.

I stopped short though. I needed to get back so I could get ready to start my day. Couldn't show up late on the first day.

I gave one last look at the sunrise, stretched as far as I could, then turned around to head back home. I had barely rounded a corner when I stopped short.

"What happened?"

A police officer stood outside the house putting up crime scene tape. The sight was so jarring that my mouth fell open slightly as I watched him.

It looked out of place. I glanced around the neighborhood; the small, brightly colored homes looked so cheerful and welcoming. It wasn't just the crime scene tape that was out of place but the ambulance and four cop cars.

The officer spun around.

"I'm sorry. I just moved into a neighborhood just a few blocks that way. I happened to be running by..."

The officer's brows knitted together as he stared at me.

"You just moved into the area?" he said the words slowly like he was trying to pick out the lie. The part of the sentence that was true.

"Yeah. I was just transferred to the Honolulu FBI field office." I fished my badge out of my jacket pocket. I was glad that I had already gotten into the habit of taking it with me everywhere I went.

He looked at the badge and nodded slowly. I glanced up at the house. It was a one-story, green-colored house with a black door.

"Mia Storm."

"Officer Dawson."

We shook hands. I glanced back at the house. "What happened here? This looks like such a pleasant neighborhood."

He leaned forward. "It's looking like a murder-suicide. Husband and wife both have bullet wounds, and the gun was close to the husband. But we are still waiting for detectives."

"A murder-suicide? In this neighborhood?"

He shrugged. "I know. Doesn't seem to fit, but you know what they say, nothing is as it seems. Just because a home looks peaceful doesn't mean there isn't a storm raging inside."

I wanted to stay. To sink my teeth into the crime scene and try to figure out what had happened before the detectives arrived. Was it a murder-suicide, or had it just been staged to look that way? Excitement bubbled beneath my skin. I tried not to look giddy. Tried not to let my excitement show. No one should be happy at a crime scene. But I had never worked on one before. Not a real one. Never had an actual case before.

But this wasn't my business, and I had no right to infringe on the local PD's cases. I offered the officer a quick smile and wished him good luck before running home.

After a shower and a quick breakfast, I headed to work. The sun was out in full force. I wasn't extra hot when I got into the car, but I could tell it was going to be a sticky day.

I stepped into the building and took a deep breath. I swiped my badge through the scanner on the wall next to the door. The small, red light clicked over to green, and there was a heavy clicking noise, signaling that the door could now be opened. And there it was. My official first entrance.

I walked down a long hallway to a series of elevators and made my way up to the third floor. I was glad no one was in the elevator with me. Glad that no one could see my forefinger rapidly tapping my thigh. It was a nervous tic. And I was beyond nervous.

My first day replacing the special agent who came before me—not technically, of course. But the senior special agent had retired, and that had opened up a vacancy, and now I was the new kid filling in his empty shoes. By all accounts, Brandon Aolani was an exemplary agent. He had the highest closing rate in the department while also being kind and helpful to the junior agents around me. He was everything you wanted in a boss and in a partner.

*No pressure.*

But there was pressure. No one said anything, but I could feel it. On account of my age and probably gender, some of the agents probably felt that I wouldn't measure up. But I had to. I had to do my best. Prove everyone wrong.

The doors dinged open, and I stepped onto the floor after taking a moment to adjust my dark-blue suit jacket. On the main floor was a sea of desks, and Kelsey gave me a quick nod as I made my way to the desk I'd been assigned. The desks were grouped together in twos. Partners facing each other. I didn't have a partner yet.

"Storm?"

I looked up. Assistant Special Agent in Charge Corrine Davies stood in the doorway of her office, waving me over. I quickly dropped off my things and rushed over. She stepped back into her office, and I followed, closing the door behind me.

"Yes, ma'am?" I asked. It was only my first day. Had I already done something wrong?

The director leaned against the wall behind her chair, brows furrowed and lips pressed into a thin line. "Take a seat," she said.

I eased into the chair in front of her desk. Something was wrong. I could feel it. Dread coiled like a snake in my stomach as a million questions ran through my head.

Were they sending me back? Did they change their minds about me joining this field office? Of course, they weren't. I was one of the best graduates from the Academy.

ASAC Davies sighed before answering. "This wasn't how I wanted your first day to start. The plan was to give you a small starter case. Something to ease you in, but…"—the director took a deep breath—"that is not what's happening. You have a new case. Your first case. There's been a murder—well, a second murder."

"Wait, a second one? What about—"

"The murders seem to be linked, so the FBI is taking over. I want you to go to the crime scene, and then when you get back, you will be briefed on the first murder. And by then, your new partner should be here."

"Yes, ma'am," I said as I stood up. My fist clenched at my sides. It was the only way to stop my forefinger from tapping my leg.

"Special Agent Baldwin has all the information you need. I'd like an initial report before five today."

"I'll take care of it," I told her as I stepped out to leave.

"And, Agent?"

I looked back.

"*Pōmaika'i.* Good luck."

I nodded. "Thanks, ma'am."

Baldwin was already waiting by my desk as I headed out of the room.

"Such an exciting case for your first one. If you need anything, just let me know. I'm always here to help. It's literally my job." She handed me a cell phone. "This is your FBI phone. All relevant information about your cases or when you have a new case will be sent to this phone. You need to keep it on you at all times. My number's already programmed in."

"Understood." I turned on the phone to find a text from her already waiting with the information about the scene.

"Head down to the garage level to check out an FBI vehicle," she went on. "Eventually you'll be assigned one, but we'll get you squared away later. They all have GPS as well, so you should be able to find it. Your new partner is from here too, so—"

I frowned. "My new partner?"

She nodded. "Yeah, he's being transferred from another division. With him knowing the island, it should be easier to get around. Anyway, I already sent the case file to your email, and I'll make copies for your desk."

"Got it. Thanks."

When she bustled, I cleared off my desk and took a deep breath. I put my personal phone in one of the desk drawers and my new Bureau phone in my back pocket.

I had my badge and gun on my hip. I was ready to go. My heart pounded in my chest so hard I was surprised no one could hear it knocking against my rib cage as I walked to the elevator.

*Deep breaths. You can do this. You have to do this.*

Turning back now wasn't an option.

# CHAPTER FIVE

I PULLED UP TO THE MOST GORGEOUS HOUSE I HAD EVER seen. My mouth practically fell open when I saw it. I would never in a million years be able to afford to live in a place like that. The paycheck from the Bureau was good, but it wasn't that good.

The entire place was angular and modern, painted a shiny black, with large front windows and a slanted roof. Even the front yard was beautiful. The contrast of the brightly colored flowers against the black backdrop of the house was just breathtaking. I got out of the SUV and stepped into the controlled chaos of the crime scene. Crime scene techs descended on the house like a swarm of locusts, deftly covering each inch, trying to figure out what was out of place and what was evidence.

Before I entered the house, I took a moment to survey the neighborhood. Whoever owned the house liked to be different. The person wanted to stand out. And they did. All the other houses on the street, though they were very nice, were pretty standard. They didn't have the same odd angles as this one did, and they followed almost the same color scheme with little variation. Some houses were white with a bold-colored trim, like blue or sage green, while others were a pastel color with a white trim.

The black house stood out. Kind of an eyesore. A beautiful one though. An officer with short dark-brown hair and light-brown eyes stood next to the front door standing guard. He glanced back through the front door before running a hand through his hair as I approached. He shook his head as if he didn't like what he saw and then turned back around, facing forward.

"Um..." His head tilted slightly as he stared at me.

I held up my badge.

"Oh, my bad." He looked back through the front door. "Coroner just arrived."

"Thank you." I shoved my badge back into my pocket and entered the house.

The foyer was sleek with slate tile, a metal console by the door, and ornate metal wall hangings. It would have been beautiful. It would have been an ideal place to come home to—if it wasn't for the smell of decay hovering in the air. The smell of decomposition was so thick, so heavy in the air, that it was hard to breathe. Suffocating almost. I was ready to run out of the house.

I walked out of the foyer and into the open living space that consisted of a living room, dining room, and kitchen. Crime scene techs hovered around the living room. Flashes from several cameras were all around me.

I glanced back at the front door, wide open, and yet none of the fresh air made its way down the hall. My hands found their way into my pockets. An instructor at Quantico told us that whenever we walked into a crime scene, we needed to make sure that we touched nothing. And the best way to do that was to keep our hands in our pockets.

It was only then I realized that I had forgotten a pair of gloves in all the excitement. Yet another thing to add to the list of things I needed to take care of.

A body sat on a sofa in the living room covered in blood and what looked like brain matter.

"What in the world happened here?" I wondered aloud. The man's head was practically bashed in. Caved in. It was hard to tell where his eyes were or where they had been. Or where they were now. The tip of his tongue touched the point of his chin, and his nose was gone.

Bile coated the back of my throat, and I tried to push it down. It was my first day. I could not throw up all over a crime scene. What would they think? My fist clenched in my pockets. Instead of focusing on the body, I glanced around the room. Tried to take in the scene.

Blood spatter coated the walls and the coffee table. There was also some splatter on the floor. Brain matter, blood, and bone were sprayed everywhere. The techs were going to have a hard time bagging and logging everything. I was careful not to step on anything. The techs had already marked spots with bone and tissue on the floor.

I stepped over the markers and moved further into the room. The kitchen was practically untouched. I looked at the countertops and the floor and checked the stovetop and cabinets. There were a few flecks of blood, but not much. And not all grouped together.

"So whatever happened started and ended in the living room."

I spun around. It was clear that someone had beaten the man to death. The parts of his face that were still visible were swollen. Underneath the blood, his skin was purple and light blue.

"Well, I think we can all agree that he was beaten to death, right?" The coroner stood over the body. She glanced at me and smiled. "FBI, I presume?"

I introduced myself.

"The new transfer? Nice to meet you. I'm Dr. Jill Pittman. I did love working with your predecessor." She turned back around and faced the body. She didn't say she was happy to have me on board or that she looked forward to working with me.

*"I did love working with your predecessor"* hung between us like a ten-pound weight around my neck. Everybody loved Brandon. Everyone loved working with him. Bile threatened to rise up again, but I pushed it back down. Doubt crept in. I had the same nagging feeling I had when I first got to the field office and learned that I was replacing someone.

*What if I'm not good enough? What if I'm not like Brandon and they all end up hating me? What if my work wasn't on par with his? What if they won't like how I do things? How do I do things anyway?*

I watched Dr. Pittman as she examined the body. The state of the victim's body didn't seem to bother her. She stared at the body carefully, examining every inch of visible skin.

After spending two weeks getting to know some of the agents that I would be working with, I learned two things about Dr. Jill Pittman. First, she was a single woman who loved flirting. She flirted with all the agents—male and female. She insisted that she wasn't into women but didn't want them to feel left out. The second thing I learned was that she was absolutely, exactingly meticulous about her work.

The doctor tucked a honey-brown clump of hair behind her ear. "Whoever did this, they *hated* this man. From what I can tell, his jawbone, orbital bone, six ribs, an arm, a leg are all broken." Her gloved fingers pressed into the man's head. "And I mean, just look at his head. Half of it is caved in."

"Is there a weapon anywhere?" I glanced around the living room but didn't see anything marked.

The doctor shrugged. "We haven't found anything so far that could have been the murder weapon. I'm going to say, this wasn't done with fists. If it was, it was a big man. UFC fighter or something. Sumo wrestler." She looked around the sofa. "No, I think someone took an object." Dr. Pittman moved her fingers around his skull. "A bat maybe. I won't know for sure until I get him on the table. And the techs just started searching the place."

I nodded. "Do we know his name?"

An officer who had stood next to the front door walked over with his notepad in his hand. "Um… the house belongs to a David Carter. He lives alone." The officer looked down at the body, and an expression not unlike my own crossed his face. "It's hard to say if that is him though."

Dr. Pittman eyed the body. "Yeah, his face is kind of mangled. We'll have to run a DNA test or use his teeth, what's left of them, to ID him."

"Is there anything else you can tell me?" I asked.

The officer held up an evidence bag with a piece of paper, and I frowned.

"Is that… is that a puzzle piece?"

He nodded. "It was cut out of a magazine. It was weird. When we walked in, it was on his chest, along with numbers." The officer handed me his notepad.

"These numbers?"

Dr. Pittman walked over to the man and opened his shirt a little wider. "Here we are."

I glanced over her shoulder and saw the numbers written on his chest—not written, *carved*. Like someone had taken a knife and etched them into his skin. His flesh. And judging by the blood around the numbers, he was probably still alive when it was done.

*Why would someone do that?*

"One nine oh one three five oh two six," I read.

The long string of numbers didn't trip anything in my head. It was too long to be a phone number or a coordinate point, and not the right format to be an IP address. I typed it in my phone and then looked up. "Are you working on the other murder too?"

Dr. Pittman nodded. "Yeah. That one is also peculiar, but I guess I'll be telling you more about that later. Unless you want me to tell you about it now."

I shook my head. As much as I wanted to know about the first case, and I did, it would be better to wait for my new partner. That way we could hear about what happened together, and nothing had to be explained twice.

For one long moment, I eyed the scene, waiting for something to jump out at me. My muscles tensed beneath my jacket. There was something about the scene that didn't seem right to me. Didn't feel right. The body was out of place. *A dead body would be out of place in a living room.*

However it wasn't just the dead body but the way he was killed. Everything seemed really controlled. There was no blood splatter or sign of forced entry. No sign of a struggle, so the victim probably knew his attacker.

But then why wouldn't he fight back? If someone was bashing your brains in, you would put your hands up to deflect some of the blows, but not him. He sat on the sofa and let someone beat him to death? That's... Why?

"Could you do a tox screen?" I asked.

Dr. Pittman nodded. "What are you thinking?"

I shrugged. "It doesn't look like he fought back. I'm thinking... well... I know if I was being beaten to death, I would at least put up some kind of struggle. It doesn't look like he did that."

She looked back at the body. "Yeah, I think you're right. It doesn't look like he struggled or tried to get off of the sofa at all, judging by the way the blood is pooled around the body."

"So maybe he was drugged before the murder. But then why do that if you are going to kill him so brutally?"

Dr. Pittman shrugged. "For effect?"

"Definitely did that."

"Oh yeah. Top marks for effect."

*Why would someone leave the numbers behind? And a puzzle piece?*

I loved a good puzzle. I loved trying to piece different bits of information together and seeing how they fit. My father used to call me the puzzler because I liked puzzles so much. I would always laugh at him when he said it. It wasn't an actual word. *Dissectologist* is the real term for a person who liked puzzles or jigsaw puzzles. But I never had the heart to correct him. He would say there was no puzzle I couldn't figure out.

As I walked back to my car, I hoped he was right.

# CHAPTER SIX

W HEN I STEPPED OFF THE ELEVATOR, SPECIAL AGENTS swarmed all around me, busy with other cases. Baldwin flitted about behind her desk, typing on two separate computers while talking to another agent. Or at least I assumed he was an agent. From my angle, I couldn't see his face.

I headed over to my desk. Baldwin caught my eye, gave a quick no, and then turned her head. I followed her gaze and saw ASAC Davies leaning against the wall.

"Storm." The boss stood up straight and waved me over.

I followed her to the conference room where a man in a dark-blue suit sat at the long conference table. He stood up almost instantly as we entered.

"This is your new partner, Tony Walker. Tony Walker, this is Mia Storm."

We shook hands. I took a moment to size him up. He was older than me, with hazel eyes. He looked like he worked out, not overly so but enough to where, if we had to chase down a suspect, he could hold his own. Peeking out from under his sleeve cuff was the barest edge of a tattoo. I couldn't quite make it out.

"It's nice to finally meet you," he said. "I heard a lot of things about you."

I smiled. "I hope they were good."

He shrugged. "I guess that all depends on whom you ask." He smiled.

My back straightened. I stood taller next to the boss. What had he heard about me? Were people talking about me behind my back? What were they saying? Did they think I was in over my head? That I couldn't replace Agent Aolani?

*Stop spiraling!*

I took a deep breath. As if he could read my thoughts by the expression on my face, he smiled and shook his head.

"Don't worry. I just heard you had a lot of promise and do things pretty well. Very by-the-book. Professional. Top of your class, right?"

"Third, actually," I corrected him. My shoulders relaxed a little. I didn't mind people thinking I played everything by the book. I did. The rules were there for a reason and needed to be followed. For a second I wondered if Brandon did the same. Or maybe he wasn't as strict, and that was why people liked him.

Tony cleared his throat. "So I hear people think we have a serial killer on the loose."

"That's what it's looking like, Agent Walker," Davies told him. "If you two wait here for a few minutes, you'll be briefed. Give you a moment to get to know each other." She gave each of us a curt nod and exited the room.

And in her wake, silence hung in the air so heavy it was suffocating. I'd always been quiet. That's to say, it had always taken me a while to open up to people. I didn't really know what to say. What to ask. I wanted him to say something. To start a conversation. Ask me anything. But maybe he was quiet too, because he didn't.

We sat at the conference table for several minutes without uttering a word. Finally, it got to be unbearable, and I decided to break the ice.

"So I take it you aren't a stickler for the rules?"

Tony's eyebrow ticked up, and a shadow of a smile touched his lips. "I think there is a time and a place to follow the rules. The rules don't work all the time. They don't work in *all* situations. At least that has been my experience."

"Well, in my limited experience, they do."

He smiled. "I think the operative word there is *limited.*"

Before I could utter another word, the door opened. Dr. Pittman and three other people spilled into the room with folders in their hands and serious looks on their faces. Dr. Pittman sat next to me.

A tall man from Honolulu PD took up the front of the room, clutching a red folder in his hand, and cleared his throat to begin. "Um… I'm Detective Ross, and I was assigned the first case in what we think would be a serial killing." He had short blond hair and a jagged scar just under his left eye. "A few days ago we were called to the scene of a murder. I have to say, it was one of the strangest I had ever seen."

He placed the folder on the table and slid it over to me. "Like your body today, the shape of a puzzle piece that was cut out from a magazine was left on the body. And there were numbers written all over his chest. We haven't figured out what they mean yet."

I opened the folder and grimaced at the gruesome photos within. A quick perusal proved that the scene from the first murder was nearly identical to the one we'd just come from. The body was sprawled out on the floor, bludgeoned and bruised, and the victim's hair was so matted with blood that I couldn't tell what color it was. His skin was purple and black.

"Jesus," I muttered.

I slid the pictures over to Tony. He took them in his hands and studied them. Detective Ross was thorough. In the folder was a handwritten note listing everything he had seen at the scene and where.

"Dr. Pittman, did you see anything notable about this first murder before we connected it to the second?

Pittman shook her head. "I've only done a preliminary exam of the body. He was beaten to death. His skull was practically crushed. Agent Storm, you had a good intuition. I did a quick check and found there were no defensive wounds, which does line up with your evaluation of the second body. If someone is beating you that badly, you are going to try to defend yourself."

Everyone around me nodded, and I fought to keep the proud smile off my face. Barely a few hours on the job and I'd already maybe figured out a crucial piece of evidence.

"Unless you were tied up," said Tony. "Maybe the guy snuck up behind him. Caught him off guard and was able to tie him up before he even knew what was going on."

"But then why beat the crap out of him?" I asked. "Was anything taken?"

Detective Ross shook his head. "Not that we could tell." The detective had the look of a man that was ready to make a quick exit. While he was thorough with his notes, I could tell he didn't want to be in the room with us. He didn't want to talk about the case. Or deal with the case at all. He wanted to leave and forget this ever happened. When they told him that the FBI would be taking over the case, he was probably relieved.

"I saw no evidence of ligature marks, but again, it's only been a preliminary check," Pittman chimed in. "I'll double-check and keep you informed."

Tony picked up one of the photos and tapped the corner on the table three times. "The only reason you would do something like this is because you needed information."

"So the guy was trying to get information from him and beat him to death?" I glanced at Dr. Pittman, who shrugged.

"That could be possible. All of his fingers were broken, and he was missing quite a few teeth. Hard to say if they were knocked out or pulled at this moment. But our second body went through pretty much the same. Fingers broken, missing teeth."

"So someone is torturing them for information," I mused. That could be a theory. But what kind of information? What did they know that would be worth torturing and killing them over?

Dr. Pittman tapped a manicured nail on the table. "Beating them to death came last. Because once the person started hitting them, they didn't stop."

Tony slid the pictures back over to me, and I tucked them into the folder.

"Is there anything else, Detective Ross?" I asked. "Anything that we should know that's not in your report?"

A lot of detectives—most, in fact—didn't put everything in their notes. Certain things stayed with you. Certain things didn't need to be written down. Clues that you purposely left out just in case a suspect could be interviewed and you wanted to make the information they gave you was genuine.

The detective looked at me and then at the door. There was a yearning in his eyes. He wanted to leave. Had this case bothered him so much?

"You really don't want this case," said Tony.

The detective's eyes went wide with surprise. His shoulders dropped a little, and he stopped playing with the hem of his jacket.

"I've never seen anything like this. And I never want to see it again. I can still smell the blood and decomp. It was so heavy in the room we could taste it. Vic had been there for a few days before someone found him. The blood had coagulated and turned black. It was everywhere. Every surface in the living room." He opened his mouth and drew in a slow, ragged breath. "There are crime scenes that just stay with you, and I think this is that for me. And I would very much like to get rid of it."

Tony nodded.

I understood what he was saying. I hadn't worked a case yet, but I had seen one. Well, the case file. When I was at Quantico, they gave us case files of old cold cases. Not so we could solve them, but so we could get used to seeing dead bodies and examining case files. So we could get used to seeing how a file should be done.

Lorna King was a five-year-old girl, and when I opened her case file one morning, the image stayed with me. No matter what I did or how I tried to erase the image, her cut-up, half-naked body lingered in my dreams for months.

There were nights when I wished I had a time machine so I could go back in time and never look at the file. I should have picked another. I should have closed it as soon as I saw the picture. I should have done a million other things that morning, but instead, I flipped through the file to figure out what happened to her.

And I learned nothing. Because the agents in charge of her case learned nothing. Because no one saw or heard anything. And little Lorna still had no justice and no one to speak for her.

But in my dreams, she spoke to me and turned them into nightmares. Nightmares filled with blood and missing organs.

I shook my head, trying to knock the thought loose.

"I think we've all been there," said Tony.

I looked up, and he was staring at me. I wondered for a brief second what case had made him wish he had never opened the file. Never gone to the scene.

"Thank you for coming in," said Tony.

The detective nodded. He was halfway out the door before he stopped and turned back.

"The numbers written on his chest… for some reason, my first thought were account numbers. I don't think it's a bank here on the island though. None of the account numbers start that way. That just stood out to me."

"Thank you," I said.

He smiled at me for a brief second before leaving the room.

"I understand his disgust," Dr. Pittman remarked.

"You're a coroner. Can you be disgusted at this point?"

She smiled at Tony's question. "I haven't worked a case that utterly disgusted me or made me want to throw up. Not yet anyway. But the day that happens is the day I can retire."

# CHAPTER SEVEN

O N OUR WAY OUT OF THE DOOR, I SLIPPED TONY THE file so he could look over it too.

"Thanks."

I could be wrong, and I really hoped I was, but he didn't seem excited or even happy about me being his new partner. And maybe he had a right to feel that way. I didn't know what department he was coming from. Or the circumstances of him being partnered with me. Maybe he didn't want a new partner.

Or maybe he was one of those agents that didn't have partners. The senior agents worked by themselves. And maybe he preferred it that way. Or perhaps I was reading too much into it. *Relax!*

I walked over to my desk and sat down. Tony sat at the desk in front of me. He flipped through the folder.

"They still don't know who the first body is. How is that possible?" I griped while I waited for him to finish.

"There was no ID on the body. And his face, much like the second guy, was pretty smashed. They're waiting on dental records so they can match them. But he was found in the home of a man named Kent Barnum."

"Showing any of his family members a recent photo to help confirm his identity would not help."

A smile tugged at the corner of his lips. "Yeah, probably better to wait for dental records."

"Or maybe… Yeah, dental records would be the best bet," I said.

"First case." It wasn't a question but rather a statement. I couldn't tell if he was judging me.

I nodded. "What about you? Where were you before this?"

He took in a deep breath. "Undercover. For a while."

His tone and the way he dragged out the words told me he didn't want to talk about it.

"So what do you want to do now?"

I blinked. He was asking me? *Of course he's asking me. I have to learn how to run an investigation.*

He slid the file over to me, and I looked through it for the second time.

"We should go down to the IT department. See what they can make of the numbers written across his chest."

Tony nodded. He didn't say whether he thought it was a good idea or not. He just went along with it.

The IT department and cybercrimes division were on the fourth floor. We stepped into the elevator, and he pressed the button for the fourth floor. The silence between us was strange. I wouldn't say awkward, but it was like we had nothing to say to each other. Like we couldn't even think of anything to say to each other.

The IT department was a whole floor of computers. There was a big screen at the front of the room that looked like a whiteboard that took up a whole wall. The constant sound of typing echoed in the room.

"Mia?"

I spun around. I recognized the voice before I even saw his face. "Eli?"

"You remember."

I should have acted like I didn't. Acted like I could remember his face but not his name. Or maybe I could have acted like I had forgotten him altogether. Like the memory of him had escaped me. Like I had been so busy doing other things that I didn't have the time to remember him. But I didn't. I just couldn't play it off.

"It's barely been a month, Eli, of course I remember."

I turned to Tony, who looked not annoyed by the interaction, but not interested either. "This is my partner, Tony Walker."

"Nice to meet you."

They shook hands, and then Tony took a step back. Behind me. As if the conversation was none of his business and he didn't care to hear it.

"You're here now? I thought you were in Chicago?"

"Uh … yeah, I was able to get a transfer out here, there was an opening for a cybersecurity specialist. I wasn't really excited about living in Chicago, honestly. Grew up there, and … I was ready to let that place go."

"Did you hear about why there's an opening in the cyber department?" Tony's voice was low and sarcastic.

I hadn't heard anything about it. I glanced behind me. The corner of Tony's mouth was slightly curved.

"Umm … no, not yet."

"He shot himself," answered Tony.

I blinked. I hadn't heard that. A million questions ran through my mind, starting with "Why did he do it?" "What drove him to it?" "Was it work-related?"

Eli blinked. "I hadn't heard that."

"Not surprising," said Tony. "You don't want the new guy to know that the old guy shot himself. New guy might not take the job."

Eli smiled tightly. "Thanks for telling me. But I don't think I'd ever get to that point."

"I think you'd be surprised," said Tony.

*That got dark.*

Tony chuckled behind me. It wasn't that I didn't like Eli. He was okay. I would like to think that maybe in the time since we graduated, he had changed. But during our time at the Academy, he had been an arrogant ass who thought he was better than everyone. He was smart though. And great with computers.

He inhaled sharply, and then his lips curved into a smile. "So what brings you two to the cyber department?"

I handed him the file. "We have two victims that had these numbers written across their chests. The detective thought the numbers might link to a bank account or something. No one has been able to figure it out."

Eli took one look at the picture before he closed the folder. "If I had to guess, I would say it's a bank account in the Cayman Islands. They start with those numbers. Follow me."

He walked onto the main floor. We followed close behind. The desks weren't divided by partners. There were six large desks in the middle of the floor, each with seven computers in long rows.

Four of them were open. Eli sat at one of the computers, opened the folder, and started typing.

"Yeah, it is a Cayman account," he reported.

"How long will it take to figure out who it belongs to?" asked Tony. He moved from behind me so he could get a better look at the screen.

"Give me one moment."

I wasn't sure what he was doing. Windows and pop-ups flashed on the screen, some black, some white. His fingers moved so fast I couldn't tell what he was typing.

"Ricky Thompson."

Tony pulled a small notepad out of his pocket and started writing what was on the screen.

"Thanks." I tapped him on the shoulder and then turned around and followed Tony to the elevator.

"Anytime." Eli's voice was low and soft. And had a hint of a smile. I didn't look back to see if he was smiling at me.

Heat rose to my cheeks. I was thankful Tony was walking in front of me so he couldn't see my reddening face. In the elevator, Tony held up his notepad to show me what he had written down. Ricky Thompson's work and home address, along with his phone number.

I glanced down at my watch. It was a little after eleven, so Ricky was probably still at work.

"You want to call him first or surprise him?" I asked.

The doors dinged, and we stepped back onto the third floor. Tony shrugged. "Probably be better to surprise him. I think it's always better to surprise people than to announce that you're coming. At least that's been my experience. If they know you're coming, they tend to not be there when you get there."

"Noted."

After informing the boss of our plans, we made our way to the parking lot. I stopped short at the SUV.

Tony stood by the trunk of the car, brows furrowed, staring at me. "Can I drive?"

My shoulders dropped a little, relief coursing through me. I tossed him the keys. "I was hoping you would ask that."

He smiled. "I always drove with my last partner."

I could drive. I mean, I had my license. But I never liked driving. I know most people loved it. When I was sixteen, an age when most teens were eager to get behind the wheel, I was dreading it. I still dreaded it. I could drive when I had to. But it wasn't my favorite thing to do. I was hoping to get a partner who liked to drive.

Ricky Thompson worked at Teletech, a tech company. We had no idea what kind of tech they specialized in. While Tony drove, I scoured their website for any inclination on what they did exactly, and I found nothing. Maybe it was just one of those things where you had to know what it was to understand it. Or something like that. We were clueless.

But it wasn't a total loss. I did find a picture of Ricky Thompson. He didn't just work at the company; he owned it. Or he was one of the owners—there were three in total.

The building looked like a typical skyscraper. Rows and rows of windows on the outside. As I stepped inside the building, a burst of cold air sent a shiver down my spine.

Inside the lobby, there was a seating area with big, comfortable chairs and plants that I couldn't tell were real or not. They were lush and vibrant but not plastic-looking. I fought the urge to yank one of the leaves as we walked up to the front desk across from the double doors. At the light-gray desk sat a blond-haired woman with a deep tan. As soon as she saw, us her brows furrowed.

"Hello, we need to talk to Ricky Thompson," said Tony.

I would have come in with a polite request, but apparently, Tony could just barge in and make demands. Before she could answer, he took out his FBI badge and placed it on her desk.

Her eyes went wide. For a long moment, she chewed on the corner of her lip. Maybe she didn't know where he was. Or maybe she was trying to figure out what to tell us.

Finally, she popped her lip out of her mouth and answered, "Top floor. He just got in."

"Thank you," I said.

She smiled tightly. She was either really loyal to her boss or afraid of him. Or maybe she really needed this job and didn't want to do anything that would cause him to fire her.

On the other side of the desk, there was a long hallway with four elevators. We picked one and got on.

I figured either because of her loyalty or her fear, as soon as we got on the elevator and the doors closed, she would call up to her boss. My heart pounded so loud in my chest that I was sure Tony could hear it. I was about to interview my first suspect. Well, he wasn't really a suspect. We didn't know how he was connected to the first murder.

But still. I was about to conduct my first interview. I was almost giddy. If it wasn't for the murders and the gruesome state of the bodies, I would have been happy. This was my first case. And yeah, it just started, and I wasn't sure I could catch the murderer, but… I was… I was a special agent.

My dream, what I had been working toward, had come true. I was going to help someone. I was going to get justice for these victims.

*Hopefully.*

If I could solve the case.

A woman was waiting for us on the fourteenth floor, and she smiled tightly as the doors opened. She smiled tightly. "Right this way."

I was right. The receptionist downstairs had called up and let them know we were there. The woman must have been his secretary. Her bright-red curls bounced down her back as she led us down a hallway and then onto the main floor.

"This is nice," commented Tony.

The main floor had one desk off to the side. There was a large seating area with five oversized chairs and big beautiful plants that were a green so vibrant I just knew they were fake. They had to be.

In the middle of the floor, there were two pillars that reminded me of Ancient Rome. Next to the desk were two double doors with gold handles. The doors opened before we could reach them. In the doorway stood a tall white man with graying light-brown hair. He wore a dark-gray suit and a light-blue shirt.

"Ricky Thompson," said Tony.

"In the flesh. I have to say, I've never been visited by the FBI before. I don't know what I could have done to warrant your attention."

I cut a glance at the secretary, who stood by her desk waiting for instructions. For a brief second, I thought I saw the woman roll her eyes at his comment. There was a story there. She might not be as loyal to him as the woman downstairs was.

"Can we talk in your office?" I pointed to the doorway.

Ricky smiled and stepped aside so we could enter. There was something about his smile and jovial attitude that didn't sit right with me.

No one was ever happy to see the FBI unless they were a victim. So either he had nothing to hide or he was up to something.

"So what exactly is all this about, Agents?"

Ricky walked over to his desk and sat down. He gestured for us to sit in the chairs across from the desk. The office space was big and grand. Floor-to-ceiling windows, beautiful palms, mahogany bookcase filled with books he's probably never read.

The chair was so plush that I bit my lip to stop from sighing. I had never felt such comfort. I wanted to lean back and go to sleep; they were so comfortable. I sat up straight. Kept my back as stiff as a board.

*Don't get too comfortable.*

Was that his game? He invited people to his office, had them sit in these chairs, and got them comfortable—so comfortable they would let their guards down and give him whatever he wanted.

"Mr. Thompson, we're here to talk about a murder," I told him.

The shock on his face seemed genuine. His eyebrows furrowed and then relaxed.

"A murder? I... You think I killed someone... Wait, the FBI investigates murders?"

"Under certain circumstances. Like a potential serial killer," said Tony.

Ricky's mouth swung open. "Now, what in the..." He leaned forward, his elbows resting on the edge of his desk. "I haven't killed anyone. I swear."

Tony pulled the picture from the file out of his pocket and placed it on the desk. Ricky blinked, and his back straightened immediately at the sight of it. He glanced down at the picture and then at them. His face slowly hardened. He pressed his lips into a hard line and stared at the picture.

"The number written on his chest is your bank account number," said Tony.

"And you think I killed him and put information on him that could link him to me?" He shoved the picture away from him. "You aren't very good at your job, huh?"

I liked to watch people. I had always been like that. Since I was a kid. I would go to the playground and just watch people. Kids. Their parents. In watching Ricky, I noticed something. His face changed as soon as he saw the picture. Most people who weren't used to seeing dead bodies turned away in disgust. They don't want to look at it.

But not Ricky. He stared at the picture, and something passed over his face. Like a dark cloud. *He recognized the body. Or he understood the message?*

"No one said you killed him, Mr. Thompson. No one accused you of murder," Tony pointed out.

Ricky scoffed. "You said you were here to talk about a murder."

"And he is dead. We never said you did it. But your banking information is etched into his skin. Now, why would someone go and do that?" Tony picked up the photo and returned it to the file.

"I don't know. I might have some enemies. Some people might not like our new technology. But I don't know anyone that would do something that crazy."

"So you don't recognize the man?" I asked.

For a brief second, Ricky's jaw twitched. "No. I don't think so. Well, it's hard to say with his face the way it was. But I don't think so."

I nodded.

"No friends missing then?" asked Tony.

He shook his head. "No. In fact, we all got together last night to play poker. And all the guys showed up."

"Have you gotten any threats lately?" I asked.

Maybe he was the target, or maybe not. Maybe someone was trying to get to him. To get his attention. Trying to frame him for murder or something. I wasn't sure, but he was definitely linked to the dead man.

"I've gotten some, but none that said they would kill me. We are just a tech company. We aren't hurting anyone."

"You know what's strange?" Tony leaned back in his chair. "You don't seem worried about your bank information being written on a man's chest. A dead man at that. Someone out there has your banking info. And yet you haven't tried looking up your accounts to see if any money was taken or—"

"Someone like you wouldn't understand, but I have a lot of money. A *lot*. Whatever they took out of that account wouldn't even begin to make a dent." Ricky looked from Tony to me and back again. "And I figured the dead body was more important, right?"

"To someone like me," said Tony. "Not to someone like you."

"Is there anything else? I don't know how I can help you, and like you said, I need to check on my accounts." Ricky stood up.

This was the telltale sign that it was time for us to leave. Tony was the first to stand up. For a long moment, I stayed seated. There was something about him. Something about the way he was acting. People process things differently, but he was hiding something. I could feel it.

I stood up, finally, and followed Tony to the door. We didn't say anything to each other until we got outside and found our car.

"You think—"

"He knows more than he's telling?" Tony opened his car door. "Definitely. We need to know who the first body is."

# CHAPTER EIGHT

A S SOON AS I GOT TO MY DESK, I CALLED DOWN TO THE morgue to see if they knew anything about the first or second victim yet. It didn't seem right that these men were dead and yet we still didn't know who they were.

Next of kin needed to be notified, but we couldn't do that until we were sure who they were. Nothing worse than notifying the wrong family that their loved one had died.

"Dr. Pittman said they still don't have anything for us," I reported. "Apparently, they are a little backed up at the moment."

"Why exactly?"

I shrugged. I was going to ask more questions. But Dr. Pittman seemed rushed. Flustered. She cut the conversation short. There was a loud thud, and then the doctor started yelling at someone in a series of expletives that I had never heard strung together.

Tony shook his head. "I wonder what's going on down there. She might be training someone new. Or they haven't been able to get their dental records yet."

"Now what are we supposed to do?" I asked the question mostly to myself. I wasn't expecting him to answer or even acknowledge it. Sometimes when I needed to work something out, I talked to myself.

*Probably not a good idea to do that in public. Especially not surrounded by your new coworkers.*

I would hate to be known as the special agent who talked to herself. But still, we needed to know who the first victim was to see if there was another link to Ricky Thompson.

"Should we just act like we know the first victim is Kent Barnum?" he asked. "The first body was found in his house."

"No. What if it's not and we've built a whole investigation around the wrong victim?"

Tony sighed. "Who else would it be?"

"We don't know. What we can do is try contacting Kent and seeing if we can find him."

Tony shrugged. He sat up in his chair and turned on the computer. I found myself staring at him. I couldn't look away. What kind of question was that? You couldn't make a notification until you knew for certain the victim's identity.

Sure, it made sense that the body was Kent's, but with the face being as mangled as it was, it was still hard to tell. What if we did notify his family and he popped up a day later?

*Would this work?* Could we be partners? Could I trust him to follow the rules?

I was worried about what my partner would be like over the last couple weeks. Special agents were not allowed to pick their partners. The higher-ups put you with someone, and that was your partner. Even if you didn't like them or you two couldn't get along, you had to find a way to make it work. Common ground. What if we couldn't find that?

*You're reading too much into this.*

I took a deep breath. It was just the first day. Just the first day.

One of my instructors had told me that FBI agents were so different. Like snowflakes, no two were the same. You just had to worry about being yourself, and hopefully, you and your partner would be able to build a good relationship. Even if it was just a working relationship. You didn't have to be best friends, but you did have to respect each other.

But we seemed so different. I was a stickler for the rules. I could admit that. I might be a little too rigid, but… I shook my head. I just didn't want to mess anything up. I didn't want to fail. I needed to follow the rules because that was what they were there for. What would happen to the FBI if no one followed the rules and protocols? If everyone just did what they liked and bent the rules to solve cases, it would be chaos.

Tony picked up the phone at his desk. He caught me staring at him, and his brows slowly knitted together.

"Did you find something?" I asked as I turned on my computer. I tried to act like I hadn't been staring at him this whole time.

"Found his phone number." He dialed the number. It rang several times before the answering machine kicked in. He left a message before hanging up.

I chewed on my bottom lip. He was probably right. The body was Kent's. But we couldn't make a move until we knew for sure.

"What about the second victim?"

"He was beaten beyond recognition too," answered Tony.

"I feel like that was the point."

"What?"

I tapped my forefinger on the desk. "Time. I think the killer knew that by beating them beyond recognition, the police would have a hard time figuring out who they were. That would give him time to—"

"Find another victim?"

"Or find what he's looking for. This just doesn't feel random. There's a meaning, a purpose behind it."

Tony leaned back in his chair. He folded his hands on his stomach. He rocked in his chair while his forefinger tapped his thumb.

"I would say you are right, especially with the *clues* he left behind."

"Yeah, what is with that? I mean the puzzle pieces. There's nothing important on them. They were just cut out of an old magazine in the shape of a puzzle piece. Why do that?"

I shrugged. "I think the killer is saying that they, the murders, are connected. I would—"

Before I could say another word, my phone rang. It was Dr. Pittman.

"Agent Storm," I replied. Still felt weird to say.

"Sorry about that, Mia. Training new people is a pain. Someone put the wrong body parts… Anyway, you don't need to hear about that."

"Uh… okay."

"I just called to inform you that we have finally identified the first body, and it is, in fact, Kent Barnum. Obviously, it was a murder, blunt force trauma. I'm going to do a tox screen for him along with the second body. We should get the second body's dental records in a couple of days, but as of now, I'm proceeding with the assumption that it's David Carter. I know you can't do anything until we know for certain, but I'm just giving you my medical opinion."

"Thank you."

I hung up the phone. A smile pulled at my lips. I tried to fight it.

"It's okay to be happy. Or excited. Whatever that look is."

I looked up and let myself smile. "The first victim is Kent Barnum."

Tony sighed. He looked at me. I couldn't tell if it was an "*I told you so*" look or not, but it felt like it was.

"Good," he said. "Now here comes the hard part."

Memories flashed in my mind of the speech that Senior Special Agent Kenneth Cole had given us on our very first day at the Academy.

"I will tell you that this job is not for the weak," he had said. "There will be days when you will feel like a failure. Days when you want to give up. Days when you wish you had listened to your parents and picked a different job. Days when you will go home, close the door, and sob so uncontrollably you will feel like you can't breathe. And then you will pick yourself up and go back out there."

Kelsey had raised her hand then. "What, for you, is the hardest part about the job?"

Special Agent Cole had sat on the edge of the desk at the front of the room. He had sighed. "Honestly, I would say the notifications. They never seem to get easier. Which I guess is a good thing. If they ever did become easy, I don't know what that would say about me. Telling someone that their loved one has been murdered is not an easy task. You have to look them in the eyes and see their pain. Hear the anguish in their voices. It's a difficult thing to do and should be done with care."

"Do you want to do it?" I asked.

Tony looked at me. He shrugged, but I could tell he didn't want to do it.

I sighed. "Okay, I'll do it." I would have to learn how to do it eventually.

After some quick research, I was able to find Kent's mother's name and address, and we made our way out to the car once again. This news was best delivered face-to-face.

Mrs. Barnum lived in a nice neighborhood close to her son. As we pulled up to the house, my heart sank into my stomach. They lived close. So close she probably already knew about the body found at her son's house.

The second my car door slammed, the front door opened. An older woman with white hair pulled into a loose ponytail stood in the doorway. She wiped her hands on her light-pink apron.

"Are you here about Kent?" she called out.

"Yes, ma'am," I said.

She nodded slowly. Her eyes were red and puffy. Someone had already told her about her son. She stepped back into the house. We followed her. Tony closed the door behind us.

I followed Mrs. Barnum into her living room. My pulse pounded in my ears. I was so nervous. I didn't want to mess it up. Or make her feel worse. But we needed information. We were here to not only make a notification but to learn as much about Kent as possible.

I sat on a sofa covered in sunflowers. Tony sat next to me while Mrs. Barnum sat in a rocking chair next to the front window. She was shaking. It was like she couldn't keep herself together.

"How do you—"

"Everybody knows everybody around here. Some people saw the police down at Kent's house. Told me about it. I called the police, and they said they couldn't tell me if it was my son until they—"

"Got his dental records," I finished glumly.

She nodded. "Right. I guess you got them."

"Yes, ma'am, we did."

"And it's Kent?" Her voice wavered on the question.

"Yes, ma'am. I'm sorry for your loss."

Whatever last shred of hope she'd been holding on to vanished, and she lowered her head as deep, heavy sobs racked her body. My heart broke for the poor woman, and I made a slight nod for Tony to grab a nearby box of tissues and hand it to her. She accepted it meekly and finally gathered herself after a few minutes.

"Who?" she finally managed. "Who would do this?"

"We don't know yet. It's actually why we are here," I told her gently. "What can you tell us about Kent? What do you want us to know about your son?"

Mrs. Barnum opened her mouth and then closed it. Tears cascaded down her face. She wiped them away with the back of her hand.

"He was a good boy. Kind. So sweet. You should talk to his girlfriend. Courtney. She would know more than me about what was going on in his day-to-day life."

"We'll follow up with her, ma'am," Tony told her.

She got up and disappeared down a hallway. After a minute or two, she came back with a piece of paper in her hand. "Here's her number."

With the paper, she handed me a picture. A picture of her and a tall man that I assumed was Kent. He had her honey-colored eyes and warm brown skin.

"He looked just like you," I said.

The comment elicited a smile from Mrs. Barnum. "People used to always say that when he was younger. He was my twin. My only son..." Her voice trailed off.

"Was he in any trouble?" asked Tony. "Having any problems with anyone?"

"Oh no. He was such a good boy. He got along with everyone. Everyone loved him. As far as I know, he didn't have any problems with anyone. But Courtney would probably know better. Even though we were close—we talked every week—there are still certain things you don't tell your mother." She smiled weakly. "He was such a good boy."

Kent was in his thirties, and yet I couldn't help but notice how she still called him her *boy*. It was like even though he was a grown man, he was still and would always be her little boy. For a second, I wondered if that was how my mother felt about me. Was that why it was so hard for her to let me go? I guess no matter how old we got, we would always be our mother's babies.

*Should definitely call my mother when I get home.*

"Did they live together?" asked Tony.

Mrs. Barnum shook her head. "I know they were talking about it, but I don't think they settled on it yet."

"Okay."

I stood up, and Tony followed suit.

"Is there anyone you want us to call for you? Someone to come by and sit with you?" I asked.

The corner of her mouth curved into a slight smile. "You're sweet to ask, but no. There is no one else now that he's gone. I guess I should get used to this now."

Tony handed her his card. "If you think of anything, don't hesitate to give us a call."

"Thank you."

I followed Tony to the front door with Mrs. Barnum following close behind. She closed the door behind us.

"Do you think that's weird?" Tony asked as soon as we got back in the car.

"Which part?"

"The part about the girlfriend. I read through the file that the detective left with us. The body was in the house for four days before someone found it. And that was because of the neighbor. He smelled something foul coming from the house. Where was she?"

I opened my mouth to say something but stopped.

"I can understand the mom not jumping to conclusions after she hadn't heard from him in a couple of days. They talked every week, okay. Maybe it was only once a week, and maybe she didn't want to be nosy and pry into his life. Some mothers are like that. I mean, not mine, but maybe she thought he would call her when he got a minute. But the girlfriend? They were talking about living together—which to me says she was spending a lot of nights over there."

He had a point. But we couldn't jump to conclusions. Yeah, it was weird that she just so happened to not be at his house— or even to have heard from him—for the four to five days Kent's body was rotting in the living room, but maybe there was a logical explanation.

# CHAPTER NINE

SENT A TEXT TO SPECIAL AGENT BALDWIN ASKING HER FOR the address of Kent's girlfriend, Courtney Fox. It took her less than five minutes to get back to me, and we immediately headed over.

We weren't sure whether she was at work or not, but we went to her place anyway. By the time we pulled into the driveway, Baldwin had sent over everything she learned about Courtney, including where she worked.

"If she's not here, we'll head over to her job and see if they've seen her," said Tony as he got out of the car.

It looked like she was home. A shiny, new BMW was parked in the driveway. As we walked down the driveway, Tony placed a hand on the hood of the car to see if it was warm. He looked at me and shook his head.

So the car had been there awhile. Maybe she hadn't gotten up yet. Or maybe she was dead. It was strange that she hadn't tried to contact Kent in the past few days.

Tony knocked on the door. While we waited, I took a moment to survey the street. It was in a nice little neighborhood, quiet and pretty empty, about twenty minutes away from Kent's neighborhood. Most people were probably at work by now. But not Courtney. Or her neighbors across the street.

She lived in a one-story house with a black door. The house was painted white with black trim. Her yard was nice and neat. Freshly cut. The smell of freshly cut grass hung in the air around her door.

Tony knocked again. This time there was the sound of heavy footsteps barreling toward the door. It opened swiftly and cut me by surprise.

The woman opened her mouth and then stopped. It was clear by the look on her face that she'd been expecting someone else. Her brows furrowed as her eyes flicked from me to Tony and back again.

"Courtney Fox?" I asked.

She looked at me, blue eyes getting darker as the seconds ticked by.

"Who are you?" There was an edge to her voice that told me she was already annoyed and it wasn't by us.

This time I got to flash my badge. "I'm Special Agent Storm, and this is my partner, Special Agent Walker."

Her eyes went wide with surprise. "Oh! Wait… what?"

"Can we speak with you for a moment? Inside?"

She looked at me for a long moment before stepping back and allowing us to enter her home. She closed the door behind us. The house was almost as hot inside as it was outside. The smell of sweat mixed with something sweet.

"Sorry for the heat. My AC went out yesterday."

We followed her to the living room, where she told us to have a seat. By the time we sat down, Tony and I had both taken our jackets off. He rolled up the sleeves of his shirt, and I finally got a proper peek at his tattoo. It looked like a row of triangles across his forearm. Maybe when we got to know each other a little better, I would ask him about them.

Courtney's living room was small and quaint. There was a sofa and a loveseat, along with a TV and a small bookcase. The sofa was by the window. Something to be thankful for. A light breeze floated in. The cool air mixed with the beads of sweat coasting down my neck sent a shiver through me.

"What is this about?" she sat on the loveseat.

"Kent Barnum."

She rolled her eyes. "What about him?"

"Well," started Tony, "he's been murdered."

Courtney gasped. Her mouth fell open. "Seriously?" She drew in a shaky breath, and her eyes brimmed with tears. She angrily blinked them away. "What happened?"

"Well, we were hoping you could tell us," I said. "He was your boyfriend."

Her shoulders dropped. "*Was* being the key word there. Kent broke up with me a month ago."

*That answers that.*

"I see. Why?"

She shrugged.

"He broke up with you for no reason?" Tony cocked his head to the side. "That seems strange."

I glanced around the room. Her house wasn't the picture of wealth or anything, but it was still pretty nice. She was gorgeous and clearly did well for herself, and to hear Kent's mother tell it, they were truly in love. Why would Kent have abruptly broken up with her?

She tucked a blond strand behind her ear. Her roots were dark—black, I think. Courtney had the kind of beauty rich men fell for. Almond-shaped eyes, full lips, and the kind of body other women would kill for.

"He said he was tired… bored, I think. He said I had nothing to offer him and I was getting older. It was time to end things." Her voice was barely above a whisper. I had to strain my ears just to make out the last of it.

"So he tossed you aside for someone new?" There wasn't an ounce of empathy in Tony's voice.

Courtney glanced out the window. "Really making me feel better right now," she griped.

I nudged Tony with my elbow as subtly as I could to get him to cut it out. Not that he was wrong, but he could use a little more tact, all things considered.

I put on a much kinder voice. "A month ago was the last time you saw him?"

She nodded slowly. "He said that, and then he left. The next morning all my stuff was dropped off at my door. And then that was it. He wouldn't answer my phone calls. Nothing."

"Was he having problems with anyone?"

She sighed. "He didn't really talk to me about business. He did have a business partner, uh… Joshua Hayes. I think that's his name. They were having some problems. They didn't see eye to eye on something, but he never told me what it was."

"Okay. And where were you last week?" asked Tony.

"Every day? I went to work, and then I came home."

"Alone?" asked Tony.

Courtney blinked back tears. It was hard to tell if she wanted to cry over his death or if she was still upset about the breakup.

"Yes, alone. Always alone. Even though I know you don't believe me. My neighbor across the street has one of those doorbell camera things. And my next-door neighbor has security cameras outside his house. You can probably see when I get home and when I left on them."

"Okay. We will check those out."

"Was anything… anything out of the ordinary happening the last few weeks?" I asked.

She shrugged. "I don't know. He had been really distant lately. But I just thought it was a problem at work. He could be an asshole sometimes and rub people the wrong way. He had a knack for that. But I don't think… I just don't see someone killing him for it."

I nodded. Tears streamed from the corners of her eyes. She wiped them away.

"He broke up with me. Not even because I did anything wrong. He just wanted someone younger. I shouldn't be crying over him." She took the sleeve of her shirt and pulled it over her fingers to wipe her tears away.

"What your brain knows and what your heart wants aren't always in sync. Your heart will catch up," I told her. "If you think of anything else, please give us a call."

I handed her my card, and she nodded.

"We'll see ourselves out."

Tony followed me to the front door. It was hotter in the house than it was outside. The cool breeze felt great against my skin.

"We should head back to the field office," said Tony.

I agreed.

Kent's girlfriend was a bust. Although usually when someone was killed, it was by someone close to him. But she seemed more hurt than angry. I couldn't picture her killing him like that. Not beating him to death.

And women didn't usually kill that way. There were more women poisoners than anything. But if she was angry enough, she could have beaten him to death. That would explain why there were no defensive wounds. Maybe he didn't think she would really go through with it. But still, it didn't feel right.

"I don't think she did it," said Tony.

"Yeah, I was just working that out in my head."

"But I'm still going to call the techs and ask them to come out and get the camera footage from the neighbors to make sure."

"Makes sense."

"Glad you agree."

We drove back to the office. I wanted to do more research into what kind of company Kent worked at. And more information about his business partner. Special Agent Baldwin could have done it for us, but when we got back, she was busy on two other cases.

"You take the company, and I'll do the business partner," Tony said as he sat in his chair.

"Works for me."

Kent had started a finance company close to seven years ago. It looked like the company was doing really well. The workers worked from home, so there was no real office space for them to go to. But Kent did rent an office space downtown where he seemed to work.

I guess working from home by yourself could be pretty monotonous. He would go there a few days a week to get some work done. His partner, Joshua, also worked there most days.

"Well, on paper, the company looks legit."

"But...?" Tony looked up from his screen. "It sounded like there was a *but* coming."

I shrugged. "I don't know. It just seems like there's more to this. I'm thinking whatever problems he and his business partner were having, it was over money."

"Well, Joshua Hayes is from New York. He worked at a finance firm there, and when they didn't make him partner, he left and started a new business. Kent joined, and thus you have Barnum and Hayes Financing."

"Thus?"

He shrugged. "You want to check the office space? Or go by his house?"

"Both."

He nodded. "Okay."

Joshua wasn't home. He lived in a nice neighborhood with large houses overlooking the ocean. I couldn't help but notice the house was much nicer than the neighborhood was compared to Kent's. I mean, both houses were nice. But Joshua's house looked like it was Kent's house's older brother or something. Bigger and shinier and much more expensive.

And that was just what we could see from the outside.

"Look," I said. I pointed to the newspapers sitting outside the front door. They were neatly stacked in front of the door, tucked in the corner so people walking by couldn't see them. A quick peek into the metal mailbox nailed to the side of the house revealed that it was full of envelopes.

"Joshua hasn't been here for a long time," I noted. "Either he's dead too—"

"Or it's possible that he killed Kent and he is in the wind," answered Tony.

"Maybe the neighbors know something."

Tony nodded, and we walked over to one of the houses. To the right was a beautiful house. Floor-to-ceiling windows in the front and a glass door.

"That makes me anxious," said Tony. "Too many windows in the front. Everybody can see in and watch you."

"What are you doing in the front rooms of your house?"

Tony shot me a look, and I stopped talking.

"Never mind."

He laughed. "Well, now we know you have a dirty mind."

The door opened then. The heat that had risen to my cheeks slowly dissipated.

"How can I help you?"

An older woman with short black hair and red-rimmed glasses stood in the doorway. She wiped her hands on a black-and-white apron.

We flashed our badges.

"We want to ask you a few questions about your neighbor."

"Oh, Mr. Franklin!" The woman stepped back to let us enter. She closed the door behind us just as I heard footsteps coming down the stairs.

"This is the FBI. They want to ask about Mr. Hayes," she said to a man walking down the hallway.

He took off his glasses. "Um… hello." He shook our hands. "Joel Franklin."

"Special Agent Walker and this is my partner, Special Agent Storm. We just have a few questions about your neighbor."

He gave a small nod before leading us into the living room. The room was so white I was afraid to touch anything, let alone sit down. White rug, white sofa, and white chairs. White walls. White bookcases. Everything was white, except for the coffee table and the side table, which was glass with a gold trim.

I was afraid to sit down. I think Tony was too, because when we stepped into the room, he stayed by the entrance.

"This will only take a few minutes," he said.

"Okay. I'm not really sure how much help I can be though."

"Not a close neighborhood?" I asked.

He looked at me for a long moment before he answered, "I wouldn't say that. Just… Josh kept to himself, you know? He didn't socialize much. It's not like we were having neighbor-hood cookouts or anything. We say hello in the morning and when we get home."

"When was the last time you saw him?" I asked.

Franklin paused. "I'm not sure. I know it's been a few days since I saw his car in the driveway."

"How long is a few days?" Tony moved further into the room.

He shrugged. "A week maybe. I just assumed he went out of town or something."

That would make sense. Maybe he just went out of town on a business trip.

"Does he go out of town a lot?" I glanced back at Tony, who was staring at the floor.

"I wouldn't say a lot. He does usually let us know. Oh, and he tells the post office to hold his mail."

"And the newspaper?" asked Tony.

He nodded. "Yeah. Definitely. This is a pretty good neighborhood, but you can't be too careful. You don't want a lot of people to know that you aren't home and haven't been for a while."

"Have you seen or noticed anything strange going on? In the neighborhood?"

He looked at me, brows slowly knitting together. "Is Josh in some kind of trouble?"

"We're just following up on an investigation, is all," Tony said smoothly.

Franklin folded his arms across his chest. "I wouldn't say strange, but… he has been a little jumpy. Or a little scared, I guess."

"What do you mean?"

"I see him sometimes looking behind him when he walks into the house. Like he's afraid someone would jump out of the bushes and get him while his back was turned. That's out of character. And the surveillance cameras outside the house are new. Within the last few weeks, I think."

"Okay." I looked back at Tony, who nodded. "Well, thank you for your time." I handed him my card. "If you think of anything else or see anything strange, or if you see Mr. Hayes, please give us a call."

"I will. Geez, I hope he's okay."

I smiled. "He's probably on a work trip and forgot to tell anyone. Happens a lot."

His right eyebrow ticked up as he stared at me. His mouth opened like he was going to ask me something, but I turned around and followed Tony to the front door.

He was probably going to ask, if Joshua was just on a business trip, then why was the FBI looking into it? And I didn't feel like having that conversation right then.

We got in the car and headed over to Barnum's and Hayes's office space. He wasn't there either.

"I'm starting to think that Joshua may be on the run," said Tony.

I still didn't want to jump to conclusions. There could have been a million explanations as to why we couldn't find him. Maybe he was already out of town before Kent was killed. Or maybe he was on a business trip and had no idea what had happened.

Even if he left after Kent was murdered, that didn't mean that Joshua murdered him. I was trying to keep an open mind. I didn't want to get too fixated on one suspect. Not this early. When you develop tunnel vision, you would miss everything else. And I didn't want to miss anything. Not this early in the case.

But it was suspicious that we couldn't find him.

# CHAPTER TEN

WHEN WE GOT BACK TO THE OFFICE, SPECIAL AGENT Baldwin put out a BOLO on Joshua Hayes, labeling him a person of interest in a homicide.

"Hopefully, we will have something in the morning," said Tony.

We were done for the day. Officially out of leads to look through. And we couldn't do anything about the second body until his identity was confirmed.

When I went home, after making sure the door was locked, I took a hot shower. As hot as I could stand it. I wanted to scrub the day away.

After my shower, I slipped into my pajamas, plopped on the sofa, and took out my personal cell phone.

My mother's voice was warm and comforting on the other line, even though a quick glance at my clock showed that it was past eleven at night back home. As soon as I heard her, the tension that had been building up in my shoulders instantly dissipated.

"Are you okay? You don't sound like it."

A smile eased onto my face. Every time I called her, she always asked me the same questions:

"Are you okay?"

"Are you eating enough?"

"Are you getting enough sleep?"

And maybe it was because of my conversation with Kent's mom today, but her questions didn't get on my nerves. Usually, I would want to remind her that I was an adult and could take care of myself. That I didn't need her worrying about me, and if anything was wrong, I would tell her and she should let me live my life. But none of those words bubbled up to the surface. It was nice to hear her voice. To hear the worry and the concern woven around every syllable.

"Yeah, Mom. I'm okay. I just got my first case today, and it's nothing like I thought it was going to be."

"Is that good or bad?"

I sighed. I wasn't sure how to answer the question. Was it a good thing? Was it bad?

Two men had lost their lives, and I had to investigate their murders. I was expecting something easy. Something to ease me into this line of work, and this case was not that. I had a sinking feeling that it was only going to get worse.

I told her what I was thinking—skimping on the gruesome details, of course.

"Well, you always did love a good puzzle. And I think you got it. You can do this."

Her belief in me warmed my heart. But I wasn't so sure.

In the morning, I went through my usual routine. I woke up, downed a protein shake, and went for a run—and was glad to not stumble upon another random murder scene this time. The run invigorated me pretty well, and I laid out a black button-down and a pair of slacks before stepping into the shower.

Before I could even dry off, my phone rang. "Yeah?"

"Officers brought Joshua into the field office," Tony said brusquely. "Figured you would want to know. I'll swing by and pick you up if you want me to."

Him picking me up would mean I didn't have to drive.

"Sure. If it's not a problem."

"Yeah. I'll be there in ten."

I hung up the phone and hurried to get dressed. By the time I was all ready and sprinted downstairs for a cup of coffee, Tony was knocking on my door.

"Hey. Come on in. You want some coffee?"

"Sure."

Tony stepped into my house, and I closed the door behind him. I led him into the kitchen.

He whistled. "This is nice."

I laughed. "Thanks."

My house was kind of small, but it fit my needs. It kind of reminded me of a cottage. Maybe that was why I liked it so much. I always wanted a small cottage by a lake or someplace quiet. I poured him a cup of coffee, and we sat at the breakfast bar.

"So how was your night?" He took a slow sip of coffee and smiled. "Not bad?"

"I came home, talked to my mother, heated some leftovers, and then went to bed."

He chuckled. "That sounds boring."

"It wasn't bad. Business as usual really."

"Yeah, but you live in Hawaii now."

"I'm still trying to get my bearings."

He shook his head. "Not a good excuse. You need to get out there more."

"You just met me."

He shrugged. "You live here now. You need to get out there and be among the locals. People around here won't open up to you if they still consider you an outsider. That's just the way it is."

I sighed. He was right. I wasn't getting out much. I was just so focused on work and trying to put my best foot forward at the office that nothing else mattered.

Kelsey told me once that I had tunnel vision. Once I was focused on a goal, I refused to see anything else or let anything else distract me.

"I'm just trying to focus on being a great agent, Tony."

"That can be a good thing. But sometimes it can mean you are missing out on the world around you," he said.

"I will try to do better," I said.

Tony nodded. "*Mahalo.*"

I raised an eyebrow at that. "And what are you thanking me for?"

"Not annoying me," he fired right back.

Despite myself, I snorted. "Finish your damn coffee."

On our way to the field office, Tony explained that the officers found Joshua at the airport trying to buy a plane ticket.

"Pretty suspicious to me," he said.

"But if he killed Kent, then why would he kill the second victim—and then wait this long to try to skip town?"

"Nobody ever accused criminals of being the smartest bunch," Tony pointed out.

He was right, in a sense. But I still couldn't square it all together.

We walked into the interrogation room, and he jumped up from his seat, visibly irritated.

"Are you serious? Finally. I've been waiting since two in the morning," he ranted. "You have no right to hold me here. I've done nothing wrong."

"Okay," I started. "Would you like to know why we are holding you, or do you just want to yell at us?"

His back straightened. His fist clenched and unclenched at his side. I gestured to his seat, and he sat down.

"Your business partner, Kent Barnum, was killed. And we were hoping you would be able to help us catch his murderer."

"Unless you did it, of course," added Tony.

Joshua jumped back up. His mouth opened, but no words came out. He was maybe in his late thirties, with a hint of gray entering his brown hair, caramel-colored eyes, and a square jaw. There was something about the way he looked at us.

Fear framed his eyes. He knew something.

"Kent… I… didn't kill him. I would never kill anyone," he said quietly.

"So why run?" asked Tony.

We sat at the table, and Joshua eased back into his chair. His brows slowly knitted together as he stared at the table.

"I knew he was dead. I knew it. Especially after I kept calling and he wouldn't pick up. And I knew how it would look. Because we had problems, I would probably be the first suspect. So I figured it best to get out of town."

He was afraid of something. But that was a stupid reason to leave. He looked more suspicious now than he did before.

"Why were you and Kent having problems?"

Joshua bit his lip. "He was…"—he took in a long shaky breath—"moving money." He said the last part so fast the words ran into each other.

"Moving money?" Tony stared at Joshua, waiting for him to explain.

"Yeah. Some of the accounts weren't adding up, and… listen, I don't know what he was doing. Or what was going on. As soon as I saw the discrepancy, I confronted him about it. He kept saying that everything was fine. He just had to cover an account that was overdrawn and he would put the money back."

"What account was overdrawn?" I asked.

Joshua shrugged. "I don't know. I couldn't tell from looking at the records, which made me think it was a personal account. And that's what pissed me off. He was playing with our clients' money, and that could ruin us. We could go to prison. But he kept saying not to worry."

"Why didn't you turn him in?" asked Tony.

Joshua sighed. "He was one of my best friends. I didn't want him to go to federal prison or something. He said he would put the money back. He just needed some time. So I gave it to him.

I told him he had until the end of next month when the quarter ends to put the money back. And he said okay."

"Was he into gambling or something that would take a lot of money?" I asked.

If he had a gambling problem, that could explain why his personal accounts were overdrawn. If he owed someone money, that could explain why he wanted to take the client's money to get this other person off his back.

Joshua shook his head. "I don't think so. Gambling doesn't really seem like him. But then again, neither did stealing from our clients, so what do I know?"

"Do you know a Ricky Thompson? Did Kent?"

"Ricky Thompson," Joshua said the name slowly, pronouncing every syllable. As if saying it slowly would draw up some kind of memory. He shook his head. "I don't think so. The name doesn't sound familiar. I'm not sure about Kent though."

"Okay." I glanced at Tony.

"How... I mean, how did he die?"

"He was beaten to death," answered Tony.

Joshua's face fell. He shook his head. "What the hell was he into?" he whispered into his hands.

"Where were you two weeks ago?"

Joshua explained that he was in New York for three days and then had to go to LA. He had just come back a couple of days ago. We would have to check his alibi, but if it held up, there was no way he could have killed either victim.

"Well, wait here. We need to check your alibi," said Tony. "If it checks out, then you can go."

Joshua nodded.

I walked back to my desk. Something deep in the pit of my stomach told me he didn't do it. He seemed so broken hearing about Kent. So sad.

"I don't think he did it," said Tony as he sat at his desk.

"Yeah, I was just thinking that. I wonder if he owed someone money or something."

Tony leaned back in his chair, his hands folded on his stomach. "Could be. But loan sharks wouldn't kill him. If they killed him, they wouldn't get their money."

"True. Not unless they have an insurance policy on him. Then killing him may be the only way they would ever get their money."

A smile tugged at the corner of his lips. He wasn't expecting me to know that. I tried not to show how happy I was to surprise him.

"That is a good point. Okay, so we should check if there are any insurance policies on him."

"And I want to know more about that personal overdrawn account. How much was it overdrawn?"

That was a job for the IT department. I was good with a computer, but when it came to getting into people's accounts and banking information, we needed help.

They got back to us just before lunch.

"Wow!" My voice was louder than I had intended. A few special agents looked my way for a moment before going back to their work.

"What is it?" Tony jumped up and walked over to my side. He looked at my computer screen and whistled. "That's a big number."

"I know. I've never seen that much money in my life. What the hell was he doing? What would you even spend that much money on? A house?"

"He already had a house. Doubt he was buying another one." Tony walked back over to his seat.

At some point, Kent's account had been overdrawn by over two hundred thousand dollars. How could someone let that happen? How could you let your account get overdrawn that much—and what was he spending it on?

"Do you think this has something to do with the second victim?"

Tony looked from his screen to me and back again. "I mean, it's clear that the cases are related. But I'm not sure if his accounts have anything to do with it."

There was a loud ding from his computer. "Okay. Give me a second." After a few minutes, he stood up. "Joshua's alibi checked out. He was in New York around the time Kent was killed."

"He could have hired someone."

Tony sighed. "That is true."

I stood up. "Still don't think he did it though."

"Also true."

I followed him to the interrogation room.

"Looks like you were in New York when Kent was killed."

Joshua nodded. "Yeah, I was."

"Did Kent have any problems with anyone? Anyone that would want to hurt him?" I asked.

Joshua regarded the question for a long moment. "He was jumping from one woman to the next. He would tell her she was his everything, and they were going to get married and move in together. And then he would come across someone younger and prettier, and he—"

"Would move on," I finished.

He nodded. "That was his MO. I told him he could only do that so many times before it backfired. I don't know if any of the women were angry enough to kill him though."

"Okay."

"He also had problems with his neighbor. Um, I can't remember his name. He lived in the house on the left. They were always getting into screaming matches about property lines and the guy making too much noise."

I looked at Tony, and he nodded.

Didn't a neighbor find the body?

# CHAPTER ELEVEN

THE NEIGHBOR JOSHUA WAS TALKING ABOUT WAS ALLEN Craster. He lived to the left of Kent in a big house with large front windows and a sage-green door.

When we pulled into the driveway, the front door opened. A huge mountain of a man with black hair and a full beard stood in the doorway. He had to be at least six feet four, and his arms were so muscular it looked like he couldn't put them down by his sides.

"That guy could have beaten someone to death," muttered Tony as we walked up the driveway.

"Definitely."

I took out my badge and held it up as we walked to the front door.

"The FBI," he said. His voice didn't match his body.

Where his body was manly and muscular and a little scary, his voice was light. Gentle. Like a child's, almost. I swallowed a laugh.

"This about Kent?"

I nodded.

"We heard you and he had some problems," said Tony.

"He was an arrogant asshole who thought he owned the street and could do whatever he wanted. The property line was wherever he said it was."

"And that pissed you off?" I asked.

"Of course. The mother—*he* cut down my trees because he said it was infringing on his property." Allen pointed to the tree stumps on the side of his property. They were close to the fence, but not that close.

"A couple of leaves fell over the fence, and he had a problem with it. It was just a couple of leaves. He said it made his property look unkempt. So he cut them down. Those trees were there before he was."

"You could have sued him big for that, you know," said Tony. "Five or six figures, easy."

Allen's eyes flashed. "What?"

"You didn't know that?" he asked. "Tree law is a real big deal. You'd be compensated for the cost not just of replacing the tree, and the firewood, but the value of several thirty- to forty-year-old trees on your property."

Allen ran a hand through his beard, clearly shocked. "Well, I... damn. Would it be too late to sue him after the fact?"

"I'm sure you can look that up, Mr. Craster," I cut in. "What other problems did you have with him?"

He finally turned to me. "He had problems with my music. Said it was too loud. Mind you, no one else on the street complained. He didn't like my friend's cars being parked in front of my house. Said it was too close to his driveway."

"He does sound like an asshole," said Tony.

"Right! I didn't say anything about his visitors at all hours of the night."

"What visitors?" I asked.

He shrugged. "I don't know who they were. But seems like every other night, there was a dark SUV pulling up to his house."

"Did you see anyone get out?" asked Tony.

He shook his head. "No, they pulled into the garage. Which was weird because Kent never did that. He always parked in the driveway. But the SUV would pull into the garage, stay for a few hours, and then drive away. The windows were tinted, so I couldn't see in. It was just strange, you know."

"Yeah, that does sound weird," I said. "Did you notice anything strange before his body was found?"

Allen looked over at the house for a long moment. "You know, there was a black car on the street. It wasn't in front of Kent's house. It was a few houses down. I say it's strange because it was there almost every day for a few weeks."

"And now?" I asked.

"Haven't seen it in a couple weeks. That was weird. But other than that, no, nothing weird."

I glanced around the perimeter of his house. He didn't have any surveillance cameras.

"Okay, well, thank you for your time. If you think of anything else, give us a call." I handed him my card.

As we walked back to the car, something just didn't feel right.

"What are you thinking?" asked Tony.

The engine turned over, and he slowly pulled out of the driveway.

"I don't know. I don't think it was the neighbor or Joshua."

"Is that tree thing true?" I asked.

He nodded. "Oh yeah. You'd be surprised by how many people get into disputes about trees. Anyway, my brain keeps landing on Ricky Thompson."

"Yeah, something about that whole situation doesn't sit right."

"I wonder if he knew Kent?"

"Let's go ask him," said Tony.

And so we did.

"You two again?" The annoyance in Ricky's voice was loud and clear when we returned to the Teletech building.

It struck me as odd. People handled things differently. What one person might find strange or worrying might not bother someone else. But even if I had so much money that I didn't know what to do with it, I would still be interested to know why my account number was written on the chest of a murder victim.

I mean, I would have questions. And I would close out that account and move the money somewhere else. But Ricky didn't seem to care. Not about the account or the dead body.

"What do you want now?" He stood in the doorway of his office. He didn't invite us in.

"We wanted to know if you knew anyone named Kent Barnum?" asked Tony.

I watched Ricky. He blinked. His expressionless mask fell for a second, and I saw surprise and then sorrow pass over his face.

And then his arms folded across his chest. The mask was back in place.

"No, can't say that I do. Why?"

"That's the body we found. Your account number was etched into his skin—"

"He didn't have ties to me," he said calmly. He glared at me, as if daring me to say something else.

"He had your account number etched into his chest. I think that would constitute as *a tie to you,* don't you think?"

He scoffed. "Can you two leave now? I have an important business meeting."

"Do you have any enemies?" I pressed. "Anyone that hates you so much they would frame you for murder? Or that would want to get your attention?"

For a split second, fear flashed in his eyes. It was so brief. If I hadn't been looking at him, I would have missed it.

"No. I don't do anything that would garner that kind of attention."

"An ex-employee maybe?" I asked. "Firing someone would make them hate you."

"No, I... well... it's nothing. It's probably nothing."

"Who?" asked Tony.

Ricky sighed. "Calvin Robertson. I had to fire him. He wasn't focusing and kept messing up the code. I told him once he got himself together, he could come back. He was angry. I don't know if he was angry enough to do this, but he was certainly pissed."

"Do you still have his information?" asked Tony.

Ricky glanced at his secretary.

She nodded. "I'll get it for you."

"Is that it? Are we done?" he complained.

"For now," I said. I moved to follow Tony and the secretary out to the main floor but turned back just before leaving the room. "Respectfully, Mr. Thompson, I'd recommend that you take this a little more seriously. This could certainly be taken as a credible threat on your life, and you seem to want to treat it like a minor inconvenience."

He smiled tightly. "Have a good day, Agent."

"Sir—"

"Close the door behind you, if you don't mind."

It was clear I wasn't getting any further with Ricky Thompson, and I didn't have anywhere near enough evidence to actually arrest him for anything, so I just gave him a nod and left. What was his deal?

Once we were back out in the main floor, his secretary handed us a slip of paper with Calvin's information on it.

"Did you know Calvin?" asked Tony.

She chewed on her bottom lip for a second before answering, "Yeah. He was nice until… his mom died. A few months before he was fired. She was everything to him. It was, like, real sudden. I think it was something to do with her heart, but I can't be sure. After that, it was just hard for him to focus, you know?"

I nodded. "Thank you."

If one of my parents died, I would definitely have a hard time trying to do my job. If he had no one else, no other tethers to this world, I could see him going off the deep end. The firing might have been the last straw. But would that be enough to brutally murder a random man who might or might not have had a connection to Ricky?

"You want to head over there now?" Tony asked.

"Yeah, we might as well. We can pick up something to eat on the way back."

The weather had been nice that morning. There was a slight breeze, not too cool and not too hot. But whatever coolness had been in the air that morning had evaporated completely. I rolled up my sleeves before I got in the car.

Calvin didn't live in the nicest neighborhood. The houses were a little run-down. Practically shacks compared to the other neighborhoods we had visited on this case.

We pulled up to his address. It was a small one-story house with a light-pink door. The rust-colored car in the driveway was dented, and part of the bumper was coming off.

"Did he get into some kind of accident or something?" I walked by the car, inspecting it carefully.

"It's not a black car with tinted windows, but he could have rented one."

The front door jerked open.

"What are you doing?" The man's voice was loud and forceful.

Tony showed his badge. The man deflated a little.

"Why are you looking at my car?"

"Are you Calvin Robertson?" I asked.

He glared at me. He was younger than I had expected. He looked like he could have been a couple of years older than me, with a mop of dark-brown curls on his head. He adjusted his gold-rimmed glasses before answering yes.

"We're here to talk to you about your boss at Teletech, Ricky Thompson." Tony moved toward him, slowly. Each step slow and purposeful. Like how you walked up on an animal you weren't sure was dangerous or not.

"You mean my *ex*-boss?" Calvin spit. "The asshole has all the warmth and decency of a cockroach."

I let myself smile at that. I was inclined to agree. "What have you been up to in the last few weeks?"

"Mostly just looking for a new job. Since he fired me." Calvin spit out the last words. He was still angry about losing his job. But his body language just didn't scream killer to me. I mean, he could have done it, sure, but…

"What is this about? Really? Did something happen to him? Because I didn't do anything. Or is this because of what I found?"

Tony and I traded a look and frowned. "What did you find?" he asked.

Calvin relaxed slightly. "I found some accounts that were strange. Someone, I don't know who, was funneling money through them."

"What do you mean?" asked Tony.

"Money would go into this account, and then it would disperse in several directions. An account over here. An account over there. But I couldn't tell where the money was coming from. It wasn't any of our investors. And then the accounts the money went to weren't any of ours either. I thought someone was doing something they shouldn't have, so I brought it to the boss."

"And let me guess," I said. "You were fired not soon after."

"Barely a week. My mother had died a little while before, and he blamed it on that. Said I was distracted, but I wasn't. I don't think I was. I know what I saw. There was something weird going on."

"Thanks for your time," I said.

Calvin nodded. His eyes darted between me and Tony. He looked uneasy. Like he was afraid to walk away. Afraid that we were playing a trick on him and weren't just going to let him go back into his house.

"It's okay, Calvin. You can go back inside." I tried to make my voice sound as reassuring as possible. It must have worked, because he looked at Tony one last time and then quickly rushed back into his house.

"That was weird." Tony looked back at me.

I nodded. It was strange. The whole thing was strange. Calvin's reaction to us and the accounts he was talking about. He looked like he was afraid of something—or better yet, someone. Was it his boss?

And what about those accounts?

We got back in the car and headed back to the field office. All the while, I kept turning over the conversation in my head. Something about Ricky Thompson didn't make sense. What was he hiding? And was it worth killing people over?

# CHAPTER TWELVE

S OLVING CASES WAS NOTHING LIKE IT WAS IN THE MOV-
ies or on TV. I knew it wouldn't be, but I'd always kind of
hoped it would. Everything seemed to happen so fast on
TV. DNA evidence was logged and identified in a day, sometimes a few hours. The detectives often had a suspect hours
after finding the body, and once the bad guy was confronted
in the final showdown, they finally cracked and said anything.

But that was Hollywood. If the shows were more accurate,
no one would watch them. No one wanted to watch people take
weeks or months to solve a case or get any leads.

Tony and I had nothing. Something in my gut told me that
everything led back to Ricky Thompson, but that's all it was.
A hunch.

"Can't get a warrant based on how you feel about someone. That's not how the justice system is supposed to work. Find something that ties him to the murders, and then come back."

While Davies was right, we were right too. It wasn't just a hunch. I mean, it was because we didn't have any evidence, but it was something else.

Ricky's attitude about the murders and his account number being on the first body didn't add up. He wasn't worried or anything. And when we asked him about Kent, he knew something. He *definitely* knew him. There was something about his expression that still didn't sit right with me.

There was just something the man him that I didn't like. And maybe it was his smug attitude. Or maybe I was right.

*They are going to trust your instincts.* I had to keep telling myself that because, in truth, I didn't have any instincts. I didn't know anything about solving cases. I had never solved one before. I had to prove myself for them to trust me.

So we had to find something that made it clear Ricky was involved in some way.

"I'm not saying he killed them," I said for the fifth or nineteenth time as we got out of the car and headed up to the building.

"I hope not, because that wouldn't make any sense," said Tony. "Why kill them and then leave behind evidence on one body that leads to you? I mean, his account number?"

"I know. But someone is using the bodies to talk to him. And he knows who it is."

"We can't prove that," said Tony.

We walked into the building. The air-conditioning was a welcome change from the heat outside.

The heat in Hawaii was different, and I felt stupid for thinking. I didn't know what I thought the climate was going to be like. I mean, it's an island.

"I know this. And I understand this. And yet, how did the person get his account number if they don't know each other?"

Tony shrugged as we waited for the elevator doors to open on our floor. The doors opened, and we stepped out into the hallway.

Special Agent Baldwin waved at us and immediately jerked a thumb to her left. My gaze followed her finger to Kent Barnum's mother. She stood up as soon as she saw us.

"What is she doing here?" asked Tony.

We both walked over to our desks to put our things down, and then we walked over to her.

Tony pulled up the sleeves of his white shirt. "Uh, Mrs. Barnum, we haven't found out anything about—"

"I know. I figured if you had learned something, you would have called me by now."

"Right," I said. "What can we do for you?"

She looked around and then leaned forward. "Can we talk somewhere?"

I nodded. Tony and I led her to the conference room. Once in there, I closed the door behind us. It hadn't been long since we had last seen Mrs. Barnum. Barely a day or two. And yet she looked like she had aged at least twenty years.

The bags under her bloodshot eyes were massive and dark. She looked like she had been crying nonstop since we last saw her.

Tony gestured for her to sit in the chair at the head of the table. She did.

"I just wanted to ask you about… well, I heard rumors about… his girlfriend maybe having something to do with it."

I blinked. We had talked to his girlfriend—well, his ex-girlfriend—but she didn't have anything to do with the murder.

"I see," said Tony. He looked at me, eyebrows raised.

I shrugged. I was curious about what was being said about the investigation. People talked. And when someone close to you had been murdered and no one had been arrested, all kinds of theories got tossed out. Some made sense, but most didn't. I wondered what they were saying.

"What kind of rumors have you heard?" I asked.

Mrs. Barnum sighed. "Someone said she killed him. Someone said she knows what happened. I heard his business partner, Josh, did it. I heard he was into some strange things…"

"Strange how?" Tony leaned forward, his elbows resting on the table.

Mrs. Barnum looked down at her hands in her lap. She bit her lip. From her reaction, I figured *strange things* meant something sexual.

"I heard something about escorts or something like that. I know he has—*had* a lot of relationships. He seemed to move through women pretty quickly. I kept telling him he needed to settle down. Find a wife. But…"—she shrugged—"he just never seemed interested in getting married and having children. He liked having arm candy, you know. A nice young girl on his arm. Some of them may have been escorts, I don't know. I thought Courtney would have been different. But maybe…"

"You think this had something to do with his death?" I asked. I mean, it was an angle, but it didn't feel right. Why would an escort want him dead?

She shrugged. "I don't know. That's just what I heard."

"Who did you hear it from?" asked Tony.

"Um… George Makaio. He's an old friend of Kent's." She wrote down George's information on Tony's notepad. "I'm sorry. I don't have more to add. I just… was hearing so many different things, and I was hoping you had some answers."

"We're sorry we don't have any. Not yet. It's still early in the investigation, and we are still trying to run down leads."

"And no one has mentioned anything about escorts until now." Tony stood up. He stretched out his hand to help Mrs. Barnum up.

She took it and eased out of the chair onto her feet with an audible sigh. She looked so tired. So drained from worrying about what happened to her son.

We thanked her for coming in. Tony followed her to the elevator. He returned a minute later, his jaw set, eyes narrowing at his desk.

"Escorts?"

He looked at me as he sat in his chair. "I don't see a link between his murder and escorts. I mean, it's the only lead we have, so we should chase it down, but…"

"Yeah, I know."

With George's address in hand, we decided to track him down. We found him at work, Nora's Beach Hut, a small restaurant so close to the ocean I could smell the salt in the air.

"We don't do breakfast," said a woman near the front door. The bright-pink flower in her hair was striking against her tan skin and caramel-colored eyes.

We showed her our badges. Her eyes went wide with shock. "Umm…"

"We are looking for a George Makaio," said Tony.

I glanced around. It was a quaint restaurant with four booths and three circular tables. The walls were littered with beach-themed decor.

"I'll go get him." The woman disappeared behind the door to the kitchen. She emerged a few seconds later followed by a tall man with shoulder-length black hair and tattoos scattered down both arms.

I stared at him. He didn't look like someone who would be friends with Kent Barnum. They didn't look like they ran in the same circles.

I stood behind Tony and nudged him with my shoulder. He nodded like he was thinking the same thing.

George smiled as he walked up. "Is this about Kent?"

Tony nodded.

"Umm… okay."

"Can we go somewhere and talk privately?" asked Tony.

George looked around for a second and then pointed at one of the booths far enough away from the hostess at the bar, who was pretending like she was sorting through receipts.

"I don't know what I can tell you," he started as we sat down.

"We heard you were telling Mrs. Barnum quite a few theories and rumors that had been going around."

George sighed. "I was just trying to figure out the truth. I'd been hearing so many things around the island. I figured she would know the truth. She asked what I had heard, so I told her."

"And what have you heard?" Tony leaned forward, his elbows resting on the smooth table.

He shrugged. "This and that. I heard something about escorts and how he was messing with someone he shouldn't have."

"Who?" I asked.

Was it the boyfriend of one of his escorts? Maybe he got angry that she was spending all her time with Kent and wanted to put a stop to it. But that didn't make sense. It didn't fit the crime scene.

"I don't know. I don't believe it."

George seemed genuine. Like he was really just looking for answers. Just trying to figure out what happened to his friend. I don't think he intended to hurt or worry Mrs. Barnum. Maybe he thought that if anyone knew the truth, it would have been her.

"He wasn't into escorts?" asked Tony.

He sighed. "Yeah… I mean, I think so. He liked women. Loved women. He loved being with them. Having a pretty girl on his arm. He loved that shit. Made him feel like a man."

"How do you know him?" I asked. It was a question that had been bothering me since he walked in. He just didn't seem like someone Kent would have associated with. Not saying that rich people and not-so-rich people couldn't mingle with each other, but it still seemed strange to me.

"We've been friends since middle school. We met when his family moved to the island. Been friends ever since."

I stared at him.

He smiled. He had a beautiful smile. Teeth so white I was almost blinded.

"Yeah, I know it seems strange. Him being all rich and everything, but he was just Kent. At least to me."

Tony slid out of the booth and stood up. I was about to follow him but stopped. George and Kent had known each other since they were in middle school. And while he might not have known everything about Kent, he was one of the only people we talked to that had known him for a long time. Almost as long as his mother. He had insight into Kent that few others had. And now was the best time to ask him questions about who Kent was as a person. But first I wanted to know something.

"One more question. Do you know a Ricky Thompson?"

"Ricky? Yeah, I know Ricky. We all went to school together. Now *he* got rich and forgot about the little people. I don't see him around. Haven't seen him around in a long time. I think he and Kent were still cool though. I guess they would be. They still travel in the same circles."

My mouth hung open. I knew there was a link. I knew it. They did know each other. I wondered for a moment if there was a yearbook or something. Something we could use to show they knew each other. But that still might not be enough. Just because you went to middle school with someone didn't mean that you would remember them over twenty years later. There were a lot of people I went to middle and high school with that if I saw them now, I would have no idea who they were. Then again, he said he didn't know Kent Barnum. But George said they all used to hang out. So he lied.

And lying to the FBI was illegal.

# CHAPTER THIRTEEN

T HE DAY STARTED MUCH LIKE ALL THE OTHERS. THE Puzzler, a name he still wasn't sure about, sat in his car watching a man leave his house.

He had been watching the man for a few days, and his routine was pretty much the same every day. He woke up, went to work, had dinner with his girlfriend, and then went home. A night or two a week, he stayed the night at her home. But she never seemed to spend the night at his. Or even come over.

The Puzzler thought that was strange. It made him wonder what he would find when, inevitably, he found himself roaming around the halls of the spacious modern home waiting for John Hargrove to come back.

Today he would find out. The Puzzler decided that he had to speed things up. The police had found the first clue he had left for them. And he was fairly sure they had found the second one. Knowing them, though, he figured they still hadn't put it together.

He shook his head at the thought. How could they be so stupid? He waited for John to pull out of his driveway. The black SUV eased down the street and then turned a corner, going left. He waited ten minutes before he started his car and then drove in the opposite direction.

He wasn't really worried about anyone seeing him. Or anyone paying attention to his car. In some neighborhoods, you could see the neighbors cared about each other.

There were neighborhoods that when you drove through them, you could tell the neighbors talked to each other regularly. Stayed outside and watched the kids play. Did cookouts, trick-or-treating, and neighborhood block parties together.

This wasn't that kind of neighborhood. He could just tell. He doubted if they even knew each other's names. The houses were so far apart that he didn't really consider them neighbors. The houses sat so far back from the street you had to get in the car or ride a golf cart to get your mail.

Sure, they probably had security cameras outside some of the houses, but they probably didn't check them every day. Or at all. Not unless something weird was going on with their house. That would buy him some time to get away.

He parked his car on another street and walked back to John's house, coming up the back way. While there were security cameras at the front of the house, there were none around the back. He also liked to keep his back door unlocked. The Puzzler found this strange. It seemed like no one locked their back door. Why was that?

He always locked his own doors. Front, back, and the windows. Was it a new trend? Or did the serenity of the neighborhood give them the illusion of safety? When nothing horrible had ever happened to you or anyone you knew, you'd start to think that it never would.

But in the case of John Hargrove, it was about to. Something horrible was about to happen to him and his neighborhood. And everyone would start locking their doors from this moment on.

He pushed open the door. The house smelled like wood. Burning firewood, to be exact. It was probably John's cologne still clinging to the air.

The house was exactly how The Puzzler expected it to be. Expensive and far too big for one person. He closed the door behind him and took a deep breath to steady his nerves. It wasn't that he was nervous. Well, maybe he was, if only a little.

It was the waiting that made him nervous. And the fact that he hadn't had as long to study John as he had the others. He'd spent a couple of weeks watching David and getting to know him. Longer with Kent. He had to make sure they were who he thought they were.

He didn't want to torture the wrong people. His plan hinged on getting it right. Getting *them* right. And he had with the first two. They were exactly who he thought they were.

And so was John.

John, the quiet man who liked puppies and helping the homeless. John, who loved his girlfriend and her ten-year-old daughter. Who always wanted to spend time together as a family. John, who donated to organizations that helped children.

Who loved helping people.

Who loved computers.

Who loved libraries and thought reading was important for a child to develop into an empathetic adult.

Who was a pillar in his community.

And who also loved to spend his free time raping and torturing little girls.

Who was able to pull the wool over everyone's eyes. Even those closest to him. But not The Puzzler. He could see through him.

For a second, when David mentioned John Hargrove, he'd been surprised. Well, maybe it was part surprise, part disbelief.

John Hargrove was well-known on the island. He was the CEO of a tech company with a heart of gold. He was always donating to organizations that helped people on the island. The ones that no one else was paying attention to.

"John Hargrove? *The* John Hargrove? Are you serious?"

But why would he lie? The Puzzler had removed the top of one of his fingers. The pain. The blood. Those were reasons in and of themselves to tell him what he wanted to know. David had no reason to lie, and yet he was still surprised, thrown off by the name.

"I'm telling you. I don't know anything. But John might know. He's more influential. More... richer. He's higher up. If anyone could tell you who runs the organization, it would be him."

"Really? You've seen him?"

Blood oozed down David's finger as he nodded. Tears streamed from his eyes. The *medication* he had given David dulled the pain. But only a little bit. He didn't scream out, but he was fully aware of what was happening to him. Maybe that was worse than feeling it completely. Like watching something horrible happening to you and not being able to stop it. To scream.

"We had a few parties a while ago. He was there." David's voice was hoarse and low. "I've told you everything I know. Please let me go."

The Puzzler had nodded. But he hadn't let him go. Afterward, his heart hammered in his chest so hard he thought one of his ribs would break. It was like his heart was trying to break out of his chest. He tried to tell it to be quiet. To calm down. To breathe as the adrenaline coursed through his veins.

He tried to tell himself that they were out of danger now. That he had gotten away and there was nothing to fear now. Nothing to worry about. But his heart wouldn't listen. His pulse was so loud it filled his ears. It was all he could hear.

It was just his adrenaline. He was so hyped after David took his last ragged breath that it took forever for his body to crash. Too quiet.

Even when he returned home, his body was still unable to quiet down. It hadn't been that way with Kent. With him, The Puzzler had returned to normal pretty quickly. With David, he'd had to work through it. His fingers pulsed with excitement. Ready to do something else.

To hit something else.

He wondered if that was why people said if you could kill one person, you could kill another. As he walked back to his car, his fingers ached to hit something.

When he returned home, he took the garbage bag with his clothes and placed them in the dram in his backyard. He took a few branches, some old paper, and wood and placed them on top of the bag. He would burn it all later. But when he got home, it was still dark, and if he was found burning something that early in the morning, it would look suspicious. David probably had neighbors that wouldn't notice, but his would.

It wasn't until after he got out of the shower that he felt normal. Not just normal, tired. He scrubbed every inch of his body in the shower. Shampooed his hair and eyebrows. Scrubbed his fingernails and every inch of skin.

When he stepped out of the shower, it was like the heat had pulled every ounce of energy left in his body. It was a struggle to slip into his pajamas and crawl into bed. But he did. Lying there for what seemed like hours, listening. Listening for something new.

For sirens.

For radio static approaching his front door.

For a knock.

No, not a knock. Pounding on his door.

The unmistakable sound of handcuffs being locked around his wrist. But nothing happened. No one came, and finally, he went to sleep.

He had a plan for John, but he'd had a plan for David too. It got a little bloodier than he'd originally planned. Once he started hitting him, it was like he couldn't stop. His arm had a mind of its own. And the only thing it was thinking about was his own pain.

He couldn't stop himself from thinking.

He couldn't stop himself from hitting him.

He was lost in a sea of blood so deep he almost drowned.

If it hadn't been for a car door slamming across the street, he would have kept hitting David. The sudden noise snapped him out of his trance and brought him back to earth. When he finally looked down, David took in a slow, ragged breath. Blood bubbled at the corner of his mouth as he exhaled.

And then nothing.

The Puzzler's arm felt so heavy it fell to his side. He wasn't sure if beating them to death was the best idea. But in a way, it made him feel better. Relaxed. He hadn't planned on beating David the way he did. But this time he did plan on doing the same to John. And he was more deserving of it.

The house was clean. The cleanest house he had ever been in. It barely looked lived in. John also had a cleaning lady, but she only came in on Fridays.

*Did he really need her?* She probably didn't have much to clean. Nothing was out of place. The hardwood floor shone bright like no one had ever walked on it.

He stepped into the open living space. He was in what he assumed was the den, because it had a large, sectional sofa and a big TV mounted to the wall. It had to be at least a sixty-inch screen, if not bigger. To his right, a few feet away, was a doorway that led to a dark hallway, and just past that was the kitchen. It was like one of those kitchens on TV. White cabinets, a big island with a white marble top, and stools on one side. On the other side of the kitchen was a sitting area. Comfortable chairs and a fireplace. Which was odd. Most homes on the island didn't have a fireplace. He must have had one built.

The Puzzler spent the day waiting for John, much like he had David. He was sure no one would come by. Like David, John didn't let a lot of people in his house. Like David, he had something to hide.

He searched the house but couldn't figure out what that something was. He found no pictures or evidence he was leading a double life. Nothing except a door—a door locked from the outside.

Now that was curious. Why would you need a door that was locked from the outside unless you were trying to lock someone in?

He followed the long hallway to the office. A spacious room with a sleek, gray desk and wall-to-wall bookcases. He searched the desk. His gloved hands touched every inch of the desk, looking for a key.

Pulled out drawers. Checked for secret compartments.

Nothing.

As he sat at the desk, a thought wandered in and made a home in his brain. The more he rolled it over and played with it, the more it made sense.

John was a man who liked control. He didn't seem like the type to leave things up to chance. No, he would have taken the key with him. Kept it on his key ring, right there next to his car key and house key. That way it was always with him. So if someone had broken into his house and seen the door, they wouldn't be able to get in. Not unless they busted the lock.

He sighed. He could wait.

A little after ten, John Hargrove walked into his home, shoved the keys back into his front pocket instead of throwing them onto the console by the door, and closed the door without looking behind him. It was his usual routine.

Only this night, as soon as the door closed and the lock clicked into place automatically, there was a prick on his neck. Sharp.

Like a mosquito bite.

His hand darted up to swat whatever was there.

"It's too late for that now."

The voice was warm and smooth. And foreign. He had never heard it before. His tongue felt heavy in his mouth. Too heavy to move so he could form words.

*What are you doing here? Get out! I'm calling the police!* These were all thoughts that flashed through his mind. Thoughts he wanted to articulate.

But his tongue was too heavy.

His sight was fading.

And the floor was inching closer and closer to his head.

When John opened his eyes, a man stood before him. His tongue still felt like a foreign object in his mouth. He opened his mouth to speak.

The man waved his hand dismissively.

"Now, really, isn't the time for you to speak. It'll take a minute or two before you can say anything. Your body still needs time to adjust."

The man sat in a chair across from the sofa. His legs crossed. His body relaxed like he didn't have a care in the world. And he didn't. He was the one with all the power. John's body tensed as the room around him came more into focus.

The blurred images righting themselves right before his very eyes.

It was then he realized where they were. His eyes went wide with surprise.

The man chuckled.

"Yeah, I gotta say, when I saw you had a room that locked from the outside, this wasn't what I pictured. A BDSM dungeon was not on my list of… uh… well, you get what I'm trying to say. But I guess I shouldn't be surprised. Given everything else you're into." He pointed to the door, which was wide open. "I presume not everyone that comes in here comes willingly. Or why lock it from the outside?"

John swallowed hard. Beads of sweat formed across his forehead like a constellation of stars. The Puzzler saw this and smiled. He wanted him to worry. To be afraid of what else he knew. Granted, he didn't know much else, but John didn't need to know that.

"What do you want?" John's voice was low, almost a mumble.

The Puzzler shrugged. "Information, mostly."

"Information? I… On what?"

"Well, I am told you use the services of a particular organization that supplies children—"

"I don't know what you're talking about." The words tumbled out of his mouth so fast they practically ran into one another.

The man shook his head. "You didn't even let me finish."

John struggled against his restraints.

"No one is coming to find you. To help you. And if they do, they will find this room. And everything you have in here. And then how are you going to explain that? Sure, adults are entitled to their proclivities, but… I mean… how are you going to explain the little outfits in the closet?"

John blinked. His back straightened almost immediately. The Puzzler got up and opened the closet doors. There he found what looked like Halloween outfits for a little girl. A fairy, Little Red Riding Hood, and a nun.

"Interesting choices. I am curious about the nun… Why?"

"What do you want?" spat John. His face turned red, and his brows furrowed in anger.

"I told you already. I'm just looking for information." The Puzzler shrugged. That was really all he was after. Just a little information. Or a lot of information. He would take what he could get.

John's eyes drifted to the far corner of the room.

"I'll have you know that I've already searched through this room and found all the knives and other sharp objects that could be used to get you out of your current predicament. Just in case you were wondering."

John blinked. A lone tear eased down his face—his last bit of hope leaving him. The Puzzler was thorough. He was always thorough. While John had been knocked out, he'd taken the time to get the keys out of his pocket and find the right one for the locked room.

Once in, he searched it. It was strange, for a BDSM dungeon. Not that he had ever been in one before, but he doubted there were supposed to be so many knives. Unless that was what he was into. Knives all over the walls like a strange art display.

"What do you want to know?"

"Well…" The Puzzler said, leaning back, satisfied that John had finally come around to telling him what he wanted to know. "Let's start with who runs the organization."

John blinked. His mouth hung open slightly for a long moment, and then his jaw clenched.

"You think I know that? Why would I know that?"

"So you *do* use their services."

"So do a lot of people. What kind of business model would that be? Huh? If everyone that uses your illegal business knew that you were the one in charge? Wouldn't make sense. And definitely wouldn't have lasted so long."

The Puzzler cocked his head. John had a point. It wouldn't be a good, lucrative trafficking ring if everyone knew the name and face of the man on the top. But someone had to know. Someone had to know something.

He stared at John. John glared at him. Why would he lie? Maybe he didn't believe him. Maybe he thought The Puzzler was bluffing. That would be understandable. He didn't know him. Didn't know what he had already done.

So he would have to show him.

§

It amazed The Puzzler how pain was such a motivator to tell the truth. He stared at John, his face slick with blood. A few fingers on each hand missing.

The Puzzler felt John's blood congealing on his face. There was a lot more blood splatter than with the last one.

But in the end, John was right. He didn't know much. If he had, he probably would have said so before he started removing his fingers.

John was much like David, a man not used to pain. Not used to feeling it. He had barely touched him before he started talking.

"Little Rose!"

"And who is that?" He positioned the shears so that John's pinky finger was caught between the blades. He squeezed a little.

"She gets the... the..."

"Children?"

John nodded, his face tight with pain. "She's the one who finds them and hands them over, I guess."

"Is she in charge?" He squeezed harder.

John let out a wail of pain. "That… that's the only name I have."

It wasn't what he wanted. Not really. She wasn't running the company. Killing her wouldn't end everything. But it would get him a step closer to what he wanted. And that was a step in the right direction.

"I'll take it. And thank you for being so upfront with me." He smiled.

He watched as John's body slowly relaxed, each muscle unclenching, one after the other.

"Now let's finish this."

# CHAPTER FOURTEEN

IT WAS PROBABLY A GOOD THING THAT I GOT A LATE START and decided to skip my morning run, because the knock on my door as I was finishing up my breakfast wasn't expected. And what definitely wasn't expected was the familiar, smiling faces greeting me when I opened the door.

"Hey!"

My mouth hung open as Dawn's arms wrapped around me. My best friend from high school squeezed me so tight I gasped for air.

"Okay, Dawn. You gotta let her go so she can breathe."

My brother Owen's voice was both surprising and confusing. *What is he doing here? What is she doing here?*

Finally, she let me go. "How are you?" asked Dawn, her deep Southern accent even more pronounced than usual.

"Good?" I opened my mouth to say something but couldn't think of what to say. Or which question to ask first. Which one was more important?

"You gonna invite us in or not?" Owen stared at me expectantly.

"Um… yeah." I backed away from the doorway. "Come on in."

They rushed into my house, eager to get out of the heat. I closed the door gingerly behind them. My mouth was dry. I had talked to Dawn a couple of weeks ago, and she never mentioned anything about coming to visit. Especially not with Owen.

"If I didn't know any better, I would say you weren't happy to see us." He wrapped his arms around me. The hug was brief.

"No, I am," I said when he pulled away. "Really, I am. I just wasn't expecting you… either of you… or together."

They traded a look and started to speak at the same time.

"Dawn—"

"I—"

They looked at each other again.

"We"—Owen looked at Dawn—"Dawn was talking about missing you. And how she wanted to see you. And I wanted to see you. So we decided to come here together. That way neither of us had to take the trip alone."

I felt my eyebrow raise. Skepticism was written all over my face as I nodded my head slowly. I had so many questions, but I didn't even know where to begin.

"Okay. Cool. Well, um… I need to get ready for work."

"Right. We figured," Dawn explained. "We just wanted to stop by and tell you we're here. We just got in forty minutes ago anyway, and I'm ready to go to sleep."

"I see. And are you staying here?" I asked Dawn.

"We got rooms at the hotel," my brother supplied. "I figured that would make it easier for you. I know you are still adjusting to your new role and you got your new case. We just wanted to catch you before you head out. Let us know when you get off, and we'll hang out."

I nodded slowly and smiled, keeping my thoughts to myself. I wanted to say a thousand things, but all I said was, "Sounds good. I'll see you tonight."

I hugged them goodbye and closed the door as they went to their hotel.

*What the… Are they dating?* The unwanted thought nestled in my brain and made a home there. It stayed with me while I was getting ready. I just couldn't shake it. *Would I mind if they were dating?*

That was a good question. I didn't have the answer. I wasn't even aware that they liked each other. If she had come down with my parents, that would have been one thing, but with Owen? And then what was that look? When they walked in, they looked at each other. There was more to this than they were saying.

I said as much to Tony when I got in the car and he asked me what was wrong.

He chuckled. "Yeah, I think that *hotel rooms* isn't actually plural."

"Right," I said. "Oh… ewww."

Tony laughed harder. "Wow. Maybe they came down to tell you. Break it to you easy."

I looked at him. "If that was the case, then why wouldn't they just say that? Before they went to their hotel. That way I have all day to sit with it."

He pulled into the field office parking lot. "You already have all day to sit with it. I mean, you know what's going on. I know what's going on. Take the day to marinate on it."

I rolled my eyes. He had a point. Maybe they were here to tell me they were dating. Did everyone else know? The way they looked at each other. There was something there. And it looked like it had been there for a while.

"Geez, I leave for a few months, and now—"

"You think it's only been going on for a few months?" Tony shot me a quick glance before getting out of the car and closing the door.

I jumped out. Had it been going on longer and they just never said anything? I shook my head. I needed to focus on work and not on them. We needed evidence to tie Ricky Thompson to the murders. I took a deep breath. I would deal with them later.

*Deal with them how? It's not really your business.*

I needed to calm down. My father always said I was like a dog with a bone when I got fixated on a puzzle. I just had to know everything. But I didn't even know if they were dating. Not for sure. Not until they said something. So I needed to stop being fixated on something I wasn't a hundred percent sure about.

I shook the thought loose from my mind and followed Tony into the building.

"How is it going?" ASAC Davies stood next to Tony's desk, waiting on us, hands on her hips. She wore a cream-colored pantsuit with a red top.

"It's not. Not really." I sat at my desk. "We have nothing. And we're still waiting for the second body to be identified."

She nodded. "Well, I asked about Ricky Thompson, and he must have some powerful friends in some very high places. I was pretty much chewed out this morning because you two keep bothering him. I was told he was the victim who had his information stolen and you two were treating him like a suspect."

I opened my mouth to say something. She waved her hand dismissively.

"I know something doesn't add up about him. I understand that. And maybe he is hiding something. But that doesn't mean he murdered those men. Not without evidence. So until we have concrete evidence saying he did it, you are going to have to keep digging elsewhere." She looked at Tony. "Do you have any other leads?"

Tony sighed. "Kent apparently was really into escorts."

Davies shook her head. "All right. Find out where he found them and who his favorites were. Maybe they know something about his life we don't."

When she walked away, I shot Tony a look. He shook his head.

"I for one find it strange that a person would call their important friends to get the FBI to leave them alone instead of helping them figure out why their banking information was found on a dead body," said Tony.

"I for one second that finding."

He laughed. "Where would he keep it?"

I shrugged. "Where does one keep their address book for high-end escorts?" I leaned forward, placing my elbow on the desk, and stared at Tony.

He leaned back. "How would I know?"

I smiled. "I don't know what you know."

He shook his head. "Well, I don't know that. Maybe we should drop by his house. I don't think it's been cleaned out yet."

Neither of us really believed that escorts had anything to do with this murder. But you never know. Maybe he and the second victim were using the same escort service. Maybe they saw something or heard something that got them killed. It was hard to say because we still didn't have absolute identification on the second victim.

Kent's house had been cleaned. I remembered the layout from the pictures in the file. The body had been found on the floor, covered in blood. It looked like someone had come in and cleaned everything up. There were no bloodstains. The house smelled like bleach and disinfectant, with a hint of lemon. A few of the windows were open to air the place out.

I walked through the house carefully. Taking everything in. By the time we got the case, the first crime scene had already been investigated by local detectives. It's one thing to see a fresh crime scene, but this one had already been worked. I doubted we would find something they hadn't.

Tony and I found ourselves in the office. It was a room near the back of the house with floor-to-ceiling windows that over-looked the lush backyard. Despite the gruesome murder that had happened in the house, it was gorgeous.

"This place is beautiful," I said.

Tony looked at me. "Yeah. It'll probably go on the market soon."

"Would they have to disclose what happened here?" I walked over to a bookcase and started searching through the books.

"Umm... I'm not sure. I know for some states you don't have to. I can't remember which one Hawaii is. But for some people, a murder would be appealing."

I rolled my eyes. "People are weird. It's a nice house, even with the murder, though."

"Yeah, well, everybody has a past."

I pulled a book out of place. "What was that?"

I heard something fall, but I couldn't tell where it had fallen. Or what it was. I set the book on top of the bookcase and then started pulling out all the books. On the second shelf from the top behind the books was a black booklet.

He must have tucked it behind the book to keep it out of sight. I opened it.

"Oh, wow. Well, I found his escorts."

Tony walked over as I flipped through the pages. It was a thin, black booklet. Inside were pictures of girls. Underneath the pictures were what the girls specialized in and the price. There was also a number for each girl.

In a booklet of about twenty pages, twelve of them had the corners turned down.

"He liked a lot of them."

Tony nodded. "Well, his friend said he was really into women. Liked having a pretty girl on his arm."

"So what do we do? Call all of them and invite them over to the house for a party?"

Tony shrugged. "Sounds good to me."

We took out our cell phones and started dialing. It was weird. Calling escorts was something I didn't think I'd ever be doing. But we needed a lead. We needed something.

Out of the twelve girls, five answered and were able to come within the hour.

Within the hour, a black SUV pulled into the driveway. Tony ran into the garage and put the garage door up. The neighbor said that he saw an SUV pull into the garage several times. He said it was strange because Kent never did that. Were those the escorts coming over?

He eased back into the house. The car doors slammed shut. The sound of heels clicking against the concrete in the garage made my heart beat faster and faster.

What if they didn't know anything? What if they tried to leave? Or better yet, what if they came with an armed guard?

As if he was thinking the same thing, Tony stood next to the garage door and drew his gun. He didn't aim it at the door; instead he aimed it at the floor.

"Kent," sang a woman, "we're here." She stepped into the house. Her eyes went wide when she saw me. "You aren't Kent."

The four other women came up behind her, and one by one, they froze. Confusion was etched into every line on their faces. They saw me first, and then they saw Tony. And then his gun.

Behind them came a man—a big guy, probably two or three times Tony's size. He must have been the bodyguard. As soon as he saw Tony, the man tried to pull out his gun, but I rushed forward and pulled out my badge and held it up so everyone could see it.

"We aren't here to hurt you. Or arrest you. We just need to ask you a few questions about Kent."

"What about him?" The guy's voice was deep and gravelly. He stared at Tony, who was still holding his gun.

"Well, since he was murdered a few feet from where you're standing, we'd like to know anything you can tell us about him."

Only then did the guy look at me, eyes wide with surprise. One of the women shrieked and tried to move closer to the door.

"Kent's dead?" The woman who had just been singing his name looked shocked. Hurt even. Like she was about to cry. "We didn't know."

"I understand that. But you all seem to be his favorites, and we are at a loss right now."

"And you ain't going to arrest us?" bristled the giant.

Tony made a show of putting away his gun to ease everyone's fears. "Look, we need your help for a murder case. Don't really care about the other stuff," he said. "Come on in."

The girls all looked up at the bodyguard, and he nodded. They all filed in to the living room. Some of the tension was gone, but the room still had a weird energy. Nobody wanted to sit down.

There was nothing to do but break the awkward silence, so I did.

"Is there anything you can tell us? Was he in any trouble? Any problems? Worrying conversations you overheard?"

The woman who had been in the front chewed her ruby-red bottom lip. She folded her arms across her chest as she stared at the floor. Her light-brown hair was pulled back in a high ponytail. Her dress was sparkly, tight, and extremely short. If she had to bend down for any reason, everything would be showing.

"What do you know?" I asked her.

"It could be nothing."

I nodded. "Or it could be everything."

She sighed. "So one of his favorites … she's not here. I haven't seen her in days actually. He really liked her. He wanted her. Not just as an escort. He wanted something more. Something permanent."

"Nothing is permanent with Kent," said one of the women. She had her arms folded across her chest. "Every girl knows it's just for a short time until someone younger and prettier comes along. But he pays really well. And if you save the money, it's definitely a way out."

"Her name is Alicia Moore. And she was thinking about it. But she had a boyfriend. And that made things tricky," the woman continued explaining.

"She was an escort with a boyfriend?" I asked.

She shrugged. "You'd be surprised. She wanted to get away from him, and Kent could have been her ticket out."

"I feel a *but* coming on."

She looked at me. "But he was never going to let her go. I think she knew that. She was just trying to find a way out."

"So you think he—the boyfriend—got wind of their plan and did something?" asked Tony.

She shrugged. "I wouldn't put it past him. He used to beat her something fierce. Black eyes, fractured jaws. Beat her with a baseball bat so bad she was in the hospital for a while."

"A baseball bat?" I looked at Tony.

Dr. Pittman said she wasn't exactly sure what the killer used to kill Kent and the second victim, but it could have been a baseball bat. And whoever beat them to death was definitely angry. It took a lot of rage to do that to them. And a man about to lose his meal ticket would definitely be angry. If he felt like he was losing control, he would have or could have done anything necessary to regain it.

But she also said that both of the victims had been poisoned with GHB, the date rape drug. That explained why they hadn't fought back. Which suggested, to me, that it was much more involved than a simple crime of passion. But I still had to ask.

"Do any of you know a David Carter?" I asked. Maybe the escort service did tie the victims together.

Two women in the back raised their hands.

"I do."

"Me too."

They looked really young. Too young to be doing this.

"What about Alicia?" asked Tony.

The woman in the front nodded her head. "I think so. His name does sound familiar. He might have been one of her regulars."

"If he was, he probably would have had the same booklet at his place," said Tony.

I nodded. "We are going to need any information you have on Alicia Moore."

I had my notepad to the first woman. She held the pen gingerly in her hands.

"And write down your name and information in case we need to get in contact with you."

She nodded. Her name was Faith Dierks. She passed the notepad back to me, and I glanced over it. She had written down Alicia's information along with her boyfriend, Seth.

When I looked up, Tony was scrolling through something on his phone. He stopped.

"Is this David Carter?" he turned to phone toward the women.

They nodded.

"Yeah," confirmed Faith. "He's one of Alicia's regulars. I've gone with her once or twice on a call when he wanted more than one girl. She liked him. He liked her too. Said she was too pretty to be doing this line of work."

Maybe he wanted to help her get out too.

"Thank you, all of you, for your help."

The bodyguard looked from me to Tony. "Can I take them back now? Wasting money."

I nodded. Tony put the garage door up. They filed into the SUV and backed out of the driveway.

I felt bad letting the women leave. What if they really wanted out? What if they were tired of their current circumstances and wanted to do something else but weren't allowed to?

Tony looked at me and shook his head. "Right now, our focus is on the two murders. If they don't ask for help, you can't help them."

I opened my mouth to say something, but he was right. Right now, we needed to focus on what was in front of us. And finally, after so long, we had a lead.

# CHAPTER FIFTEEN

"**S**O WHAT ARE YOU THINKING?" I ASKED AFTER WE got into the car.

"More importantly, what are you thinking?" countered Tony.

I sighed. "Okay, so if Alicia's boyfriend thought that Kent and David were trying to take her away from him, maybe he killed them."

"I could see it. Taking her out of his control would have been a dangerous thing for everyone. If he was as bad as Faith said, he never would have let her go."

I nodded. Now we just needed to find her. I glanced down at the piece of paper with her address on it. Tony knew where it was. It was nice having a partner from the island. Someone who knew where everything was so I didn't have to hear the annoying voice taunting me on the GPS system. It was also nice having a partner who liked to drive.

Alicia lived in a nice neighborhood. It wasn't as nice or as expensive as Kent, but it was nicer than the one I lived in. Her house was a two-story house with a soft-pink door and matching shutters.

"That's cute."

Tony followed my gaze to the cow mailbox out front. He rolled his eyes. "So does not fit the neighborhood," he said as he got out of the car.

He was right; the mailbox was out of place. If she lived in a neighborhood with an HOA, she probably wouldn't have been allowed to put it up. The rest of the houses were painted in muted colors. White, cream, with black or light-green shutters. The pink made her house stand out. And if you didn't notice the pastel shutters and door, you definitely saw the mailbox in the shape of a cow's head.

"Well, I like it. Although I probably would have gone with a pig to match the pink on the house."

Tony shook his head. As we walked up to the door, I looked over to a neighbor's house. The blinds in the front window moved. Someone was watching us. Tony knocked on the door while I looked around the neighborhood. It was quiet. People were probably at work already.

He knocked twice. Nothing.

He knocked again. And then rang the doorbell a few times. There was no car in the driveway. And no one came to the door. But I did hear a door open. I backed away from the house. A woman with long black hair stood on the porch of the house next door, puffing on a cigarette.

Tony rang the doorbell again. He pounded on the door. Nothing. I walked over to the neighbor.

"Excuse me, have you seen Alicia Moore lately?"

Her eyes narrowed. "Who's asking?"

I showed her my badge. Her attitude changed. Well, a little. She seemed less standoffish. She even put out her cigarette.

"I thought you might'a been with Seth. I heard he was lookin' for her."

"Does he live here too?" Tony asked from behind me.

I shifted so he could move forward. The woman's porch was small, and all of us could not fit on it. I stood on one side of the stairs leading to the front door, and he moved over to the other side.

"He did. I think she put him out or something. One night a few weeks ago, they had a fight to end all fights."

"They do that a lot?"

She looked at Tony and nodded. "They were always fightin' about something. I don't know what he was so mad about. He stayed home playing video games while she went out and worked. He had it made, and it still wasn't enough." She leaned forward and whispered, "You guys know about what she did, right?"

"She was an escort," I said.

She nodded. "I'm Patty, by the way. But yeah, she went out every night, and he stayed home. And yet *he* was the one that was angry. She told me once that she didn't even want to do this anymore. But it was him. He talked her into it. Said it would only be for a little while until they got themselves together. Five years later…" Patty shrugged.

"When was the last time you saw her?"

She looked at Tony as she tapped her forefinger on her chin. "I'm not sure. I'm usually working. Today's my day off. I think it's been a week or two. I figured she might be staying away to let him cool off. That's usually what happens after they have a fight."

"Where does she go?" I asked.

"Umm. Well, one night after a fight, she asked if I would take her to a friend's apartment. Umm… Laura something. I can't remember her last name. But I can give you the address."

"That'd be helpful, thanks."

She wrote the address down on Tony's notepad. We thanked her for her time. Tony gave her his card just in case Seth or Alicia showed up at the house.

Laura *something* lived in apartment 512 a few blocks from Alicia's house. As plans went, it wasn't a good idea. If she was trying to get away from Seth, Laura lived far too close to make that possible. He probably knew where she lived and knew that her apartment would be Alicia's first stop.

"She lives too close," I said as we got out of the car.

"I know. If she was trying to get away, she should have gone underground. Or picked a friend Seth wasn't familiar with. If she lived this close to them, he knows her. But maybe she didn't have any other friends that she could turn to."

The apartment complex was nice and clean. Palm trees towered over the courtyard. There was a sitting area close to the pool and the unmistakable scent of decomposition wafting from the fifth floor.

My stomach twisted in knots. My heart hammered in my chest. I felt like I couldn't breathe. No, I didn't want to breathe. I swallowed, and I could taste the bile threatening to rise up my throat.

I looked at Tony. And he looked at me. The closer we got to Laura's apartment, the stronger the smell. Tony paused a few feet away and took out his phone. He called for backup and the coroner.

We didn't have to see to know. The smell of a decomposing body was a smell you could never forget. No matter how much you wanted to wipe it from your memory.

We should have waited for backup. For the coroner. Whoever was dead in the apartment was beyond our help. But I couldn't.

My feet pulled me toward the door. I turned the doorknob, and it was unlocked. I drew in a deep, shaky breath and pushed open the door, and my heart dropped into my stomach when I saw a woman's body on the floor.

The door skimmed the bottom of her feet as I pushed it open further. Her face was black, as was most of her skin that was exposed. Black with gray edges. Flies buzzed around her head.

And then I heard something.

Soft and mournful.

Crying.

I looked back at Tony. His eyes went wide, and he tucked his gun back into his holster.

"Wait here." He rushed into the apartment, carefully side-stepping the body. After disappearing down a dark hallway, he emerged a few seconds later with a crying baby girl.

Tears pricked the corners of my eyes. I had to back away.

From the body.

From the smell.

From the crying baby.

How long had she been there crying for her mother? Who would do that to a child? Tony walked out of the apartment and closed the door behind him.

"From what I could tell, the only dead body is the woman on the floor. But there is blood on the wall down the hallway and in the bedroom across from the baby's room. Looked like there had been some kind of struggle."

He saw a lot to have been in there for what seemed like seconds. I could hear his voice, but the words were a jumble. I just kept staring at the baby. She had stopped crying. She rested her head on Tony's shoulder.

Like she was thankful to have been rescued.

To see someone. Feel someone. To be held. To be away from that smell. And even though she was probably hungry, maybe being held was enough for right now.

Tony wrapped his arm around her while I called and told dispatch to send an ambulance. The baby was probably dehydrated and would need fluids. It was hard to say how long she had been in there by herself. The woman on the floor was... Her body was so... She was *rotting*. Her skin was black from decomposition. She had to have been there for a long time.

It felt like it took backup forever to find us. In truth, it probably took less than ten minutes. Backup arrived with the coroner and an ambulance close behind.

Dr. Pittman strolled up with a white lab coat thrown over her lilac form-fitting dress.

"I thought you had a dead body." She glanced back at the paramedics unloading the ambulance.

"We do," said Tony. "Paramedics are for the baby."

Dr. Pittman blinked. Her body stiffened as she stared at the child. "How long has she been in there?"

She was quiet in Tony's arms. He held her like he was used to holding babies. Confidently and gingerly. She played with his fingers as he bounced her.

"That's for you to find out," he said with a nod toward the body.

Pittman's face fell. "That's just cruel. She looks dehydrated."

Not wanting to waste any more time, Tony rushed out to the ambulance to get the baby looked at.

And despite the unimaginable horror of the scene, Pittman burst into a smile. "Look at you, finding dead bodies all on your own."

I could only grimace. "Wasn't looking for it. Was really just looking for information. A link between our victims, and I think we found another one." I pushed open the door.

Dr. Pittman eased into the apartment, her eyes glued to the body. "Oh, I was told that the second body will finally be IDed any day now. They had a backlog or something."

I nodded, but she didn't see me. She couldn't take her eyes off the body. I lingered in the doorway. The smell was strong, and while there wasn't much fresh air, it was more than inside the apartment.

"She's been dead for days." She shook her head. "That poor baby. Was she who you were looking for?"

"I don't know. She's either Alicia Moore or her friend Laura. Laura is the one who lives here. We are going to talk to the property manager and see what he can tell us. But I think... something is telling me the woman is Laura. And Alicia is missing, she might be dead, or her boyfriend has her. Tony said there was a struggle and blood in the room across from the baby's room." I pointed down the dark hallway.

She nodded. "I'll get techs on it right away. With the condition of this woman's face, I can't tell you if she's Alicia or not. Or Laura. But you might be right. If her boyfriend was after Alicia, I doubt he would kill her and take Laura."

I sighed. I backed away from the door and bumped into something hard. I spun around. Tony took a step back.

"Sorry. The baby is okay. Dehydrated though. They're getting her started on fluids and then taking her to the hospital."

He looked at Dr. Pittman poking at the woman's caved-in skull. "Can you tell how long she's been like that?"

Dr. Pittman looked up. "I would say maybe a week. Although it is awfully hot in here and the heat can mess with the time of death. More than three days. It's not an exact science. Although if it was a week, that baby probably wouldn't be alive right now."

My mouth opened and then closed. She was right. The baby couldn't have survived more than a week without food. She looked like she was maybe, at absolute most, a year old.

Tony nodded. "The property manager is downstairs in the courtyard."

I followed him down the stairs past crime scene techs dragging their gear up the stairs.

A man in a floral short-sleeve shirt and khaki shorts stood next to a tree. The officer next to him gestured for him to sit down on one of the dark-blue chairs.

The officer looked at us as we walked up and shook his head. He walked over to us. "He… uh, Mr. Wilson, is a mess. A bit dramatic. I can't tell if he's faking it or if that's just the way he is. So have fun with that."

The officer stepped away, and we walked over to Mr. Wilson.

"Are you detectives?"

"FBI," said Tony.

Mr. Wilson's eyes practically bulged out of his head.

"The FBI investigates murders?"

Why did everyone seem surprised by that? Mr. Wilson wasn't from Hawaii. His country accent was thick. He couldn't hide it if he tried.

"We do. And we are investigating this one. What can you tell us about the woman who lives in apartment 512?"

"Well, uh… Laura Stinger. She was nice. Quiet. Didn't have many friends. Just her and her baby girl Zoey really. Never had a noise complaint or anything about her. She…" He trailed off.

"She what?" I prompted after several seconds of silence.

"She did seem like she was hiding out or something. Hiding from someone."

"What made you think that?" I sat in the chair across from him, and he leaned forward. It reminded me of my mother when she had gossip about the neighbors.

"Well, she acted like it. How can I explain? She reminded me of those battered wives hiding from their husbands. She didn't give her number out. She kept a bat by the front door. And she just seemed anxious."

"Was there anyone else living with her?" asked Tony.

"Wasn't supposed to be. But a woman—Alicia something—came by from time to time. Sometimes she would stay a couple of nights. Sometimes when she got here, she was covered in bruises. I figured Laura was just trying to help out a friend. So I never said anything."

"Laura worked at a women's shelter."

I spun around. An older woman with long brown locks stood next to a palm tree smoking a cigarette.

"She did?" asked Mr. Wilson. "Well then, I guess that makes sense. This is Shirley. She lives down the hall."

Shirley waved. "Yeah. She was hiding out from an ex, Zoey's father. But I don't think he lives on the island anymore. She was real careful. But her friend Alicia ..." She sighed. "Laura was trying to help that girl, but I told her Alicia wasn't ready for help. She was still in love with that man. She wasn't ready to get out and leave everything behind."

"Did Alicia come by recently?"

Shirley took a long drag from her cigarette. Smoke billowed in the air as she spoke. "A few nights ago, I was walking to my apartment. I just come home from work. As soon as I reach my door, I hear crying. I try to mind my business, but I looked towards the courtyard, and Alicia was walking behind Laura. They were in a hurry. And I think Alicia had blood on her leg. She was wearing jean shorts, and there was something dark on her thigh. Alicia was sobbing. Laura put her arm around her and hurried her into her apartment."

"Was the baby with them?" I asked.

She shook her head. "No. I think Zoey was already inside. Laura pushed Alicia into her apartment just as I was opening my door. She looked at me"—Shirley closed her eyes and shook her head—"her eyes looked so sad. She smiled, but it wasn't her usual smile. It wasn't bright, it was sad. She gave me a short wave and then went into the apartment. I heard the locks, and then I went in mine. It was so weird, you know. Usually, she sees me, and we just get to talking. Standing out there all night, just talking with Zoey laughing or sleeping between us. But..."

"Did you hear anything? Any noise after that?" asked Tony.

She shrugged. "Once I fix me something to eat and put my feet up, I'm asleep. And I sleep hard. I didn't hear anything."

I nodded. "Did Laura have any tattoos?"

"Or scars?" added Tony.

Shirley put out her cigarette. "She had a butterfly on her hip. She said she got it after her divorce. And a mockingbird on her wrist. I don't know about scars, but the way she said he used to beat her, I wouldn't be surprised."

We thanked them for their time and gave them our cards in case they thought of something we should know. Mr. Wilson provided Laura's rent agreement, which had her contact information and next-of-kin information on it.

We went back up to the apartment. They were just loading the body into a body bag.

"Does she have a mockingbird tattoo on her wrist?" I asked.

Dr. Pittman pulled both of her arms out of the bag. She examined one wrist. It was hard to tell if something was there or not. It was black, and it looked like her skin was peeling. On the right wrist, she pulled up the sleeve of her dark-green long-sleeve shirt.

"Yes, she does." She turned her arm so I could see it. "This arm was protected because the sleeve was down."

"So this is Laura," said Tony.

I nodded. "Now where is Alicia?"

# CHAPTER SIXTEEN

W E SPENT THE REST OF THE DAY TRYING TO CONTACT Alicia's next of kin and figure out what to do with little Zoey. We had to call her ex-husband. Neither of us wanted to. If he beat her as badly as they said, he shouldn't have custody of Zoey. But he was her father. And he needed to know about his daughter. He had rights and all that. So even though I hated to do it, I called him.

"Mark Stinger?"

"What do you want?"

*Sounds like a nice man.* "I am Special Agent Storm with the Honolulu FBI. Is this Mark Stinger?"

He went silent for a moment. "Whatever she says I did is a lie. I don't even live there anymore."

"No, sir. I'm calling to tell you your wife was murdered."

I heard him take in a long, deep breath. And then he chuck-led. "Huh. She always said I would be the one to kill her some-day. Guess she was wrong. What does this have to do with me? Am I a suspect? 'Cause, like I said, I don't live there no more. I live in Kentucky. And I haven't left the state since I got here months ago."

"Are you going to ask about your daughter?"

"Oh yeah. Zo okay?"

"She is still alive. Even though she was left in her crib for a few days while her mother's body was decomposing on the floor."

"Damn, that's rough. Do I have to take her? Laura didn't want me around her, and you know what? I prefer it that way. She'll probably end up a stuck-up bitch like her mother."

"Sir, this—"

"Look, do what you gotta do, lady. I don't care."

Before I could even say anything else, he hung up. My blood was practically vibrating beneath my skin. Boiling in my veins. How could he be so callous toward his own wife and daughter?

At least Tony had had more luck with his calls.

"We need to head to the women's shelter downtown," he told me. He looked down at his watch. "Evelyn Witt was on Laura's paperwork as her next of kin. She runs the shelter. She said she'll be there in the morning to talk with us. Also said she wasn't surprised but didn't elaborate."

I nodded and leaned back in my chair. I was ready to go home. I was ready to ease into a hot bath and then crawl into bed.

I needed to change my clothes. Wash my hair. Even at my desk, miles away from Laura's body, I could still smell her. Every time I moved, I smelled her decomposing body as if I were still in the room with her.

Tears pricked the corners of my eyes. I shook my head to get rid of them.

"Come on. Let me take you home. You can take a shower and get something to eat and talk to your brother and your friend."

My mouth swung open. I had completely forgotten about them. I pulled my personal phone out of my desk drawer. Four missed calls.

When we reached my house, there was a car in the driveway. I jumped out of the car, and Tony followed. Dawn jumped out of the car, arms up.

"Oh!" I glanced at Tony, who already had his hand on his holster.

Dawn stared at him, her hands still up. Owen got out of the car and walked over to her. He positioned his body between Dawn and Tony, but I rushed out to defuse the situation.

"Tony, this is my brother, Owen, and his girlfriend, Dawn. Guys, this is my partner, Tony Walker."

Tony smiled. He nudged me with his elbow before taking his hand off his gun.

"Sorry. I, uh… wasn't expecting to see you guys in her driveway. Can't be too careful." He looked from them to me and back again. "Nice to meet you two. I've heard a lot about both of you."

They shook hands. Dawn kept staring at me in surprise. She wasn't expecting me to call her his girlfriend, but I didn't feel like pretending I didn't know. Then they had to tell me, and then it would be awkward. I have had way too long of a day to deal with that.

"All right. Everyone come inside so we can have a drink."

Tony turned to walk back to the car, but I grabbed his wrist.

"Everyone means you too," I insisted.

He pulled back for a second, but I shot him a look that was somewhere between pleading and ordering.

"All right," he finally relented.

I pulled him to the door, and we all went inside. I headed straight to the bar. Maybe if I drank enough, I wouldn't smell the body anymore.

"Shouldn't you get some food in you before you start drinking?"

Tony walked over to my fridge. There wasn't a lot of food in it. I was more of an order-out person. I could cook, but I didn't feel like it.

"I can work with this."

"Okay. You make the food, and I will make the drinks."

"Long day?" asked Dawn.

She stayed close to the bar while Owen joined Tony in the kitchen. Owen was a good cook. He could make anything.

"It wasn't great," I admitted as I mixed tequila with lime juice and some pineapple juice. "How long is Owen on leave?"

"He goes back in a week." She was quiet for a long moment. I knew she was waiting for me to say something. Waiting for me to yell. And I could. I could scream and rant and let myself get so pissed that they kept this secret from me. I could play out a conversation I had been having with myself all day.

*How could you date my brother? Why didn't you tell me? How long has this been going on?*

I could have done that. And maybe if my day hadn't gone the way it did, I would have. But I was too tired to care. Too tired to be so invested in their lives.

I didn't tell them everything that was going on with me. Granted, nothing was going on with me, but still. Everyone was entitled to their secrets.

I handed her the drink and made three more.

"It's only been less than a year," she finally said. She took a long sip.

I simply nodded my head. "Okay." I turned over to where Tony and Owen hovered over the stove. The smell of onions and garlic filled the air. "What are you two making?"

"Just something to snack on," said Tony.

I had some packs of ramen in the cabinet, and Tony turned it into a five-star meal. He added garlic, onions, soy sauce, thinly sliced steak, and a fried egg on top.

"Oh my god, this is amazing," I marveled as we sat in the living room at the coffee table each slurping down our bowls. "My ramen never tastes like this."

Tony laughed. "We ate it a lot when I was a kid. It got kind of boring."

"Yeah, I ate it a lot in college," said Dawn. "Never came up with anything like this though."

"Right?" I stuffed a piece of steak in my mouth. It was so tender I barely had to chew it. "If it wasn't the seasoning packet, I wasn't adding it."

Everyone laughed.

"So," started Dawn, "what's the big case you two are working on that has you both stressed?"

Tony looked at me. "Is it that obvious?"

"You two look very tense," said Owen.

It wasn't until he said it that I realized how tense my shoulders were. I tried to pull them down, away from my ears. It didn't last long.

I took a deep breath and then told them everything—well, almost. I kept some things back. Part of me wasn't sure if I should have been telling them anything. If it was even allowed. But once I started talking, and Tony didn't stop me, the words somersaulted out of my mouth.

Dawn's mouth hung open. I think a fly flew in.

"We really need to identify the second body so we can really start digging into his life."

"But you guys have an idea who he is, right?" asked Owen. He shoved the last piece of food in his mouth and chewed slowly.

"Yeah, babe, but they have to be certain. If it's not him and they alert the next of kin and it turns out they are wrong, or they are chasing the wrong leads this whole time because they thought it was someone else." Dawn shook her head. "It's better to be sure first."

Tony sat on a pillow to my right. I poked him in the thigh when my best friend called my brother *babe*. He chuckled.

"And the tech department still hasn't figured out the numbers on the second victim's chest," said Tony.

Dawn shook her head again. "Oh, that whole thing sounds like a mess."

I had almost forgotten about the numbers on the second victim. The number on Kent's body was Ricky Thompson's account number. I wondered for a brief moment if the second number was linked to Ricky too.

But where did Alicia and Seth fit in? Did they know Ricky Thompson too? To me, it seemed like Seth was trying to get rid of people who were trying to take Alicia away from him. People trying to help her find a new and better life.

Kent and David wanted Alicia for themselves. They both thought she was too pretty to be stuck being an escort. Kent wanted her with him. He was willing to take care of her.

Even Laura wanted to help Alicia find a better life. I think that was why she kept taking Alicia in when she ran away from Seth. She would probably take the time to try and talk her out of going back. Tried to tell her that there was another way. A way out.

But Alicia was in love with Seth. And maybe she couldn't picture her life without him. Laura was trying to get Alicia away from Seth, and maybe that was why he killed her. And maybe that's why he didn't kill the baby, because she had done nothing wrong.

And then an idea—a thought—wandered into my head and started moving things around. Shaking things up. Moving puzzle pieces into the correct places. I shook my head. Could it have really been that simple? Wouldn't someone have figured that out by now? I was sure the IT techs had already tried it and just didn't say anything.

I turned to Tony. "This whole time we've operated as if the numbers on the second body were just one long number, like the number etched into Kent Barnum's chest. But what if they're not? What if instead of it being one long number, it's several numbers?"

# CHAPTER SEVENTEEN

TONY LIKED MY IDEA, ALTHOUGH HE WAS SURPRISED NO one in the tech department had thought of it. I was surprised too, honestly. After dinner, we sat around and talked for a bit. And then Tony had to go home, and my brother and his *girlfriend* went back to their hotel a little while later. It would be hard to start thinking of Dawn as his girlfriend and not just as my friend. I guess I would have to get used to it, for however long it'd last. And if it did end, I hoped it wouldn't ruin our friendship.

She said it wouldn't, but I wasn't so sure. I thought it would depend on who was at fault. With the house quiet, I did my usual after-work routine. I finally got to take the shower that I had been longing for all evening. I wanted to feel clean. New. But more importantly, I wanted to get the smell of Laura's decomposing off of me. I could still smell her. I could still smell that room.

I wanted to forget the events of the day and start over in the morning. I wanted to find Alicia, and I wanted her to be alive. I wanted Laura's sacrifice to not be in vain. I wanted to scrub my face and my nose and go to bed smelling like vanilla or lavender or some kind of flower. I wanted to feel clean.

So that was what I did. I took a shower and scrubbed my face and my nose and slathered lavender lotion all over my body and went to bed.

The next morning, getting out of bed was a challenge. I woke up tired and in dire need of caffeine. I followed my usual routine, but I cut my run short. I wanted to see more of the neighborhood, but Tony was going to come and pick me up so we could go to the women's shelter Laura worked at.

As I got ready, I could see the case unfolding in front of me. Something was telling me the cases weren't related. Not really. Kent and David might have wanted to help Alicia, but that wasn't what got them killed. Laura, who knew what it was like to be a battered wife, was trying to help. Seth was looking for her after she left him, and he might have followed her to Laura's house.

I wasn't sure that was the case. But something in my gut, deep in my bones, told me that was what happened.

I had time to drink one scalding hot cup of coffee before Tony pulled into my driveway. When I got in the car, he just stared at me.

"Am I supposed to be saying something?"

Tony smirked. "How did it go after I left last night?"

After talking about the case, my brother asked what it was like living in Hawaii. He asked if I liked it. But who didn't like living in Hawaii? It was literally paradise even with the dead bodies.

"I do. I love it," I'd told him.

After we'd finished eating, Tony and I had washed dishes. I'd watched my brother and my best friend making googly eyes at each other, and my stomach had soured. We'd talked for a little bit after Tony left, but then they'd left too.

I shrugged as he backed the car out of the driveway. "It was okay. Not awkward at all."

It was a little awkward. It was like, without another person there, we didn't know what to say to each other. It was awkward, and the conversation was clunky and shallow, and it never used to be that way.

"Are you upset or annoyed that they are dating?"

I sighed. I wasn't upset. I did wonder how long they had been dating and if they had been telling me the truth about when it started.

But I knew I shouldn't care. Their love lives were none of my business. It shouldn't have mattered. Whom they were dating shouldn't have bothered me, but it did. I didn't know why it did, but it did. It felt like they had this big secret that I wasn't a part of. Like everyone knew but me, and now I knew, and I couldn't help feeling like they'd been lying to me this whole time.

"I'll get over it. I just hope it doesn't mess with my friendship with Dawn or my relationship with my brother."

Tony nodded. "It shouldn't. Sometimes you just have to let people live their lives. Whatever happens, happens. It'll all work out."

"Yeah, I guess. I just never pictured them together. I didn't even know they talked to each other like that. I didn't know they had a reason to hang out. I think that's what's bothering me. It feels like they were hiding it from me. And I don't like that."

"I don't think they were hiding it really. Maybe they just wanted to know that it was serious before they told everyone."

I shrugged again. I understood what he was saying. And he was right. I just had to let it go on my own. And I would.

We pulled into the parking lot of the shelter. It wasn't what I was expecting. I was not sure what I had been expecting, but it wasn't this.

The one-story brick building was plain on the outside. The branches of a large tree obscured the name of the building: Hope.

While plain, it made sense. If you were running a women's shelter, you wouldn't want a building that drew a lot of attention. It was a place women would go to get away and feel safe.

It wasn't hard to find, but you would have to know where you were going.

The door swung open as we walked up the concrete walkway. A woman stood in the doorway with perfectly styled red hair, bright-red lipstick, and a forest-green pantsuit. Something about her just didn't scream *I run a women's shelter.* She was too put together.

"Special Agents." She smiled and stepped back so we could enter the building.

"Are you—"

The woman waved her hand dismissively. "No, I'm not Evelyn. I'm her attorney, Paula Sheppard. She called me soon after you called her and asked me to sit on this conversation."

Tony looked at me. "I find it curious that we called to talk to her and she called an attorney. Makes me think she's hiding something."

Paula smiled tightly. "Evelyn has nothing to hide. It's just a matter of protocol. Many of the clients of this shelter have never had a reason to trust law enforcement, so whenever they come by, there's always an attorney present."

I nodded. It made sense. I hated to admit it, but even though I was brand-new on the job, I already knew that not everyone in law enforcement was in it for the right reasons. But that was why I wanted to do this job in the first place—to make the system better from the inside.

She looked us over and then led us down a series of hallways away from the sounds of children playing and women talking. We came to a door, and Paula knocked twice before opening the door.

A woman who looked like she could have been Paula's twin sister sat at a small, black desk. They had the same red hair, the same nose, and the same eyes.

The woman who I assumed was Evelyn had a stronger, more pronounced jaw and large bags under her eyes.

"Sisters," said Tony.

A weak smile touched Evelyn's lips and faded. Unlike the bright, put-together Paula, she looked so tired. But I guess this kind of work would do that to you. Constantly having to worry about whether everyone was safe or not or if someone was going to give away your location. Or if you were going to have enough funding to take care of the people that needed your help.

"You are here about Laura Stinger?" asked Evelyn. She gestured for us to sit in the two vacant chairs across from her desk. Her sister leaned against the wall.

"Well, yes and no," said Tony.

He explained how we were looking for Alicia Moore and that led us to Laura's apartment, where we found Laura dead. But we still hadn't found Alicia.

Tears welled up in Evelyn's eyes. She drew in a shaky breath, and her sister walked over and patted her on the back. She whispered something to her so low I couldn't hear.

"Laura was a good woman. She was so kind and was always eager to help. Especially women who were in the same situation she had been some years ago. I assume you've talked to—"

"Her ex?" I asked. "Yeah. Great guy. Real concerned with his daughter's well-being."

"Is he going to take her?"

I shook my head. "I'm not sure what's going to happen to her, but he's made it clear that he doesn't want her."

"Good. She deserves better."

"What can you tell us about Alicia Moore?" Tony took his notepad out and turned to a blank sheet of paper.

Evelyn sighed. "Well, Laura really took a liking to her. I think she saw some of herself in Alicia and really wanted to help her get out of her current relationship. I told her. I told her that Alicia wasn't ready."

"What made you say that?" I asked. How would she know if someone was ready to get out or not?

She was quiet for a moment. "I've been doing this for a long time," she said finally. "A long time. You can tell. Some women want to leave, but they just aren't ready."

"How do you know when a woman is ready?" I asked.

"When she can't be sucked back in. When he can't talk her into coming back—then, and only then, is she ready to leave. When she's had enough and knows that if she doesn't get out now, he'll kill her. Then she's ready to get out. Alicia hadn't realized that yet. She still believed Seth when he said he was sorry and that he would change. But Laura thought that she could get through to her. She was really trying to get through to her. And I think this last time, she did."

"What makes you say that? Did you talk to her about Alicia?"

She looked at me. Her eyes looked so tired. Like she hadn't had a good night's sleep in days.

"Yes, we talked about Alicia. But she didn't want to come to the shelter. She wasn't ready to make that step yet. So Laura suggested she stay with her. I told her that wasn't a good idea. She wasn't sure if Seth knew where she lived, and if he did, that could have been dangerous. But she kept saying she had to get Alicia, and this was the only way she could do it. She kept saying everything would be fine ..." Her voice trailed off.

I nodded. "Where do you think Alicia and Seth would go?"

She shrugged. "I didn't know her well enough. The only person that did know is dead now. I don't know where he'd go. I wish I did though."

I nodded. So that was a bust. There was nothing she could really tell us. Nothing that we didn't know already.

"Do you know Seth's last name?"

"Drake, I believe. Seth Drake."

Tony got up and took his phone out of his pocket. By the time I thanked them for their time and followed him to the front of the building, he already had an address for Seth.

"That was fast."

He smiled. "Well, we are the FBI."

I chuckled.

"Don't read too much into that though. Sometimes it doesn't happen as fast."

Seth Drake lived in a small house that looked like it was just barely hanging on. The carport had a dent in it. One of the shutters was partially hanging off. The front door was dark green. But even with that, I could still see the dark stains all over the bottom.

"Tony," I pointed as soon as I saw the stains.

His shoulders slumped a little. We got out of the car, weapons drawn. Tony called for backup, but we didn't want to wait. What if Alicia was inside waiting for us to rescue her? What if she was injured and needed an ambulance?

We only hesitated for a second, gave each other a nod, and then headed toward the door.

I touched the concrete step on the porch and stopped. My heart sank into the pit of my stomach. Bile rose up my throat, and I swallowed hard to push it down. The nauseating smell was so thick, so heavy it made my stomach bubble. It was almost worse than at Laura's house.

I stumbled back into Tony. My hand covered my nose. I moved away from the house, trying to get as much fresh air as possible. She was dead. I knew it.

We had gotten to her too late.

"We need to check the house," said Tony, his voice barely above a whisper.

I nodded slowly. I followed him. He knocked on the door and then tried the doorknob when there was no answer. The door wasn't locked.

"FBI," he announced.

The smell inside the house was so heavy I couldn't breathe. We moved through the living room, following the smell down the hall and into the main bedroom.

There were two bodies in the room. One was lying on the bed, the other slumped on the foot of the bed. Both looked like they had been dead about as long as Laura.

This wasn't how I wanted the case to end. I was hoping for a happy ending. We would find Alicia beaten up but alive, and we could arrest Seth for Laura's murder. And then we could ask Alicia about Kent and David and understand what the connection was between them.

Or maybe we would find Alicia after she got the courage and killed Seth. We would find her covered in blood, sobbing. Seth's dead body on the floor with a bullet hole or maybe a stab wound.

I could think of a million other scenarios I would have preferred to see. Dozens of outcomes that didn't involve Alicia dying. She could be safe and sound and ready to start a new life maybe away from Honolulu. Away from all the bad memories.

Maybe she could have even taken Zoe with her and just started their lives over.

A million different scenarios, but this was what we had.

I backed out of the room. "I guess we found Alicia and Seth."

# CHAPTER EIGHTEEN

W E STAYED AT THE SCENE LONG ENOUGH FOR CRIME
scene techs to start working the scene. We noted the
placement of the gun, which was next to the second
body. It looked male, and if I had to make a guess, I would have
said it was Seth.

"I'm going to go out on a limb and say that these two have
been dead about as long as the other body. The decomp is
extensive," Pittman reported.

"Do you think they were dead before or after our other
victims? Kent and the second victim." I asked just outside the
doorway of the main bedroom.

The house was small and felt cramped with all the crime
scene techs moving around and looking for evidence. I noticed

that there was no note by the body. I guess Seth wasn't the type to leave behind a suicide note.

Dr. Pittman eyed the bodies. "They may have been alive when Kent was killed, but definitely not the second victim. I'll have to get them on the table to confirm, but we're looking at maybe three to four days at most."

"Thank you," I said.

Then I rushed out of the house, ready to gulp down some fresh air. Sweet, fresh air. I had to move away from the house to take a deep breath. I leaned against the car and waited for Tony, who was speaking with an older woman next door.

After a few minutes, he joined me at the car.

"Neighbor, Mrs. Covington, said she saw Seth and Alicia entering the house a while ago. She said it could have been a couple of weeks ago, she's not sure. Alicia had a busted lip, but that was normal for them."

My heart sank a little at hearing how the neighbor saw them but didn't try to help Alicia. But I guess she was used to it. She was used to hearing them fight and argue and the police being called. She was used to seeing her covered in bruises.

Getting involved in domestics sometimes didn't end well, as Laura had found out. So helping her probably wasn't a good idea.

"Did she say anything about hearing a shot?"

"She said she may have heard something. She can't pin down when she heard it. It was sometime in the last week or so. At first she thought it might have been fireworks or maybe a car backfiring or something. She said she really didn't think anything of it."

That made me a little angry. If the neighbors had been paying closer attention, maybe we… I shook the thought from my head. From the looks of it, Alicia was shot in the head. There was nothing we could have done for her. She was dead the second he shot her. But maybe her body wouldn't have had to lie there next to the bastard that shot her for so long.

I sighed. "So Seth's angry that Alicia has finally gotten the courage to leave him and he goes looking for her."

"Stalking really."

"Right. He starts stalking. Figures out where she's staying and goes over to Laura's house to persuade her to come home. And maybe Laura intervenes and talks her out of it."

Evelyn mentioned that Laura might have seen a lot of herself in Alicia, and that was why she was so desperate to help her. She wanted her to get out like she had and move on with her life. But he just couldn't let go.

If Laura had just let Alicia go with him, she might still be alive. Her daughter would still have a mother. And maybe Alicia would have been alive too. And then they could have tried to get her out another way.

I shook that thought out of my head. That wasn't her fault. She was trying to save her friend's life. How could she have ever known that this man would be so monstrous?

Tony nodded. "And then seeing that he's not getting through like he wants, he kills Laura. Maybe he felt like she was trying to poison Alicia against him. Laura was the problem, not him, so he dealt with it. But now Alicia is frightened, and she's too scared to get away, because if he killed Laura, he could kill her too. He forces her to go with him. And when he gets back to the house, he sees that she's still trying to get away from him and decides that if he can't have her, no one will."

"He keeps his control over her by killing her," I finished the scenario.

Tony sighed. That was probably how it happened. Or close enough, at least. We didn't know for sure, and we probably never would with the way her body was decomposed. But it was pretty clear.

To say I was angry was an understatement. We should have gotten to her sooner. We should have… I shook the thoughts from my mind. How were we supposed to know? How could we know if she didn't go to the police?

And we weren't the police. We didn't work on domestic abuse cases, so how could we have helped? There was nothing we could have done, and I needed to keep that in mind.

"We need to get back on the case," said Tony finally. "We need to get back to…" He waved his hands around searching for the right word.

But I knew what he meant. Alicia Moore was a detour, and now it was time to get back on track.

I nodded. "Right. Back to the problem at hand."

We chased the Alicia Moore angle down because we thought she and her boyfriend had something to do with the murders. But now we know they had nothing to do with it. So now we needed to refocus.

"We should go to the IT department and see if they've made any progress," I said.

"Right."

We drove back to the office in silence. As soon as we entered the open space, a woman jumped up and waved us over. I looked back at Tony, who shrugged, but walked over anyway. I followed him.

"Hello. Special Agent Love. I was told to look into what you said about the numbers."

"Oh," I said.

Love looked new in the same way I was new. Like she had just gotten out of the Academy. She was still fresh-faced and doe-eyed, and a little shorter than me with light-brown eyes and black hair.

"It was a good thing you suggested it. I mean, we might have come around to the same conclusion eventually, but this definitely saved time." She sat back down in her chair and pulled up her screen on the large monitor on the wall.

"You were right. You see, we had been running it as one long number. I mean, we figured since the first one was one number, why would this one be any different? I thought it might have been another account number, but they aren't. It's several numbers written to make it look like it's one number."

"You think the killer did it on purpose?" I asked as I inched closer to the screen.

Love shrugged. "Maybe, maybe not. They could have done it because they were writing on a body and it was a little difficult. Or they were running out of time. Or they knew it would take us longer to figure it out if we thought it was one number. Gave them more time to do whatever. But anyway, like I said, it is several smaller numbers."

"Have you figured out what the numbers mean?" asked Tony.

"They are driver's license numbers," answered Love. "And one of them belongs to Ricky Thompson. I think he was picked out first because we were already looking into him. We took the number and divided them into eight numbers. The database is cycling through the numbers now. I'll let you know when all the numbers have been accounted for."

I sighed. "Thank you."

I followed Tony back to the elevator. This had to be a sign. A clue or something that Ricky Thompson was linked to these murders. But why wouldn't he help us? I don't think he was the murderer. It seemed very unlikely. I mean he was smug and arrogant, but he wasn't stupid. Killing people and leaving clues behind that linked to you was... less than smart.

Someone was trying to frame him or get his attention. But why? And why wouldn't he tell us what he clearly knew? Maybe he was scared. Maybe they had something on him and he wanted to remain absolutely silent.

When we got back to our desks, Tony made the call to tell Ricky that we needed to see him at the field office. He said he would come by in the morning with his lawyer. We agreed it was fine. Waiting a day gave us more time to figure out how we were going to get the truth out of him.

He knew something. I could feel it in my gut. He knew something, and he was either afraid to tell us or—no, he was just afraid to tell us. There was no other explanation. What I couldn't figure out was why. I mean, if someone started killing people that I knew and leaving behind clues that linked to me, I was going to wonder what those people wanted. What were they going to do to me? And wouldn't it be better to tell law enforcement what I knew so they could catch the person? That way the person couldn't kill me?

Was whatever secret he was hiding really worth dying over? He seemed to think so. I just couldn't understand why he would be so standoffish. It was like he knew the goal wasn't to kill him but to get his attention. But why would someone want to do that?

"I feel like we're missing something," I said.

"As in one thing?" Tony's eyebrow ticked up, and I chuckled.

"You're right. A few things. I think we're missing a few things."

He nodded slowly. "Ricky is linked somehow, but his driver's license wasn't the only one written on the second victim. So this isn't just about him."

"I wonder if he knows the other people."

"Probably. Maybe this was about a deal gone wrong or something. He was supposed to do something, and he didn't, and now someone is out to get him."

"What kind of deal?"

Tony shrugged. "Rich, powerful guy like that? You never know. Probably something shady. But we shouldn't be jumping to conclusions. His account number was the only one written on the first body, so he's definitely at the center of everything."

We spent the rest of the day digging into Ricky's life. He wasn't a nice guy, but he didn't seem particularly evil. Sure, he was an asshole, but I couldn't find anything that would drive someone to kill people and link them to him in some way. At least I wouldn't. But maybe he pissed off the wrong person.

That was what my mind kept coming back to. He had made someone mad, and this was their revenge. They knew something about him and were leading us to find it. Why couldn't they just call in anonymously? Why did they have to kill people?

It did get our attention faster. Or maybe this was about getting his attention.

Before we left the office, Dr. Pittman stopped by.

"The bodies were definitely Alicia's and Seth's."

"Can you tell what happened?" I asked.

I wanted to know, but I didn't. I was half hoping she said no.

"No, the bodies are too decomposed for us to tell."

"No, we can only surmise what may have happened."

I felt so bad for her. She had finally tried to make her way out of it. To leave him behind and now she was dead. And not just her, Laura, who only wanted to help, was dead too. All because of the actions of one vile, cruel man.

Dr. Pittman sighed. "From what we can tell, after he killed Laura, he took Alicia back to his house. We aren't sure exactly what happened or what was said. She must have said something or done something, like trying to get away, that really set him off. Her skull was fractured in three different places. Two ribs were broken. Her right arm was fractured, and so was her jaw."

"Damn," muttered Tony.

"She was naked under the blankets. Hard to say whether that happened before or after the beating, although there was no blood on her clothes, which we found in the corner of the room."

*He probably raped her.* I didn't say it out loud, but I knew we were all thinking it. My stomach soured when I thought about it. Had he done it before he beat the shit out of her or after? I shook the thought from my head.

"He shot her twice in the head. Then he covered her with the comforter, sat on the edge of the bed, and then shot himself."

Tony sighed. I put my head in my hands.

"I figured you two would want to know. And while Seth was still alive when Kent died, he was already dead when David was murdered. So I would say he wasn't your killer, and I doubt he was working with someone. He doesn't seem like the type that works well with others."

"Thank you," I said. My throat was so dry the words scraped against my throat like sandpaper.

She nodded and then turned to walk away. We had already figured out that Seth wasn't our killer, but it was good to hear it out loud. But that meant we wasted... No, we didn't waste anything.

We should have been working on the serial killer case, but in the past couple of days, we had taken a detour because we thought Alicia might have been the link between the bodies. While we might have taken a detour, that didn't mean we had wasted our time.

There was no telling how long Alicia and Laura's bodies would have gone unnoticed. We found them. We found Zoey too and saved her life. And while it wasn't what we were looking for, it was something.

When we walked into the field office the next morning, something didn't feel right. Wrong. I felt like something bad was going to happen.

Unease settled into my bones, and I just couldn't shake the feeling. We walked onto our floor, and the first person I saw while I walked to my desk was Special Agent Baldwin.

She rushed over to us before I could get into my chair.

"Have you two heard?"

Tony and I looked at each other and back at her. We both shrugged.

"Ricky Thompson killed himself this morning. Jumped off his building."

# CHAPTER NINETEEN

Y MOUTH SWUNG OPEN. IT TOOK ME A LONG MOMENT to get myself together. For the words—the right words—to come out of my mouth. Of all the things I was expecting, this wasn't it.

I wasn't expecting him to come in and tell us *everything* we wanted to know, but I wasn't expecting him to kill himself.

He just didn't seem like the type. I shook the thought from my head. No one seemed like the type. You never knew what someone was going through. It's difficult to say whether someone would kill themselves or not.

When I was in high school, the most popular girl in school hung herself in her bedroom closet. Daisy was *popular*. Everyone liked her, from the teachers to the janitor. It was hard to find someone with a mean word to say about her. She had shown no signs of being depressed or wanting to end it all. She went to school one day. She finished cheerleading practice and then went home and hung herself in her closet before her parents got home from work.

It was months before we understood why. Months before everyone in the school knew that she had been keeping a big secret. The perfect girl who seemed like she had the perfect life had been raped by her father, got pregnant, and was forced to have an abortion. And nobody ever knew.

Our English teacher made us write in a journal every day before class. That was where they found her suicide note months later when Mrs. Long was cleaning her classroom. She had left the note there, because if she'd left it at home with her body, her parents would have destroyed it before they called 911.

And while you never knew what someone was thinking or planning, I didn't think Ricky Thompson would do that. I wondered for a brief moment if he had a secret like Daisy.

The word that finally came out of my mouth, after a long period of dumbstruck silence, was, "Seriously?"

It wasn't the right word. But it would have to do.

Tony sat down and leaned back in his chair. His brows knitted together slowly. He looked how I felt. Annoyed. Frustrated. Angry. Ricky was our only lead. He was our link. Why did he have to kill himself?

"When?" I asked.

"I just got the call a few minutes ago."

Tony was already getting to his feet and putting his keys back in his pocket. I stood up too.

"Yeah, I figured you two would want to take a look," Baldwin said. "I told the local police to expect you."

She walked away from our desk, and we headed toward the elevator.

The ride to the Teletech building was a quiet one. Neither of us knew exactly what to say. I was at a loss for words. I didn't see him killing himself. We should have gone to see him yesterday. We should have forced him to come in.

"We didn't have probable cause," said Tony. "We couldn't force him to come in." He sighed.

I nodded. We had been thinking the same thing. And while I knew he was right, it didn't make me feel any better. I wondered if this was what the killer wanted.

Did he want Ricky to kill himself, or did he think it would go another way too?

We pulled up to the building. It already was swarmed by cops. Crime scene techs were everywhere outside.

Dr. Pittman was already examining the body as we drove up. As soon as the car came to a stop, I jumped out and rushed over to her.

"Can't walk three paces in this town without running into you two," she said. "Are you on this one too? It's definitely a suicide."

I explained the link between the other case. Her eyes went wide.

"Oh." She looked down at the body. "He jumped. Not only is the angle right for a suicide, witnesses saw him do it."

I shook my head. Tony joined us. And then an officer walked over. We flashed our badges and asked to speak with the witnesses.

There was only one witness, his secretary. She had been at her desk and just happened to look out the window at the exact moment Ricky's body passed by.

"Are you sure he jumped?" I asked.

His secretary, Cora, was distraught. Her mascara was running. Her eyes were redder than the curls on her head, which were a mess. She nodded slowly.

"We were the only ones here. We're always the only ones here in the morning." She stifled a sob. "I have to get in before him, so around six… I'm here every morning around six, and he gets in thirty minutes after me, usually."

"And there was no one else here?" asked Tony. "No janitor or…"

She shook her head. "No. Just us."

"How was he acting when he got in?"

She dabbed her eyes with a tissue. "It was weird. I mean, you've met him. He wasn't a nice man. He was rude and very short with people and… but this morning he was nice. It… well, it caught me off guard. He told me I looked pretty today and that he hoped I had a good day. He had never said anything like that to me before. Not even when I first started."

"What did he do before he went up to the roof?"

She glanced at Tony and then chewed on her bottom lip for a moment. "He came in. Went into his office. He was there for twenty minutes, I think. Then he came out, um… he stopped by my desk and told me to hold his calls this morning and that he hoped I had a wonderful day. And that he was going up to the roof for a minute." Cora shook her head. "I should have known then that something was wrong. The way he looked at me. And he never goes to the roof. There's nothing up there."

I glanced at Tony and then headed into the building. He went into his office. If he had already made up his mind to kill himself, then why go into the office? Why come to work? Why couldn't he have done it at home?

"Maybe he had to get something off of his computer." Tony pressed the button for the top floor.

"You think he left a note?" Even as I said the words, I couldn't picture Ricky Thompson leaving behind a suicide letter.

He shrugged. "Some people do. Some people don't."

"But we are definitely thinking suicide, right? No foul play?"

Tony pressed his lips into a firm thin line. "I want to say yes. It's not exactly our killer's MO, is it?"

"The question is, was he more afraid of what the killer would do to him? Or of being arrested for… something?" I asked.

"All depends on what that something is."

The doors dinged open. The floor was filled with crime scene techs and cops. While it looked like a suicide, and it probably was, they still needed to gather evidence. Just in case.

We flashed our badges to the officer keeping watch. In Ricky's office, there were two techs and two officers looking around.

"Did anyone find a note?" asked Tony.

A female officer with dark-brown skin and caramel-colored eyes sighed. "I'm not sure if it's a note or what it means exactly, but his computer was on when we walked in." She pointed to the screen:

"I am not a monster."

"Any other context?"

She shook her head. "It was the last thing he wrote, so it had to mean something. Does this mean the FBI is taking over the case? You want us to have the computer and electronics transferred to the field office?"

Tony nodded. "Will do."

"Anything else?" I asked.

"His phone." She pointed to a pile of electronic pieces on the corner of the desk. "He broke up his phone, and from what we can tell, the SIM card is not here."

Now that was strange. He was going to kill himself, and even left behind a message, but he destroyed his phone so we couldn't see what was on it after he died. What was the point of that? I mean, he was dead; what did it matter now?

"Send that and all its pieces to the field office too."

The female officer nodded.

We checked the roof before we left the building, but there was nothing there.

"'I am not a monster…,'" Tony mused. "Whatever the killer had on him, he was afraid it was going to get out. He just didn't want to face it."

"But what could that have been?" I asked.

We already did a deep dive into Ricky's life and came up empty. He wasn't the nicest person in the world, but we found no evidence of him doing anything illegal. So what could he have been into that made him think killing himself was the only option?

As soon as we got back to the office, my phone got two alerts. And I was thankful for them both. With our only suspect dead, we had to start from square one. Anything he could have told us about the killer or what they wanted out the window. Or off the roof really. We needed another lead.

The first alert was from Dr. Pittman. The second body had finally been confirmed as David Carter. The second alert was from the IT department. They had finally gotten all the names attached to the driver's licenses.

We headed to the IT department before we went to our desks, and Love was waiting for us.

"Wow, you guys got here pretty fast," she commented as she was pulling up her computer.

"Well, we were just getting in," replied Tony.

Eli stuck his head around a corner, saw us, and walked over. "How's the case?"

I sighed.

"That bad?" he looked at Tony.

"Our prime suspect... well, not suspect, really, but the one connection between these two bodies just killed himself. He was supposed to come in this morning with his lawyer, but instead, he went to his office and jumped off the building," answered Tony.

"Damn. You sure it's a suicide and not made to look like that?"

Tony shrugged. "Could be, but it's pretty different from our killer's MO. They're still processing the scene. We're thinking more like he didn't want his secrets getting out."

"Damn," said Eli again. He sat on the edge of the desk across from Love's desk. "That's... I guess he really didn't want to talk to the FBI."

"Most people don't," I said. "But they don't kill themselves. And leave behind messages that say 'I am not a monster.'"

"And the plot thickens. What the hell is that about?"

Tony and I both shrugged.

"Okay. So these are the six license numbers that were written on your second victim. One of them was Ricky Thompson."

"Can you print these out?" I asked.

She nodded. Ricky was no longer an issue, so we needed to focus on the other five. We would have to divide and conquer. Hopefully, we could get a few other agents to help.

Special Agent Love printed out the names with their contact information and handed them to us. Eli wished us luck. He said he was curious about the case. I told him we would let him know how it all worked out before we headed back to our desk to make some calls.

"We just need to ask you a few questions about Ricky Thompson. Did you know him?"

Every person I asked that question did know him and was saddened to hear about his suicide. All four people agreed to come in and talk about their friend.

One person didn't answer the phone. John Hargrove. I left him a voice mail and then waited for him to call back. After a few hours, the four men who had answered showed up. Louis, Travis, Harris, and Corey.

We could have spoken with them separately and then compared notes at the end of our interview. But an idea popped into my head. I glanced down at the sheet of paper on my desk, where John Hargrove's name was highlighted.

"I think we should give them to four other agents, and we should try and find John Hargrove.

Tony's brow ticked up. "They guy who didn't answer? Why?"

Sometimes it felt like he was testing me. Like he was pretending to be clueless so he could see if I knew what I was talking about. If I knew how to stand by my decisions and my convictions. If I knew how to back up a theory. This felt like one of those times. Like he had the same idea but wanted to see what had gotten me there.

"It's just a feeling really. I'm more concerned about the guy who didn't show up. He never even called back. It just feels strange to me."

A smile tugged at the corner of his mouth. "Yeah, it feels strange to me too."

We had Special Agent Baldwin hand off the four men to agents who had been briefed on what questions to ask, and then we set off to find John.

I called him again while we were in the car and still didn't get an answer. My heart sank a little. Something was wrong. Either he had skipped town or he was already dead.

John's house was nice and luxurious on the outside. Well-manicured lawn and a Lexus in the driveway. The house was beige or light-brown with black trim. If he was home, why wasn't he answering his phone?

"I got a bad feeling about this," I said.

We got out of the car and eased up to the door, our hands on our holsters. As soon as we neared the door, I smelled it. The unmistakable scent of a decomposing body.

The door was locked. Tony kicked it in. We cleared the living room and the kitchen and the office. I followed the smell to a room. A room with the door closed—and with a lock on the outside of the door.

"Why would you have a lock on the outside of the door?" I wondered

"You want to keep someone in," answered Tony.

I pushed the door open. And there it was.

A body. Just like the others, it had been beaten beyond recognition. Just like the others, there was a newspaper clipping tacked to his chest.

# CHAPTER TWENTY

STUMBLED OUT OF THE ROOM, MY HAND REACHING FOR MY phone automatically. I didn't think I would see this many dead bodies as an FBI agent. When I think about it now, that thought seems so stupid.

How could I be an FBI agent and not see a dead body or two? That came with the job. But we had seen so many in the last few days. It felt like it was never ending. Body after body.

Fat flies swarming around dried blood. Eyes beaten out of sockets. It was just too much. When they first told me where I would be stationed, it was my understanding that I would be eased into my job. Smaller cases at first. Learn the ropes and all that. But no.

I was surrounded by dead bodies looking for justice, and I was unable to deliver. I wondered for a brief moment if Brandon

Aolani would have solved this case by now. I wondered if they missed him. If they looked at me and thought I was lacking. If they called him and talked about the case and how I still hadn't solved it yet.

For a brief moment, I wondered if he was better than I would ever be and I would never be able to fill his shoes.

My mind flashed back to something my mother said when I first told her about my new case and how I was trying to fill someone else's shoes.

"You can't do that. No one sees the world like you do, and that's what you need to bring to your new job. You won't be him, and he could never be like you. Of course, he would have solved cases faster, he had more experience. You're just starting out, and it's going to take a little while for you to get your bearings. So don't be too hard on yourself."

Even though she had made it clear that she didn't want me to join the FBI, her little speech really made me feel better. I wasn't sure if it was just something moms said to their children to make them feel better or if she really believed it. But it worked. It made me feel better about myself, and that was something that I needed to hold on to now.

Brandon Aolani had retired. He'd done his duty to the FBI and to the people of Hawaii. And now it was my turn to step up. And I had to speak for these victims.

I called Dr. Pittman once I got to the living room. There was still the smell of decomposition, but it wasn't as bright as it was in the hallway.

"You okay?"

I nodded, hunched over and trying to catch my breath.

Tony took a deep breath. "This probably wasn't the best first case for you to have. The Bureau was supposed to ease first agents in. Get them used to the job. They kinda threw you in the deep end."

"Without a floaty or those arm things that stop you from drowning," I complained.

Tony chuckled. "I'll be your floaty."

"Thanks."

"The body looks like it's been here for a while. Although not as long as the others. And it seemed like he really hated the guy."

"What was the thing on his chest?" I asked now standing up straight.

"A newspaper clipping of an old case. I think it was worked by the local police, but I remember hearing about it."

It didn't take long for backup and the crime scene investigators to arrive. Tony showed them into the room, and the techs started working the crime scene.

"I want you to take pictures of the body now so I can get that off his chest."

I can see the flashes from the camera from the hallway. A few seconds later, Tony emerged with the clipping in his gloved hand. I slipped on a pair of gloves so I could touch the paper.

"Jayden Sheppard," I said the name slowly.

"Ten-Year-Old Boy Goes Missing on Family Vacation," read the headline.

"That would be heartbreaking. You take your family on vacation, and then your son goes missing."

Tony rocked back on his heels. "I vaguely remember the case. He was playing or something, and then he was just gone. Parents never found out what happened to him. As far as I know, it was never solved. And it wasn't an FBI case. It was the local police."

I read through the article. How was this linked to the murders? Were the murders about Jayden Sheppard? How did this puzzle piece fit with the others? Nothing was making sense.

"You two have really been working me the past few days." Dr. Pittman sashayed into the house in a bright, almost-neon pink dress that looked so skintight I don't think she could have bent over a body if she wanted to. Her hair had been pinned back with flowers, and she was already snapping on gloves and shrugging on a white lab coat.

"Have somewhere to go later?" I asked.

She shrugged. "Not yet. Now point me toward the body."

There was a flash in the hallway, and she turned. "Never mind. I'll follow them."

We had been racking up the body count lately. It wasn't intentional though. The killer was trying to send a message, but now with Ricky dead, it didn't feel like the message was for him but for us.

John was killed before Ricky killed himself. At least that was how it looked. I only saw the body for a few seconds, so I couldn't say for sure.

I wondered if the killer knew Ricky was already dead. If he had any idea what his plan had caused. If he cared. Or if that was part of the plan all along. Make Ricky so distraught and fearful that he had no choice but to kill himself. If he wanted to keep his secret, he had to die.

"So John Hargrove is dead."

"Are we sure that's who that was?"

Tony cocked his head to the side. "I think it was, but we still need to make sure."

"It is," said Dr. Pittman. She walked toward us with a picture frame in her hand. She pointed to a man next to a woman in a bikini. "This is John Hargrove. You see that tattoo on his side? I just checked the body, and it has that tattoo. Same placement. Same everything."

In the picture, the man with short strawberry-blond hair had a tattoo of an anchor on his side.

"That's a weird tattoo. And a weird placement," I remarked.

Tony. "I guess he loved the water. Or wanted to be anchored to something. To himself."

"Okay. So our victim is John Hargrove. Now we need to figure out how he is connected to the first two victims and what that has to do with the Jayden Sheppard case."

"Well, that means we need to go to the local precinct."

"See you next crime scene," Pittman joked as we headed out.

I shook my head. How that woman managed to keep her stomach straight astounded me.

Tony and I drove to the local precinct. I had a million questions roaming around my head. I was hoping we could find the answer to at least one. Just one.

How were they connected to Jayden Sheppard?

We walked in, and the smell of lemons hit me. Across from the door was a large wooden desk with a man sitting behind it, looking completely bored. We badged him, and his expression somehow got even more uninterested.

"What do you want?" he sighed.

I raised an eyebrow. I knew that local law enforcement and the FBI didn't always get along, but most of the officers I'd run into on this case had been pretty all right to work with. But maybe that was why this guy was behind a desk and not out catching bad guys.

I fixed my most professional smile on my face. "We aren't here to take over a case, we just need to speak with the detective who worked the Jayden Sheppard case. Missing ten-year-old."

"Mhm." He picked up his phone and asked for a Detective Kalani, then returned to idly staring off at whatever he was looking at before.

Tony leaned in to whisper, "Real warm reception here at the HPD."

I had to bite down a laugh.

A few minutes later, a large Hawaiian man, who looked a little too young to have his hair so gray and so thin, emerged from the hallway to the right.

"So the FBI wants the Sheppard case?" he asked instead of saying hello.

"I'm not sure if we want it exactly," I told him. "But we would like to know how it ties in with our current case."

This seemed to pique his interest. He stared at me for a moment like he was waiting for me to elaborate.

"Can we go sit down and talk?" I asked instead.

Detective Kalani gestured for us to follow him. We followed him down a short hallway to an open floor filled with desks and detectives all busy staring at computer screens, writing something down, or scrolling on their phones.

We followed him to what looked like a conference room. It wasn't as nice as the one in the field office, but it was nice enough. Long table, comfortable-looking chairs, and a closed door for privacy. We took our seats, and he cleared his throat.

"So what do you want with the Sheppard case?"

We explained what we knew so far and the last clue we found. The newspaper clipping.

Kalani's brows furrowed. "That is strange. None of those names came up in my investigation. I mean, I don't have the case file right now. I'll have to get it out of storage. It's a cold case. All of our leads dried up years ago."

"I see," I said.

He sighed. "I can go to storage today. If you'll come back tomorrow, I'll have the case file and my notes for you to look over. I can't be too sure—I'm a lot older now—but I don't remember John Hargrove, Ricky Thompson, or the others even being interviewed for this case."

"Did you have a prime suspect?" Tony asked.

He stared at the ground for a long moment. "Levi. Levi something."

"Okay," I said. "Call us when you have the case file, and we will come over and get it." I handed him my card, and he nodded.

"Will do."

We left the precinct with no answers. And I was a little irritated.

"How long ago was the Jayden Sheppard case?" I asked when we got back into the car.

"Three, maybe four years."

Why wouldn't he be able to remember a case from three or four years ago? He wasn't that old. I mean, he was still working, wasn't he? This whole thing was frustrating. We were so far behind the killer we would never catch up before they killed someone else.

I had the feeling that the killer was trying to tell us something. He was trying to lead us somewhere; I just couldn't tell where.

It was a puzzle. Only we didn't have all the pieces and didn't know where to find them.

We spent the day looking into John Hargrove. Much like Ricky Thompson, he was the CEO of a tech company. A nice guy who loved giving to charity and helping with his community. And while some of that could have been true, I couldn't help but wonder if there was something people didn't know about John.

I mean, nice guys didn't end up beaten to death in a room that locked from the outside.

"What was up with that room?"

"Yeah, I was thinking about that," said Tony. "Not only did it lock from the outside, but there were whips and chains and strange outfits in the closet."

"So a BDSM dungeon."

Tony shrugged.

"That locked from the outside. So whoever he had in there couldn't get out even if they wanted to."

"It looked that way," he acknowledged.

"So maybe John Hargrove wasn't such a great guy after all."

An hour before the day ended, we got a call from the front desk saying Detective Kalani was here to see us. He was escorted to the conference room where we met him.

He set a box on the table, but the bright-red notebook, he kept in his hand. He held it close to his body like he was afraid he was going to lose it.

"These are my notes on the case. You can make copies of them, but I need them back. I have other cold case notes in the notebook."

I nodded. "I thought you were going to wait until tomorrow?"

He shrugged. "I couldn't get it out of my mind. And since I couldn't focus on anything else, I figured I might as well go ahead and look for it."

"Okay," said Tony.

We all took a seat at the table.

"Umm. Levi Whitman was the name of the prime suspect. He lived two houses down from the Airbnb that the Sheppard family was staying in. The way things are now, you stay in a strange person's home because you don't want to pay for a hotel room. You don't know the people in the neighborhood. Anyway, he was a registered sex offender. Raped two kids when he was early twenties. So naturally, we looked at him. But we could never pin it on him."

"He had an alibi?" I took the top off the box and started going through the evidence.

"Airtight. He was at work. We talked to his boss and coworkers. Everything checked out. But I still felt like he knew something. There was something he wasn't telling us."

In the box were a backpack and a towel.

"Those were found on the street where Jayden had been playing. They were his. It was like someone just scooped him up and took him away. Like he was never there. And we never found a body or anything to say he was hurt or murdered. Just... nothing."

"The family still follow up?" I asked.

He sighed. "I still get calls from them asking if there's been any movement on the case. Sometimes I don't want to answer... I never have anything to tell them. But I do anyway. And I let them vent and talk about their son. It gets harder and harder every time. But I don't know how his case could have been linked to yours. The father was in construction. Mom was a teacher. And he was ten. They probably never had a reason to cross paths."

I nodded. He was probably right. But there had to be a link. There had to be something. The number on the first body led us to Ricky. The numbers on the second body led us to Ricky and John Hargrove. The news clipping had to be leading us somewhere even if we couldn't see it.

I took his notebook and made copies of his notes before thanking him and sending him home.

"There has to be a link," I said. "There just has to be. This has to be important, or why leave it tacked to the body?"

"Your guess is as good as mine," Tony replied glumly.

I could only hope that guess would be good enough to put a stop to this killer. Before he struck again.

# CHAPTER TWENTY-ONE

L ITTLE ROSE SPENT HER LAST DAY LIKE SHE ALWAYS HAD. To her, it was no different from all the others, so there was no reason to do anything different. It wasn't spent trying to better herself or helping someone. It wasn't spent trying to contact her family and make amends. No, she spent her day like she had every day since she was sixteen—high and in the back seat of someone's car.

When she was done for the day and had made all the money she was going to make, she went home. A small run-down motel that was trying to be an apartment complex. She stumbled up to the door, fished her keys out of her purse, and opened the door. The smell of weed and heroin mingled. It was a smell that she loved. A smell that she had come to savor. A smell that meant escape and happiness all rolled into one.

She closed the door behind her, stumbled over to the sofa, and collapsed. To Little Rose, it was just any other day. And this was her normal routine. But it wasn't. The Puzzler sat at the small kitchenette across from the sofa, shrouded in darkness. While she closed her eyes, he watched her. Debating on what to do now.

The Puzzler was puzzled, to say the least. He didn't have to go through his usual routine of watching and waiting. No one paid attention to her. No one was looking for her. Or would notice if or when she went missing. She had no one. And that was new to him. She had no neighbors that would say something about a strange man entering her home. That was normal for her.

He watched her and waited. Until her chest rose and fell and light snoring came from her direction. He knew she was sleeping.

Now that she was asleep, he could go through with his plan. She was high—that he knew. But he gave her a little of his serum anyway so she would stay knocked out. Just long enough for transport.

He waited ten minutes to make sure she was really out. He then stuffed her in the large piece of luggage that he had brought with him. Little Rose was not a large woman. She looked like a teenager. Short and thin from drug use and not eating enough.

It was easy to tuck her inside the roller bag. Too easy. The Puzzler zipped it up. He stood in her small apartment and stared at the bag for one long moment.

It was strange. A person stuffed in a piece of luggage like a pile of clothes. He didn't dwell on it too much. Her current predicament wasn't his fault. This was a hell of her own making.

He made sure he got everything he came with before exiting the apartment. The roller bag trailed behind him. Outside it was dark and quiet. He walked down the stairs and to his car without seeing anyone. That didn't mean no one saw him, but he was careful. He pulled his hat so low it hid his eyes. He gently placed the bag in the trunk of the car.

He looked around for a moment before he got in his car and drove off. The spot where she would have to answer his questions had already been picked out.

A place where no one would hear her scream. He could have done it in her apartment. He thought about it. But there were too many people around the building. People hanging outside at all hours of the day. People who weren't always high.

Someone would hear her screams. Someone would grow a conscience and think about calling the police, and then all this would have been for nothing. And she, out of all of them, *she* deserved everything that was about to happen to her.

The Puzzler pulled up to the abandoned warehouse and parked. It was an old factory that had been closed down and then turned into a warehouse that was then closed down a few years later.

No one was using it now. He had sat in front of the building for a couple of days just to see if anyone ever came by.

No one ever did. There had been some runners that passed by. Or people walking their dogs. But no one ever went into the building. And no one passed by after dark.

He pulled the bag out of the trunk and hauled it inside. The main room branched off into hallways and closed doors. He didn't need the endless hallways or the tucked-away rooms. The middle of the floor was more than enough.

The windows were frosted, so even if someone did walk by, they wouldn't be able to see in. The chair and his tools were already set up. All he had to do was take her out of the bag and tie her to the chair. It was easy enough. He couldn't get over how light she was.

Like picking up a small child. She was still sleeping. He threw her over his shoulder, walked over to the chair, and placed her in it. She didn't make a sound.

All he had to do was wait.

The Puzzler wasn't sure if it was the drugs she had taken or the ones he had given her, but he had to wait longer than usual.

He smacked her a few times, and yet she still wouldn't open her eyes.

It was an hour or two later when she finally came around. He watched her go through all the emotions that the others had when they had first woken up.

She woke with a jolt. Her eyes blinked rapidly as she looked around, trying to gauge her surroundings. When her eyes settled on him they went wide with surprise.

"Do you want me to call you Little Rose or Maggie Woods?"

She opened her mouth to speak and then closed it. She opened it again.

"I don't do bondage, and you're going to have to pay me up front."

The Puzzler laughed. "That's not what this is. I'm going to ask you a few questions, and you are going to answer them."

"And if you don't like my answers?"

He played with the pliers in his hand and shrugged. Whether he liked her answers or not, this would all end the same. She was going to die. She deserved to die.

She was worse than the rest, and she would pay for it. He thought better of saying what he was thinking. He needed her to be calm for a little while longer while the drugs worked their way out of her system.

This time it didn't matter if she screamed. They were in a warehouse in the middle of nowhere. No one would hear her.

"I don't know anything."

All the others had said the same. And while some knew nothing, some knew a little more than he did. He would have never looked for Little Rose if it wasn't for John Hargrove. He had led The Puzzler to her. And now she would lead him to the next person.

"Do you know a man named John Hargrove?"

She pressed her lips together as if to stop herself from talking. Which told him everything he needed to know.

He sighed. "I see. Well, he's the one who told me about you. Said you could help me in my quest for information."

She rolled her eyes. "You think you're the first to ask about them? You're not. I didn't say anything when the cops asked, and I'm not saying anything now. I'm not dying because you want information."

The Puzzler chuckled. He stared at her and thought about whether that was irony or something else. She was, in fact, going to die because he wanted information.

Was it irony? Or was it a self-fulfilling prophecy?

He knew, deep down, that just asking wasn't going to get him anywhere. Little Rose had been around for a long time. While her frame was small like a child, her eyes were older than his.

She was a woman who had *seen* things. Some good. Some she wanted to forget. She wouldn't give in so easily.

He knew he was going to have to torture her, and he knew he was going to enjoy it.

When he snapped off her pinky finger, the scream that erupted from her mouth made him jump. She had been so quiet before. So soft-spoken. He didn't know her voice could be that loud. She screamed even louder when he cauterized the wound.

She was bleeding everywhere, and he couldn't have her pass out before he got what he wanted.

"You son of a—"

"Name-calling will not help you. Not now." He pulled his chair closer to her and then sat down. "You know what I want to know. So just tell me already. This will be much easier if you just spill everything."

Tears streamed down her cheeks, and that, for some reason, surprised him. Maybe the drugs were wearing off. The constant throb in her finger working down the length of her arm must have been painful.

"Who runs the organization?"

"What organization?" she croaked.

"The one you supply children to."

She was quiet then. So quiet that he almost thought her heart had stopped beating. Her whole body went still like she was a bear and if she could just stay still long enough, the threat would go away.

But The Puzzler wasn't going away. Not without the information he needed. He needed the next rung on the ladder so he could get to the top.

So he could be done.

So the police could see the bigger picture.

She shook her head.

"I see."

The Puzzler sighed. He hated when they were stubborn. He tried to give them a way out. If they just told him what he wanted to know, there would be no need for torture. There would be no need for these theatrics.

He would just take the information, kill them, and be on his merry way. He didn't like the act of torture, but that didn't mean he wouldn't do it. And so he did.

When he sat back in his chair to catch his breath, Maggie Woods was covered in blood, and her answers came a little faster.

She told him everything he wanted to know. Everything she knew.

"I just get the children. Children no one cares about. Children left outside to play with themselves. Where no one is watching them. I take the ones I think they'll like, and they pay me," she explained, her voice hoarse and tired from screaming.

"Just because a child is outside—"

"If you loved a child, you wouldn't leave them alone. Not even for a second. Their parents weren't watching them. No one was. It took them a while to even notice they were gone. What kind of parent does that? What parent doesn't care? And so we take them."

He could have gotten more information. He could have. He could have removed a few more fingers. An eye. After all, she didn't need her hands or her eyes to talk. But he couldn't.

Her words… her words had gotten to him. Crawled beneath his skin and made a home there. Burrowed into his bones. Children were loved. Their parents loved them. They deserved to be able to play out in the streets and then come home to be with their families.

But she stole that away from them. She ruined their families. And while he wasn't sure if Maggie was the one who had torn his own family apart, at that moment she was.

He could have gotten more information from her. But instead, he picked up the metal pipe and walked over to her chair. And he hit her.

Again. And again. And he kept hitting her until his arm was so tired, so numb.

The pipe was so slick with blood that it slipped from his fingers. The hard metal hit the ground, shaking him from his trance. When he looked up, Little Rose was dead.

When she had died, he wasn't sure. He couldn't say when she stopped screaming. When her screams had been replaced with the soft, wet sound of pipe striking flesh, breaking bones.

It didn't matter. Not really.

He slumped back into the chair to catch his breath. His chest heaved. His arm was so tired he couldn't lift it. The sound of blood rushing in his ears blocked out everything else.

There was nothing else. Just him and Little Rose's broken, mangled body.

He sat there for a little while. Usually, he didn't stay with the body. There was always a chance that someone would come over and knock on the door. Or that someone had seen him slip into the house.

But not here. There was no chance of someone just walking into the warehouse. So he could take his time leaving. He could catch his breath. Give his nerves the chance to settle. Give his heart the chance to return to a normal rhythm before he jumped into his car. He hadn't been able to do that before.

He took a deep breath. The smell of blood hung heavy in the air. He wondered for a moment how long it would take someone to find her. It took a while with the others, and he was okay with that.

But no one would be looking for Maggie Woods. No one would notice if she didn't turn up to her corner the next day. Or the next.

And that was sad. But fitting.

He wondered, as he stared at the pool of blood, how many children she had stolen. She wouldn't say how many.

He had asked her twice. This made him think it was a pretty big number. A number so high she was ashamed, as she should have been.

The Puzzler would never understand how a woman in her position could do what she had done. How could she take those children, all those children, and hand them over? Knowing what would happen to them. How could she do that?

She knew what they were going to do. She knew what kind of men they were, and yet it didn't matter to her. She didn't care as long as she got her cut.

He hated her. He didn't know her, and yet he hated her. And now she was dead.

And now he needed to get cleaned up and search for the next name on the list.

# CHAPTER TWENTY-TWO

L EVI WHITMAN NO LONGER LIVED IN THE HOUSE NEXT
to the Airbnb, so it took a while to track him down.

He was a short man. He looked like a child himself.
Well, a teenager, with dark-brown hair, brown eyes, and thick
wire-framed glasses. There was a curve to his back, like he sat
behind a computer for long periods of time.

There was something about him that said creepy. My
mother believed that she could tell if a person was a killer or
not by the way they looked.

"It's all in the eyes," she'd said when I told her about my first
case. "I'm telling you. You know I watch a lot of true crime. And
every time they show the mug shot, I just know. The eyes are
shifty and creepy-looking."

I tried to explain to my mother that just because some people were bug-eyed didn't mean that they were murderers. She didn't want to listen.

"I'm telling you, just look at them. Creepy people kill people."

She made me laugh, and I needed that. If she saw Levi Whitman, she would have arrested him on the spot. He was a little creepy-looking. I don't know if it was killer-creepy, but there was something about him that just didn't sit right with me. But we couldn't arrest him just based on his looks.

"Why is the FBI in my living room this time?" he asked.

He had invited us in. Maybe he thought he had nothing to hide or that we wouldn't find anything. But it was his idea for us to come in and sit down. So we did. The living room had a sofa, a chair, and a TV on the far side of the room. That was it.

"We wanted to talk to you about the Jayden Sheppard case."

Levi jumped up. The abrupt action made my hand reach for my holster.

"I didn't do anything to that boy," he snapped. "I've gotten my shit together. I haven't done anything in years to anyone, especially not kids. I made two mistakes, and now you guys are just going to come here and think I'm guilty every time a child goes missing."

I would have felt sorry for him if it wasn't for the so-called mistakes he made. That being said, it must have been hard to live with. And whenever the police had a missing or abused child, they always found themselves on your doorstep. Regardless of how you turned your life around, you would always be the first suspect. No matter what.

That must have been hell. But it was a hell of his own making.

"No one is saying that you did it," I assured him. "Jayden Sheppard came up in a homicide we are currently working, and since you lived right down the street, we figured you were the person to ask."

His shoulders dropped a little, but he didn't sit down.

"FBI investigates murders?"

I glanced back at Tony. Why did everyone ask that?

I nodded. "We do. And we have a murder victim with the newspaper clipping of Jayden's case tacked to his chest. A John Hargrove?"

Levi slid back into the chair across from me. "John's dead?"

I blinked. My back straightened. "You knew John Hargrove?"

He nodded slowly. "We went to school together."

Tony frowned. "What about Ricky Thompson, David Carter, and Kent—"

"Barnum? Yeah, we all went to school together."

Was he the link? The thing that tied them all together?

"They're all dead."

Levi stared at me, mouth wide open. "I... I can't believe it. Why?"

"We don't know," I answered. "Can you think of any reasons someone would try to kill them?"

Levi shrugged a little. "I mean we might have been assholes in high school. But I don't think we did anything that was worth killing us over. Or them over."

"Were you all still close?" asked Tony.

Levi ran a hand through his hair. "Not really. Not with my scandals. I lost a lot of friends. But I still saw Kent from time to time. We would say hello. I can't believe they're all gone..."

Levi wasn't able to give us much more information. But all the victims knew each other from high school. That had to mean something.

Before I got back into the car, there was an alert on my phone from the IT department.

"Eli from IT wants to see us," I announced.

"Better be something good," Tony said.

"Okay, so after our last conversation, I had been thinking about your victims," Eli told me as soon as we stepped off the elevator.

"Well, we have another one for you," I said. "John Hargrove. He was one of the driver's license numbers that you all searched for. He was the only one not to show up to the field office, and when we went to see him, he was dead. And had been for a little while."

"Damn. Okay. I got to thinking about the link among the victims. And maybe it wasn't that they all knew each other."

"They did though," I said.

His face fell.

"Found out today. All of the victims and a sex offender went to high school together."

Eli's shoulder dropped a little. "Good to know. But anyway…"

I chuckled a little. He seemed so eager to show us what he found. Like a little kid wanting you to look at the drawing. He turned toward the computer and pulled the screen up onto the big screen.

"So I was thinking maybe there was another link. I took the license numbers and did a search. I looked for places or transactions they all did."

"Maybe what they had in common wasn't each other but places they frequented," offered Tony.

"Exactly," said Eli, the excitement in his voice bubbling up to the surface. "When we did the search, we found they had a few transactions in common."

"Why would they stand out? I mean, everyone has to go to the store or out to eat, so it would make sense if they shared some common transactions," I pointed out. "Especially if they all grew up around here."

"It would make sense. And you're right they did. But these"—he highlighted pieces of text on the screen—"are to a shell company. This company has no office, no board of directors, and no CEO. It doesn't exist, and yet here it is, and they all have transactions to it."

I moved closer to the big screen. Not only did they all buy things from this company, but they also had recurring transactions once a month. Like a subscription or something.

"We looked up the company and can't tell you what they sell or what they do."

"That is strange. I wonder what it's for."

Part of me was saying to drag back in those other four people and make them tell us. But how could we make them do that? We were the FBI, but we had nothing concrete saying this company had anything to do with the victim's murder. But this had to be our link. There had to be something to it.

I was so tired of going back and forth. Of looking for something and not knowing what I was looking for. I was tired of searching for links and then being disappointed when they didn't go anywhere. I was tired of finding dead bodies and wondering if we could have done anything to stop it.

Tony's phone rang, and he stepped aside to take it. When he returned a minute later, his face had fallen, and he was sighing.

"Hate to break it to you, but we've got another body."

I groaned.

The drive to our next crime scene was a silent one. I didn't know what to say. I didn't know what else to do. Solving murders… I felt like I was way over my head. Like they had pulled in the wrong person for this case. I could never replace Brandon Aolani. I could never solve this puzzle.

We pulled up in front of the crime scene tape. The warehouse before us was run-down and old, practically crumbling. I almost worried it would collapse on us when we stepped inside.

Blood covered the floor, and there was a woman slumped in a chair, with crime scene techs taking pictures all around her.

"She is definitely the freshest one you've brought me," said Dr. Pittman. "And she was tortured like the rest. Only—I don't know how to say it—he *really* took a distaste to this one."

I looked at the body. This time I wouldn't cower or run away. I wouldn't step outside searching for fresh air. I wouldn't run. This time I was going to stand my ground and look at the victim. Regardless of what my stomach had to say about it. I took a deep breath and swallowed hard.

Dr. Pittman was right. The victim was beaten savagely. There was blood spray all along the wall and on the ceiling. Her skull was crushed. Half of her head seemed to fold in on itself. One of her eyes was missing.

He'd beaten her over and over again with something. Her nose was pushed inward. I drew in a shaky breath. She wasn't fresh, but she hadn't been sitting as long as the others, so the smell wasn't as bad.

"Do we know who the victim was?" asked Tony.

"Maggie Woods."

I looked up at an officer standing next to the body. He was Hawaiian with thick, black hair and light-brown eyes.

"Everyone at the precinct knows her."

"Why?" I asked.

He glanced at her body for a long moment. "She's called Little Rose. She's been collared a lot for solicitation. She's been in and out of jail since before I started."

Dr. Pittman peeled the newspaper clipping off her chest and handed it to Tony, who was putting on gloves.

"CHELSEA WESLEY STILL MISSING," read Tony.

"Do you know the case?"

He shook his head.

"I don't think the FBI helped with that one," said the officer. "I vaguely remember when she went missing. I think Detective Kalani had the case."

"Fun coincidence," I noted with a sigh. This was a lot of back and forth and not learning anything. What was the killer trying to tell us?

"You two again?" Detective Kalani jumped up from his desk when we arrived at the precinct. "Did you find Jayden?"

I shook my head. "We have another murder."

"I heard. Someone is really keeping you two busy. Do you think it's linked to Jayden's case? Did you talk to Levi?"

I nodded. "We did talk to him, and we learned about a connection between our victims. Well, the victims before the last one. Maggie Woods. And she had a newspaper clipping of another missing kid case. Chelsea Wesley."

Kalani stumbled back. His hands landed on the back of his chair. His grip tightened on the chair.

"Haven't heard that name in a long time. Um..."—he looked around—"let's go to the conference room."

We followed him into the same room as before.

"Chelsea Wesley was a sweet girl," he explained. "Her adoptive family lived here on the island. Brother still lives here. She was taken when she was playing in the front yard. I mean, it was like she just disappeared. We never found her. Not her body, alive or dead, or any trace of her anywhere."

"How long ago was this?" I asked.

"Fifteen years ago. It was the first case I had as a detective."

"Were there any suspects?"

He sighed as he looked at me and shook his head. "No. No suspects. I mean, fifteen years ago, this was before Ring cameras and all the techy stuff people put outside their homes to catch thieves. No one on the street saw anything. She was there one moment, and the next she was gone."

"Were the parents ever suspects?" asked Tony.

He nodded. "We did suspect them. And I think some people still do. It was strange that the little girl went missing days after the adoption was final. And the parents didn't really seem that upset about it. But that could have been because they had just adopted her and didn't have that familial bond yet."

"What did you think?"

"Honestly, I don't know." The detective stared at the wall, clearly reliving those days. "Some days I thought it could have been the parents. Taking care of two children was more than they could handle. But some days I just couldn't see the mother hurting that little girl."

"Was there a connection between Jayden's case and Chelsea's?"

The killer had to be pointing us in this direction for some reason. There had to be something that they wanted us to know about both missing children.

"I don't think so. I mean, other than them disappearing without a trace, I don't see any connection."

"Well, maybe that's it," I said. "How they disappeared. It's hard to just pick up a child and make them disappear. Not just that, but if they were dead, then where was the body? Surely Chelsea's body would have been found by now."

"You would think," said Tony. "Is all her family gone from the island?"

"Her brother, Dane, still lives here. He calls me every once in a while. Just trying to keep his sister's case fresh in my mind."

"Can we—"

"Sure. I'll write down his information for you." Kalani walked back to his desk, wrote down the information, and brought it to us.

"I know you don't owe me anything, but if you find out who did these kidnappings, or if you need any help at all, please call me and let me know. I would love to close these cases."

I nodded.

I handed Tony the address on the way out the door, wondering, what was the point? How were missing children connected to our murdered victims? And did it have anything to do with the shell company that the victims paid monthly?

A million questions ran through my mind. Over and over. The puzzle kept turning. Pieces moving. Pieces trying to fit in the wrong places.

There was something we were missing. There had to be. The killer was doing this for a reason, but I just couldn't figure out what it was, and that irked me.

Maybe that was why they kept killing people. Maybe the killer felt like we should have put it together by now. And since we hadn't, they were going to keep killing people until we solved the puzzle.

But the pieces they left behind hadn't added up to anything yet. None of it made any sense. How were we supposed to put it together if we didn't know everything?

And were they just going to keep killing people until we figured it out?

I was beyond exhausted. I just wanted to take my brain, plop it on the kitchen counter, and then go to bed. Where I didn't have to think for a few hours.

That would have been nice.

# CHAPTER TWENTY-THREE

D ANE WESLEY WAS ANGRY. THAT MUCH WAS OBVIOUS from the moment he opened his door. We flashed our badges and introduced ourselves, and he went completely still.

"The hell do you want?"

He didn't move to let us in, nor did he step outside to bar us from entering his home. He waited. Waited for us to say something else.

"We are looking into your sister's case and would like to talk to you about the day she went missing. Anything you could remember would be helpful," said Tony.

After a long moment, Dane stepped back into the house and allowed us to enter. We followed him into the small, three-bedroom home with a separate dining room and a spacious living room.

The place looked like it hadn't been updated in years. Floral furniture, wood paneling, and one of those plastic runners that my grandmother had in her hallway. The place looked like an old lady lived there. Or used to anyway.

"Why do you care now?" he spit. It was obvious from the way he looked at us and the way he answered our questions that he was harboring a deep, simmering rage. Everything he said, every word he uttered had an edge to it—a sharp one.

"We believe her case is linked to another case that has just come to our attention," answered Tony.

Dane glared at him. He looked like an older version of his sister. Detective Kalani gave us her case file, and in it were a few pictures of her.

They had the same honey-brown skin. The same dark eyes and the same dimpled chin.

He was the male version of her if she'd been allowed to grow up. We weren't sure if she was dead or not. But she had been missing for fifteen years. Chances were, she was dead.

"So now you care," he said softly. It wasn't a question. It was a statement. "Where were you fifteen years ago?"

I wanted to say that fifteen years ago, I was in grade school, but I didn't think it was going to help at all. It would have just made Dane angrier than he already was even though Tony might have gotten a chuckle out of it.

"The point is that we're here now. And we could use your help," said Tony.

He wasn't going to help us. Fifteen years ago, Dane was fourteen. He spent his teenage years living in the shadows of his sister's disappearance. And that probably made him bitter and angry, especially when she was never found. I didn't blame him for being angry at us and not wanting to help us. It made sense. If it were me, I would have been angry too. But we didn't have time for that. We didn't have time for his bitterness or his anger. We had our murders to solve. And right now, that was what really mattered.

Tony pretty much explained all this. Dane sighed, and his shoulders dropped a little. And his glare faded away. All that was left was sadness and pain. He had the saddest eyes I had ever seen. So sad I could feel myself about to cry whenever I looked at him, so I had to look away.

We would probably never find Chelsea, but we could learn how her case was connected to the others.

"What do you need to know." Like before, it wasn't a question. Dane's voice sounded weak and small.

"What do you remember from that day?" I asked.

Dane drew in a shaky breath. "Not much really. I wasn't even here. I was at the park playing with my friends. When I got home, she was gone. And my mom is crying and the police are there asking all kinds of questions. But no one could tell us where she had gone or who had taken her. It was like she just vanished. But people don't just disappear."

He made a good point. People didn't just disappear. Somebody had taken her. But what had made it so strange, at least to me, was that no one had seen anything. Chelsea had been playing in her front yard during the day, and yet no one saw anything strange. No strange cars. No strange people walking around.

So it wasn't some stranger walking around the block. Maybe it was someone that everyone knew. Someone that no one would look at twice.

"Did you notice anything strange that day?" asked Tony.

Dane shrugged. "It was a long time ago. I don't think so. This was a quiet neighborhood. Until that day, nothing had ever happened, not like this."

"Did anything strange happen after she was taken?" I asked.

"Everybody was just sad. Just… sad. I don't really remember anything beyond that."

They were still sad. He was still sad. It looked like his life had stopped when he was fourteen and he could never get past that point. He could never get past his sadness. And I suspected that neither could his parents, and that, of course, did not help him.

We thanked him for his time and left. There was nothing he could tell us. And his parents were no longer alive. His father had killed himself shortly after Chelsea went missing. And his mother basically drank herself to death. That could have been a sign that they were guilty. That they couldn't live with the guilt of doing something horrible to Chelsea. But it could have also been that they couldn't deal with their family and friends suspecting that they hurt their child.

Even though Dane and Chelsea were adopted, the Wesleys still viewed them as their children. Detective Kalani had shown us newspaper clippings from that time. A week or two after Chelsea went missing and there were still no leads, the press turned on the parents. Saying that they were the only ones home and that they had to have done something to Chelsea, because children didn't just disappear. It was brutal. I couldn't even imagine what their family and friends were saying to them. It was probably just as bad, if not worse.

We got in the car and drove back to the field office having exhausted all our leads in the field. There was nothing else for us to do. I slumped in my desk chair and leaned my head back. I was tired of feeling like we were several steps behind the killer, of feeling like this was a puzzle I was never going to be able to solve, and that if someone else had been given the case, it would have been solved by now.

Tony disappeared into the break room and came out a few minutes later with two steaming mugs of coffee. He set one on my desk and then sat in his chair. The FBI did not make good coffee, but I was thankful for the gesture.

A million thoughts ran through my head, and none of them made sense. I couldn't make sense out of any of the clues that the killer had left behind. There was something we were missing. But we had no idea what it was. How can you solve a puzzle when you didn't have all the pieces? When you didn't know what the picture was supposed to be? Were we going to have to wait until another body dropped to figure everything out?

I set my mind to work to figure everything out, but not even ten seconds later, I sat up in my chair, feeling like I'd been struck by a bolt of lightning.

"What if this case is more about the children than the adults?"

Tony had just pressed the black mug to his lips. He looked at me and stopped. "What?"

"What if we've been looking at this case wrong the whole time?"

Tony's eyebrow ticked up as he slowly sipped his coffee, waiting for me to explain further.

"I've been trying to figure out how these pieces fit together. It's like… it's like the killer is trying to give us a puzzle. Remember the puzzle pieces from the beginning? They're trying to give us a puzzle and give us the pieces to put it together. When you have a puzzle, some pieces are more important than others. Like, once you have the corner pieces and the outside perimeter put together, you can easily fill everything else in. But if you start at the center it's, much more difficult."

I don't think I was explaining it correctly because Tony was just staring at me like he was waiting for me to get to the point.

"What if the clues that were left with the victims had a differing level of importance? Like we were still focused on Ricky Thompson's account number being on Kent's body. We were focused on the driver's license numbers that were on David's body. All of these were important, but what if the newspaper clippings on the last two bodies were *more* important?"

Tony set his mug down on his desk. "So you think someone is using these murders to bring our attention towards these missing child cases?"

I nodded. We were more focused on the first two bodies because those clues seemed more important. But what if they weren't? What if the missing children led to the other cases?

"I mean, I guess it could make sense," Tony finally admitted.

There had to be something about both Chelsea's and Jayden's cases that connected to the serial killer case. I just knew it. Because if it wasn't, then why leave those clippings behind?

For the rest of the day, we made our game plan. People we needed to talk to, files that we needed to get, and things that we needed to look into. There was something about the last victim that didn't sit right with me. For starters, our only female victim. And the way her body was beaten and mangled, there was a lot of rage there. Possibly even more than the others. The killer seemed angrier at her than the other three victims. There had to be a reason for that.

I made a note to go see Dr. Pittman in the morning and ask her about the last victim and the state of her body.

"Okay, you two," said Special Agent Baldwin. "It's my birthday tonight, and I expect to see you both at *pau hana* with us."

I blinked. "Um… what's *pau hana?*"

Tony laughed. "Happy hour. We'll be there."

I looked at him. *We.* What did he mean *we?* I wasn't really feeling going out and drinking at the bar. Not now. Not with the case still being open and us having no leads. I wanted to stay home and think. Maybe do a puzzle.

She smiled and walked away. When she was out of earshot, I looked at Tony and folded my arms across my chest.

"*We* will?"

He chuckled. "First, it will be great for you to get to know your coworkers. Outside of me. Second, my dad used to always say that when you are stuck on something when you can't figure it out, take a break. Focus on something else for a while, and then it will come to you."

"So going out with them is our way of focusing on something else for a while?"

He nodded. "And from what I hear, Eli will be there."

My shoulders dropped a little. What did that have to do with anything? Why would it matter that Eli was going to be at the party?

Tony smirked. "He likes you." Tony started packing up his desk.

"No, he doesn't."

He nodded slowly. "Okay. Sure." His tone was flat, and I could tell he didn't believe me.

Eli didn't like me. He never liked me. He was a pain in the ass when we were in school, and I tried my best to stay away from him. I shook the thought from my head. He wasn't interested in me. And even if he was, I wasn't interested in him.

I got my stuff together and followed Tony out of the building and to the car. It wasn't a "go home and get changed" kind of night out. Everyone was going to the bar straight after work.

The bar was just around the corner from the field office, and it was the main place all the agents went to after closing a case. It was the closest, and they didn't water the drinks. I guess the owner figured if you were in law enforcement, you needed something strong.

The Shaka Lounge had a minimalist kind of decor. There were flowers and traditional Hawaiian artifacts all over the walls. There was a bar near the door, stools, then booths around the perimeter of the room and round tables and chairs in the middle of the room. Toward the back of the room was a pool table and a dart board on the wall.

We walked in, and the place was already jam-packed. Special agents were everywhere. A few guys I had seen around the office were already playing a game of pool. Kasey Swift was hustling all of them, it looked like. She waved to me with a smile and immediately slammed two balls in two different pockets at the same time.

Tony pointed me toward a booth where Eli and Special Agent Love were nursing two beers. Love waved us over.

We sat in the booth with them just as a waitress was passing by the table. Tony stopped her and ordered another round for the table.

"So… how's the case going? Did we help any?" asked Love.

I sighed. This was supposed to be us getting away from the case. I wanted a mental break, not to be drunk and still talking about work.

"You did, but right now, we're nowhere. Honestly… I don't know what to say."

Tony chuckled. The waitress brought the drinks to the table. As I nursed my beer, Tony explained what we had learned so far.

Eli shook his head. "Makes me happy to be in the IT department."

Love agreed.

"You'll get it," he said. "You were one of, if not *the*, smartest graduates we had. If anyone can figure this out, it's you."

I looked away as the heat rose to my cheeks. Tony nudged me under the table, but I didn't look at him. Instead, I glanced around the room.

Baldwin had joined the festivities, and I finally learned her first name was Hattie. Everyone was drinking, talking, and having fun. Three people were in line to play darts, and a handful of agents sat at the bar.

"But it is interesting," said Love. "The clues. The puzzle pieces left behind. But the ones with the children seem to be more important."

"I was thinking the same thing. It's like he's trying to show us something. The last two victims with the missing children tacked to their chests were beaten more savagely than the first two."

"Especially the last body," Love replied. "Dr. Pittman uploaded her findings an hour ago, and I had to take a look. This case is so weird. Whatever problems or grudges that the killer had, they definitely had it with the last two victims."

I glanced at Tony. We needed to see Dr. Pittman in the morning. I needed to know what was in her report.

# CHAPTER TWENTY-FOUR

HEN TONY PICKED ME UP IN THE MORNING WE went straight to the coroner's office.

"I was told you two had questions for me about Maggie Woods." Dr. Pittman looked like her usual self, bright and put together with immaculate makeup. She wore a black-and-blue hip-hugging dress with purple flowers pinned in her hair and black pumps. She was so cool that I wanted to be her.

"Have you had the chance to examine the body yet?"

"I finished my exam yesterday evening." She handed me a folder with her findings. "Whoever did this to her really, really hated her. I mean, she was a prostitute for a very long time, so her body had the usual trauma for one in that profession. But when your killer got a hold of her... basically, he beat her to death. But first, he tortured her. He cut off six fingers, removed her eye, and cut off her ear. And that was all before bashing her in the head with a pipe. He beat her so viciously there were no remnants of her brain left in her skull."

My mouth fell open as I listened to her. The other victims had been beaten too. They had been tortured too. But it was nowhere near what Maggie suffered. It was like once he started hitting her, he couldn't stop himself. It took a lot of rage to do that to her. But what made him angrier at her than the others?

"She also had heroin in her system mixed with GHB. The same substance we found in your first three victims."

"The date rape drug?" asked Tony.

The doctor nodded. "I would say the heroin, she took herself before she met up with her killer, and then the second was likely injected into her, if the pattern holds. And the only blood we found at the scene was hers. Nothing from your killer was left behind. This guy's careful."

She was right; the killer was careful. Too careful. We hadn't been able to find anything from the killer in any of the crime scenes unless it was something that they had left behind for us to find. Like the clues and the newspaper clippings. They wanted us to find those so we did. But hair, blood, saliva, anything else of theirs was nowhere to be found. Not even a footprint. It made me think that they had done this before. That they had practiced being somewhere without leaving any trace that they were there.

"What do you think?" Tony asked once we headed to the office.

I wanted to tell him he was doing it again. He was testing me. He had already drawn his own conclusion from our conversation with Dr. Pittman, and now he wanted to know if we were on the same page. But were we?

"I have no idea," I admitted. "This is all so much."

"Trust your gut."

I rolled my eyes. People kept saying that to me. I had heard that phrase a thousand times at the Academy, and it never made sense. Everyone's gut was different.

I took a deep breath. "How can we get a list of children that have gone missing in the area in the last ten years?"

"I'm sure the IT department can look that up."

I nodded. "Well, in that case, we could go to them, ask them for the list, and then see if there's a correlation between when a child goes missing and when there is a transaction from the victims to that shell company."

Tony smiled. I guess I gave him the right answer.

Love's excitement was palpable from the moment we emerged on the fourth floor.

"I was hoping you would come to see me today. Any news? Suspects?" She wiggled her light brown eyebrows.

"Can you get us a list of children who have gone missing in the last ten years? In the state."

She almost cheered at the prospect of helping us but wisely kept it under wraps. "Sure, I can do that."

She set to work on her computer. Her fingers moved so fast over the keys it was amazing. I could never type that fast. My fingers ached just looking at her. Several minutes ticked by, and then she stopped.

"Okay. In the last ten years, 250 children have gone missing," she reported.

"Jesus," Tony muttered.

"Can you filter out any that were later found, or whose cases were closed?"

She nodded and typed in a few more things. "That puts us at 193."

"That's still too many," I groaned.

"What about by age? Can you filter out anyone, say... above the age of thirteen?" Tony offered.

I frowned as Love turned back to check.

"Both cases are pretty young—a ten- and an eleven-year-old," he explained. "It's possible the older kids might have just run away from home, instead of being, well..."

"Makes sense."

"That gives us 112 cases," Love said. "Now what?"

I couldn't think of any further way to narrow it down, but there was clearly much more work we had to do.

"Let's try a different tack. We need you to look at the victim's bank accounts and their transactions with the shell company."

Love blinked. "Um... Sure."

I could tell by her tone she was trying to follow the conversation but was a little confused about what I was asking.

"See if there is a correlation between when a child was taken and any transactions from the victims to the shell company."

She paused for a long moment before realization dawned on her face. "I get it. You think the company may have been stealing children."

Hearing it out loud like that just set something off in my brain. I didn't know if it was right; I was still sorting through my thoughts and hadn't settled on anything just yet. But something was telling me that I was much closer to the right track than we had been before.

"That's going to take me a little while to comb through everything," said Special Agent Love. Her fingers were already working the keys.

"*Mahalo*, Agent Love," Tony said as we headed back out. Then he turned to me. "Now where do you *want* to go?"

*He's testing me again.* Trying to see if I know what the next move was. It was the way he said *want* like I was supposed to know we needed to go somewhere. We needed to go interview someone.

I paused for a moment before we got on the elevator. My mouth opened, and then I closed it. It opened again. I knew where I wanted to go, but I wasn't sure if we were thinking the same thing.

*Stop second-guessing yourself.*

"I want to go to the local precinct. I want to know more about Little Rose."

Tony smiled. I guess that was the right answer. There was something about the way she was so brutally beaten. The killer took out her eyes. He cut off her fingers. He was torturing her for information. But what kind of information could she have had? What could she have known that the others knew too?

We headed down to meet with Detective Kalani. The moment he saw us, he threw his hands up.

"You two again? You come here to open another one of my cases?"

"Not today, Detective. But we could use your help."

He waved us back to the same conference room we'd been using. We could have asked someone else for the information we needed, but we had already built a relationship with him. He might not know what we needed, but I felt like it was still better to ask.

As he was closing the door behind us, a few detectives and officers walked by and took not-so-surreptitious glances through the windows. They were probably wondering what two FBI agents were doing in their precinct and why we were stopping by so much.

"So how can I help you today?"

Tony let me talk first. He had been doing that a lot lately. I wanted to say it was because he trusted my instincts. But the paranoid part of me, the part of me that thought I wasn't good at this job, thought that maybe ASAC Davies wanted him to keep her briefed on my progress, and the best way to do that was to let me take the lead.

"We just ... Have you had any dealings with Maggie Woods? Also known as Little Rose?"

It was subtle, but his right eye twitched, and then he blinked rapidly. That was weird, and I made a mental note of it. There was a story there, and I really wanted to hear it.

He gestured to the chairs around the table, and we sat down.

"Maggie ..."—he shook his head—"she had been in and out of not just this precinct but others since she was sixteen. Her mother threw her out because the mother's boyfriend liked her more. Can you believe that?"

The tale of mothers choosing their boyfriends over their children was a common one. It happened a lot. I never understood it. How could you give birth to a child and then choose a man over them?

My mother would never. Sometimes I think she loved us more than my dad anyway. He said so a couple of times. Not in a mean way. He was just making an observation.

"Anyway. She ... she just got in with a bad crowd. The same boyfriend her mom chose over her left her. Found Maggie on the street and became her pimp."

I tightened my jaw to stop it from dropping. I wondered what the mother thought of that. Or if she knew. She probably did. I wondered if she hated herself after it went down. Or tried to make amends at any point. If I were Maggie, I didn't think I would have forgiven her.

"A few times we tried to get her to change her life around. I was in vice at the time. She was smart. She really was. She could have finished high school and gone to college. Maybe not a four-year, but a community college or something. Learned a trade."

"She didn't want to do that?"

He looked at me and shrugged. "We tried. I tried to get her to see she had more options—better options. That she didn't have to live like that. But every time I thought I had gotten through to her, he came around. And he ruined it. He had a hold on her that she just couldn't shake. He was killed a few years ago. But—"

"That life was the only thing she had ever known," I finished.

He nodded. "I think so. She didn't think she could do anything else. And by then she was already strung out on drugs. I think she used them as a way to forget the things she'd done."

"Being a prostitute?"

He opened his mouth to say something, partly formed a word, and then stopped.

"That could have been it," he finally said. "Or it could have been all of the other girls she handed over to the asshole. We had no proof, but I think she was persuading girls to work for him… What was his name?" The detective sat silently for a long moment. "Derrick Jensen. Yeah, that's it. I think he used her to get other girls to work for him. Talk him up, you know? Like he was the greatest pimp to ever walk the earth. And it worked. When Derrick died, he had a lot of girls, some no older than fourteen."

Tony grumbled under his breath.

"You couldn't arrest her for that?" I asked. "For getting the girls to stay with him."

"Like I said, we had no proof. It was a hunch. These girls were brainwashed. Whenever we asked about Maggie or about Derrick, they would never say anything bad about them. They were there of their own free will. And we'd arrest them for solicitation, but just to talk. Try to get the girls to turn on them or at least go home. But as soon as we released, they went right back."

"What happened to them after Derrick was killed?" asked Tony.

Kalani shrugged. "Some of them did finally go home. Some started working for themselves, and others were taken in by other pimps."

"How did he die? I mean, who killed him?" I was hoping he was going to say one of the girls got tired of his crap and shot him, stepped over his body, and went home. That would have been a great ending.

"Rival drug dealer. Turf war of some sort. When it went down, a lot of the girls ran before Derick died. They knew what was coming. Some weren't so lucky, they either didn't think Derrick would die or they were too high to understand what was going on. Ever since, Maggie's been in and out of lockup practically for some petty crime here or there. Never anything big enough to keep her longer, but she'd be back in a month or two anyway."

We sat in complete silence for a moment. The weight of Maggie's life story weighing down on us. She had a hard life and an even harder ending. What was the killer trying to tell us about her? What had she done?

I blinked. "How did she get the girls? I mean, she had to find them somewhere, right?"

He shrugged. "I don't know. She could have seen them in the grocery store or on the street walking home. In the park."

"Were any of them there against their will? Like were they kidnapped?"

The detective furrowed his brow but then looked up as if an idea had just popped into his head.

"It's funny you should say that. Because there was a time when we thought the same thing. There was a girl named Bella Swanson. She was walking home after school one day, and then she went missing. A year later, we raided the girls on the corner, and there she was. She was sixteen then. She swore up and down that she had run away from home of her own free will, but I never bought it."

"What made you think she was lying?" I asked.

Kalani leaned forward and placed his hands on the table. "Bella was a good kid. She was smart and funny and helped her mother take care of her siblings. She was at the top of her class. I mean, she aced everything. She was also a cheerleader and already thinking about college. A girl like that doesn't just decide one day that she's going to run away."

"Maybe being perfect was too much for her?" I wondered. Maybe she was tired of being the perfect child. Maybe she just wanted the chance to rebel.

He waved a hand dismissively. "I'm not saying it couldn't have happened. Kids run away all the time. But not this girl, and not like that. She would have planned her escape. She would have packed a bag, taken it to school, and then just disappeared. She was smart. We checked her room, and there was nothing missing—no clothes, no toiletries. Nothing. And then we traced her route from school, and we found her backpack with her school books in it, her phone, and her wallet."

Now it made sense. She was a teenage girl; she would have definitely taken her phone. Someone must have grabbed her as she walked home.

"I knew she was lying. But when it comes to the law, what you know and what you can prove are often two different things. We couldn't prove she didn't leave willingly. She said she didn't need her backpack anymore, she had taken the money out of her wallet, *and* she left her phone because she knew we would be able to trace it."

She was a smart kid. She was also lying. That must have been so frustrating to know that she was lying and not be able to get the truth out of her.

"Where is Bella now?" asked Tony.

She might be able to tell us something about Maggie that no one else can.

"I can get you her info. No idea if she'll talk or not. After the raid, she went home with her parents."

"Maybe that's it," I said as Kalani went out to grab the girl's information.

Tony turned in his chair to face. "What?"

"Maybe that was why the killer hated Maggie so much. What if she was the one who nabbed the children?"

# CHAPTER TWENTY-FIVE

A RMED WITH NEW INFORMATION, I LEFT THE PRE-
cinct ready to speak with Bella Swanson. I had a feeling
I was at least slowly getting an idea of what was going
on. The puzzle was slowly taking shape.

But I hadn't figured out how Kent and David fit into the picture. If the murders were about the children, how did the others
fit in? And did it have something to do with the shell company?

Detective Kalani was only able to give us the information
for Bella's mother—and said she might speak with us or she
might not, he wasn't sure. He wasn't sure if Bella even still lived
on the island. But Mrs. Swanson lived in a quiet neighborhood
with nice yards out in the suburbs.

Her home was white stucco with pretty pastel-blue shutters that matched the front door. There was a red Camry in the

driveway, so someone was home. Tony knocked on the door. We waited a couple of minutes, and then the door opened.

A woman with grayish-white hair pulled into a ponytail stood in the doorway. She looked from me to Tony and back again, waiting for us to say something.

"Hello, Mrs. Swanson?"

She nodded. Her brows slowly knit together as she pressed her thin lips into a hard line.

"I'm Special Agent Becket, and this is my partner Special Agent Walker. We'd like to talk to you about your daughter, Bella."

At the mention of her name, Mrs. Swanson's eyes welled with tears. I wanted to wrap my arms around her, but I stopped myself.

She took a step back, allowing us to enter the home. It smelled like something was in the oven or on the stove. Meat, I think. There was a hint of garlic and onions in the air. She closed the door behind us and led us to the kitchen where we sat at a round wooden table.

"What about my Bella?" She used her forefinger to push her silver-rimmed glasses up her nose.

Mrs. Swanson was an old woman. She looked older than she should have been. Her hair was more white than gray. The wrinkles and bags under her eyes looked like they were fighting for space.

"Do you know where she is?" I asked.

She blinked. "What are you talking about? I know exactly where she is." She pointed into the next room. "She's always with me."

I craned my neck to look into what I saw was the living room from my scent. On a table next to the window was an urn. Bella's picture was in a light-blue frame next to it.

"I'm sorry," said Tony. "We didn't know. What happened?"

Mrs. Swanson sighed. "She killed herself." She grabbed two napkins from the napkin holder in the middle of the table. "A few years—not even a few years after she finally came home. She just couldn't live with it. But she never said what it was."

"Do you think she ran away?" I asked.

She shook her head. "She wouldn't have done that. And after she came back, there were so many nights she woke up screaming. Begging someone to stop. She could never move past it."

"The police—"

She waved her hand dismissively, cutting Tony off. "They couldn't do anything. They had no proof she had been taken, and she kept saying she ran away. I think she said it because she was scared. Of someone. I don't know who though."

"Did she ever talk about a Maggie Woods or Little Rose?"

Mrs. Swanson rolled her eyes. "Bella mentioned her a couple of times. At first she seemed like she missed her. Like Maggie was a friend or something. But as the months went on, she seemed to hate Maggie. And then one day she was across the street."

"Maggie?" I asked. She nodded.

Why would Maggie come see Bella? Unless she wanted her to come back with them. Maybe that was her job: try to get the girls to come back. All the ones that had broken free and gotten away from them.

"She looked scared. And she didn't want to talk to her. I watched them from the front window. Bella turned around and started back toward the house, and Maggie grabbed her. Tried to pull her back. Bella got out of her grip, said something, and then ran inside."

I sighed. "Did you ask her about their conversation?"

"I tried. But she would never want to talk. I asked her what Maggie wanted, and Bella just ran up to her room."

"How soon after did she kill herself?"

"A couple of months. I don't know what she said, but Bella just couldn't let it go. She couldn't move past it." She shook her head. She dabbed the corners of her eyes with her napkin. "Why are you asking about Bella and Maggie?"

We explained that Maggie was killed, and we thought it had something to do with her job. Mrs. Swanson nodded and said she wasn't surprised that Maggie had been killed. She wondered how many children she had hurt through the years.

I wondered about that too. How many little girls did she hand over to Derrick, knowing what he was going to do to them? Mentally, I shook the thought from my head. I needed to remember Maggie was dead. Maggie had been murdered. She was our victim. I couldn't linger on her past for too long. That being said, I couldn't help but think that her past was why she was murdered.

Maybe one of the little girls she had turned out was coming back for revenge.

We thanked her for her time and left the house. There was a tense silence in the car. Tony's fingers gripped the steering wheel so hard his knuckles turned white.

"Are you okay?"

He looked at me for the first time since he started driving.

"Sorry. I hate cases like these. When children are involved. There's a special place in hell for someone that hurts a child," he said.

I nodded. All I could do was nod. I didn't know what else to say. What could I say? I had never worked a case before, not really. I didn't know what it was like to work a case involving children. How devastating it could be. Not just to the parents but to the officers who found the bodies or took statements.

I stared out the window. Mrs. Swanson's face flashed in my mind, and I tried to tuck it away. To cast it out. I didn't want to think about her. I wanted to focus on the clues. I wanted to force the puzzle pieces together so we could figure this case out and be done with it.

She looked so broken. So many years later and she still looked broken. A million fragmented pieces that she was never able to put back together. Especially not after Bella killed herself.

"What are you thinking?" asked Tony as we pulled back into the field office parking lot.

I shrugged. What was I thinking? Part of me wondered what all this had to do with Maggie or Little Rose. It seemed like this case had more to do with her than anything. The murderer hated her and wanted to make sure she suffered. They tortured her. I mean, they tortured the others too, but they really took pieces off her.

This had something to do with children. It had to. I thought popped into my head, and I jumped out of the car as soon as he parked. I waited for him to get out before I said anything. He moved slowly. I think he did it on purpose.

"I think you have an idea," he said when he slammed the car door.

"Maybe."

"You going to tell me what it is?"

I opened my mouth but then swallowed my words. I shook my head. "I want to wait until I make sure I'm right. I just need to check the crime scene photos."

"On Maggie?"

"John Hargrove."

We headed back upstairs to our desks. The John Hargrove file was on his desk. He handed it over, and I flipped through it until I got to the pictures.

John's body was a mess from any angle, but that wasn't what I was looking for. I flipped through the pictures until I got to one of the closets.

I had noticed it before, but for some reason, it didn't register. I took the picture out of the file and then handed it to Tony. He stared at it for a moment and then looked up.

"What am I looking at?"

"It's a picture of the closet in John's dungeon."

"Okay."

"Look at the costumes. They seem pretty small, don't they?"

Tony looked back down at the picture, eyes slowly widening the longer he stared.

"We need to check the costumes to make sure they were children's costumes," he said.

Naturally, we would have to make sure. Just because they were small didn't mean they were made for children. Could have been made for little people. Maybe he had a fetish or something. But they looked like they were children's costumes.

There was a fairy costume with bright-pink wings. A princess costume that was a mix of light pinks and purples. They looked like something a child would wear for Halloween or to a birthday party or something. And the door locked from the outside.

Had he been keeping little girls there? The little girls that Derrick and Maggie stole? My phone vibrated in my pocket, and I pulled it out to a message from IT.

"Love's got something," I said.

We rushed upstairs, not even wanting to wait for the elevator. We tried to make it seem like we weren't running, but we were. Well, it wasn't really running but power-walking. A weird power walk to Love's desk.

"Is there a link?" I said the words fast so maybe she wouldn't notice that I was out of breath.

She smiled. Boxes popped up on the screen. Numbers and transactions were highlighted in different areas.

"What am I looking at?"

"The links," answered Love. "I did what you asked, and what I found was more than interesting at first. So then I broadened the search. You remember the driver's license numbers?"

I nodded.

"Well, I got my hands on their information and added them to the search. I looked through their transactions to see if there were any links to the other victims and to the shell company. And there were."

Tony stepped closer to Love's chair. He stood behind her, and I was off to the side. Both of us stared at the screen, trying to make sense of everything.

"So what did you find exactly?" asked Tony.

Love took a deep breath. I could tell she was trying her best to figure out a way to explain everything without getting extra techy and confusing.

"Okay, so basically, all of these people are linked by the shell company. They have all made transactions with the company. All once a month. That being said, while there are monthly transactions, there are also other ones."

"What do you mean?" I asked.

She pulled up two screens and moved them side by side. "For instance, John Hargrove paid the company a sum every month for the last seven years. But a few times a year, he pays the company a separate amount. See here."

I whistled. "Wow, that's a lot of money."

Love nodded. "That's more than the three of us make combined."

Once a month, John paid the company twenty thousand dollars. But four or five times a year, he paid an additional *fifty* thousand dollars or more. All told, he was transferring about half a million dollars to this company every single year.

That was a lot of money for a company that had no building or CEO and could not be found online. What were they doing? What service could they have been providing that was worth that much money?

"They all have those kinds of transactions. The monthly payment is the same, but the other transactions vary."

She highlighted several numbers on the screen. Some were fifty thousand, some less, and some more. David Carter spent thirty thousand every other month. Kent spent seventy thousand or more a few times a year. Sometimes they even topped the six-digit mark. And that was on top of the twenty thousand coming in from each man like clockwork every month.

My mind flashed back to what Joshua had said about Kent. He said Kent was moving money. That his personal account had been overdrawn and he moved money from a client's account to cover it.

Tony was already staring at me like he was waiting for me to say something.

"Kent," he said.

I smiled. I guess we had been thinking the same thing.

"Right. Joshua said that he was moving money to cover his personal account. And remember, it was overdrawn by two hundred thousand?"

Tony nodded. "Yeah, it was. So that was why he needed to scramble to find more money. He probably picked a client he knew wouldn't miss it to give himself time to put it back."

"But to steal two hundred thousand dollars," said Love. "He must have been desperate. Gambling maybe?"

I stared at the screen. It could have been gambling. Gamblers did get pretty desperate. Especially when they owed people money. If he owed for a bet, it could explain why he needed that money. The twenty thousand could be a membership fee.

And then the rest of the money could be to buy into a game or something.

That could make sense, but then how did Maggie fit in? How did the missing children fit in?

"I mean, that's possible," I acknowledged.

"You don't seem convinced," said Love.

I wasn't. Not really.

"Yeah, I wasn't convinced either when I first looked at it. And then I saw this."

She minimized the two big windows and brought up a local news article.

"Zak Iona went missing five years ago. He was playing at the park, and he never came home. Parents went looking for him, and his bike was still at the park, but he was nowhere to be found. He went missing March 10."

"Okay," I said.

"Now." She brought back up the finance records and zoomed in. "Two days before he went missing, David Carter paid the company an extra hundred thousand."

My jaw clenched.

"Same thing here." She pulled up Ricky Thompson's account and then the newspaper clipping of Chelsea Wesley. "Two days before she went missing, he paid the company a hundred and fifty thousand. And it goes on and on. I've been able to find ten correlations so far, always two days. And I think that's only because we only have these names."

"So if we could find more people that pay the company, you think there would be more correlating transactions?" I asked.

"Yes. I mean it could be a coincidence, but—"

"There's no such thing," said Tony.

I was inclined to believe them. "Can you look up Jayden Sheppard?" I asked.

She nodded. Jayden Stuart had disappeared on August 7, and on August 5, there was a transaction from David Carter's account. A hundred and eighty thousand dollars.

My stomach tightened. Bile threatened to rise into my throat, but I pushed it down.

These people, these *victims*, were buying children so they could do whatever they wanted with them.

# CHAPTER TWENTY-SIX

**M**Y MOUTH WENT SO DRY THAT TRYING TO TALK WAS near impossible. The words felt like sandpaper. We stood there in silence watching the screen, staring at the missing reports of children of varying ages. Some as young as three.

Now we were getting a fuller picture of the situation. Ricky Thompson liked little girls while David Carter liked little boys. Kent Barnum liked both.

The thought made my stomach turn. Were we really supposed to solve their murders? I mean, was the world a sadder place without them in it? Or was it a better place?

It felt like a better place to me, but... I closed my eyes and shook the thought from my head. When I opened them, I caught Tony staring at me.

"I know," he said. "We have to put that out of our minds. They're disgusting monsters, but we still need to solve their murders. They are still our victims."

"But what about *their* victims?" I asked.

Silence nestled between us. Tony sighed. "That's the job. We can't assume every murder victim is perfectly innocent. We have to take our own judgment out of it and do what we can."

"He's right, I guess," added Love.

"Thank you for your approval," said Tony.

He was right. Our job was to solve murders. Solve crimes and bring people to justice. I liked to think that David and the rest would pay for their crimes in hell. That would have to do for now, I guess.

But I still had two questions: How did Maggie fit in, and what about those other names?

As if he had been reading my mind, which he had been doing a lot lately, he said exactly what I was thinking.

"We need to call those people back in."

That was easier said than done. Because we didn't know all the pieces of the puzzle. We didn't know what we didn't know. And because we didn't know the right questions and what was really going on, when we called them in the last time, we basically tipped them off.

We tried to call them back in, but they were no longer on the island. They were no longer in the United States at all actually. Louis Bennet, Travis Laurence, Harris Daugherty, and Corey Mendez. All gone. And with no signs of coming back.

In fact, they all left pretty much immediately after we had agents speak with them. They weren't all on the same flight or anything. But they were gone all the same.

I slumped in my chair. If we had known... I couldn't help but think we had handled everything the wrong way. We should have been the ones to talk to them. We would have seen something in their facial expressions. And because we didn't interview them, they were gone.

"Stop doing that," said Tony.

I grumbled. Was he psychic or something?

"Stop playing the what-if game. Nothing about this case, in the beginning, pointed to child molesters and trafficking children. We didn't have that clue until Maggie, and that was well after we were investigating Ricky. This isn't our fault. So stop thinking about what we should have done and focus on what we can do now."

I took a deep breath. He was right. There was no point in dwelling on the past. It was over and done. We didn't ask them the right questions because we didn't know the right questions to ask. Not until we started investigating Maggie's murder. Not until we found the shell company.

"Do you think Maggie was being used to get the children?" I asked.

Tony cocked his head to the side. "I think so. At least at first. Maybe she and Derrick worked with the company. And maybe he used her to get close to the children."

"With Derrick dead, maybe they went to someone else."

He looked at me. "You don't think she was still working with them?"

I sighed. "No, I don't."

After we found her body, we had gone to her apartment. It wasn't really an apartment building though. It reminded me of an old run-down motel that was trying to be an apartment complex so it could make more money. But it had none of the amenities that an apartment building had. It definitely wasn't safe. It was filled with junkies and prostitutes and people walking in and out. There was no kind of security.

It wasn't exactly a shock to see that it was completely filthy and filled with drug paraphernalia. Moldy food on the kitchen counter. Trash everywhere. It looked like she just went home to do drugs and sleep.

"If the company had been paying her, then she would have had enough money to move out of that hovel. Or to stop being a prostitute," I pointed out.

"But you forget. Why would she leave? She didn't know any other life. And she had a serious drug habit. Maybe they did pay her, and maybe that's where the money went."

"Point made."

I wanted to feel sorry for Maggie. She'd had a hard life. Her mother threw her out, and her mother's boyfriend pimped her out. She was the product of her environment. But she knew what was going to happen to those children. She knew because the same thing happened to her. And yet she still went along with it. She still stole them from their parents and handed them over.

I wanted to feel sorry for her, but she had opportunity after opportunity to tell the police what was going on, and she never did. She and Detective Kalani had a relationship. He knew her and was trying to get her to go to rehab and leave her pimp. She could have told him.

But she didn't.

Maybe it was because of the drugs. Maybe it was because of Derrick's hold on her. But whatever her reason, children were molested and raped because of what she did. And now she was dead.

I couldn't spare any sympathy for her. Not when there were still so many children suffering.

"What do you think their end game is?" I had the habit of referring to the killer as a man, and I needed to get out of that habit. It could have been a woman. It was unlikely because the *victims* were tortured, but it was still possible.

It would take a lot of rage to do what they did. And a mother whose child was taken away by Maggie and brutalized by one of the other victims would have that kind of rage.

It would explain why Maggie was tortured and beaten the way she was. Because it started with her. She took the children and handed them over. They really hated her. If I had a child, I would hate the person that took them. I probably wouldn't be able to stop myself from hitting them either.

Tony shrugged. "Maybe they just want to kill everyone that was involved."

I chewed on my bottom lip. Did that mean that they were done? Was Maggie the end of it? I sat with the question for a moment.

"I was thinking if that was the case, then maybe they were done. Maggie stole the children. With her being dead, then maybe it would be over. But that's not it. She wouldn't be the end because she was nothing to them."

"What do you mean?" He leaned back in his chair and folded his hands and rested them on his stomach.

"Look at the way she lived. They didn't care about her. As long as she delivered, they had no other use for her. With her dead, they would just find someone else to do it. That would be easy with that kind of money."

"So you think ... See, I was thinking this was about revenge. But you think it goes deeper than that?"

"Revenge how?"

"Like maybe one of the children they trafficked, one of them that got away, came back and decided to get revenge."

I tried to fit that scenario into the puzzle I had been creating in my head. It might fit, but my gut was telling me no. It wasn't right. I thought back to Bella. Bella had gotten away, and she was so afraid of Maggie she wanted nothing to do with her or Derrick. She was so afraid she killed herself.

In my mind, anyone that was able to get away stayed away. As far away as possible. They would never come back. I know I wouldn't.

"I don't think that fits. I think the killer is looking for information. That's what the torture is for. And they are killing people associated with the organization while looking for information."

Tony opened his mouth and then stopped. "They're looking for who runs the organization."

"Exactly. Killing the person who takes the children does nothing. They can get another Maggie. They probably have already. What they want is the person on top. You shut them down, and everything else falls apart."

"Okay. So who has the motive to do this?"

Now that I didn't know. At first I thought about Mrs. Swanson, but that didn't make sense. Sure, her daughter was taken. And then her daughter killed herself. And she probably blamed Maggie for her daughter killing herself. If she hadn't been taken, maybe she would still be alive.

But Mrs. Swanson was an old woman. The last time we saw her, she looked so tired and run-down. Although that could have been because she had just gotten done killing people. I'd imagine that would take a lot out of you. And she wasn't exactly sympathetic when she heard Maggie had been murdered. Could it be her?

Or someone else. Someone we hadn't talked to yet. Or maybe someone we had.

"You know who is still angry about their missing loved one?" I asked.

Tony, who had been staring at his computer screen, turned to look at me. "Who? Mrs. Swanson?"

I shook my head. "She doesn't feel angry to me. She feels resigned. Like this is her life now and she's just waiting to die and then she can be with her daughter."

He nodded. "I get that. And I don't think she would have the strength to beat them like that. I mean adrenaline can do a lot, but I don't know if it can do that much. Who?"

"Dane Wesley."

Tony blinked. "The brother. Chelsea Wesley's brother?"

I nodded. "Think about it. When we went to talk to him, he was still, after all these years, so very angry. I mean, that is understandable. But he's angry and bitter, and maybe he wanted the people responsible for tearing his family apart to suffer."

Tony leaned back in his chair. He did that whenever he was thinking about something.

"I mean, I guess I could see it. He does seem angry enough. We should question him again."

The last time we went to see Dane, we only asked him about his missing sister. It never dawned on us to ask about the murders. Truth be told, this was not where I thought the investigation was going to go.

At first I thought someone was after Ricky Thompson. That for some reason they wanted to get his attention, and in a way, I was right. They did want to get his attention. They wanted him to know he was next. He was next, and all his secrets were going to come out. And instead of facing it, he jumped off a roof.

Then we thought that it had something to do with Alicia Moore and her abusive boyfriend. She wanted out, and he wouldn't let her go. David and Kent wanted to help her get out of being an escort, so we thought the boyfriend killed them. But that was a bust. Alicia Moore and her boyfriend were dead along with the woman that was trying to help her, long before David was killed.

So many false leads and the bodies kept coming. Although it had been quiet since Maggie was killed, he wasn't done. I didn't have any proof of that, but somehow I knew. I could tell. So either he got what he wanted from Maggie, or he was still searching for it.

"Yeah, we need to find him, and fast."

Instead of calling, we jumped in the car and headed back to Dane's house. The car was in the driveway, so at least he wasn't on the run.

Tony knocked on the door several times, but no one answered. We would have loved to kick it in, but we didn't have probable cause or a warrant.

We turned to head back to the car, and one of his neighbors stood on her porch watching us.

"Are you two with the police?"

"FBI," I answered and flashed my badge.

She looked startled. "Dane in trouble?"

"Have you seen him?" asked Tony.

Slowly we made our way over to the fence that divided their properties. We didn't want to spook her and tried to keep the conversation as casual as possible. We definitely shouldn't tell her we were looking to talk to Dane about a serial killer who killed child traffickers.

She might have helped us if we told her. Or she might have thought he was doing the Lord's work and kept her mouth shut. It was better not to say anything.

"I haven't seen him in a while. A few days actually. He packed up, jumped in a rented car, and left."

"He packed up?" Tony leaned on the fence.

"Yeah, he had a couple of bags with him when he got in the car."

"Did he say where he was going?" I asked.

She shook her head. "Dane... I mean you know about his sister, right?"

We both nodded. I was surprised she knew; she looked like she was around my age. Pretty, with long, jet-black hair and several tattoos down both arms.

"I was a little girl when it happened. My mom wouldn't let me go outside by myself for months. It really shook up the neighborhood. Dane was never the same after that. He was withdrawn. Really angry, you know. But I guess that's understandable."

"So he's the kind of neighbor that doesn't talk much?" I asked.

"Or at all really. There's a wave here and there, but that's about it."

"Thank you. And if you see him, give us a call." Tony handed her his card.

We walked back to the car.

"We need to find Dane. We talk to him, and then all of a sudden he's packing and leaving in another car? Doesn't feel like a coincidence to me."

"Just like I said," Tony replied. "They don't exist."

# CHAPTER TWENTY-SEVEN

COULDN'T SLEEP. I HAD BEEN TOSSING AND TURNING ALL night until finally, at two in the morning, I decided to get out of bed.

The case weighed so heavily on my mind that nothing else mattered at this point. It had been a few days, and we still couldn't find Dane. He wasn't on the island, or in the state, as far as we could tell, and his BOLO hadn't turned anything up.

We were able to get a warrant and search his house, but we didn't find anything. There was a drum in the backyard that looked like clothes and other stuff had been burned inside. The contents were taken to the lab for analysis.

There was nothing else in his house. He must have been a gamer or something because there was a room that looked like it was part office, part game room. We took his computer too, but so far, it had been so encrypted that not even Eli and Love's best combined efforts could get anything off it.

In his closet, it looked like he'd just ripped clothes off the hanger. Drawers were left open, clothes spilling out of them.

Tony and I figured that Dane was worried or panicked after we came to visit him. And so, in order to finish his mission, he split.

The neighbor was right when she said he was quiet and withdrawn. He had no friends, at least no one that we could find. He also didn't have a job—or at least no record of one. But he was still paying the mortgage on the house and paying utilities.

How was he doing that if he didn't have any income?

Something wasn't adding up about Dane. He had a lot of secrets. And we had no way of figuring them out.

What we didn't find in his house were the murder weapons or his cell phone. We tried to track the latter, but either he took the SIM card out or turned it off.

At this point, we were just waiting for it to be turned back on. And really, I didn't have a problem with that. I tried to keep my feelings on the case to myself. We still needed to close it and everything, but who were we kidding? Dane had no one to call. He had no friends. So the only reason he would turn his phone back on was so we could find him.

When, or *if*, he wanted us to find him. And that would probably be after he killed the next person. We would have to wait until then.

And I was okay with that. What he was doing was wrong. I understood what got him there—I shouldn't say that. How could I understand? I had never lost someone like he had. They stole his sister from him, and then his whole world fell apart. His parents died, and then he was alone again.

His biological parents had died when he was younger, but then he wasn't alone. He had Chelsea. But now he had no one. So yeah, he would want to kill the person who had stolen her from him. That didn't make it right. But it made me okay with waiting until he was done. And that was wrong. That whole thought process was wrong. I shouldn't feel that way.

But it wasn't like we had any other way to track him down. We spent every day trawling every inch we could of Oahu, but it was getting to be tourist season, meaning millions and millions of people were streaming in every day. We couldn't exactly stake out the packed beaches and hope we'd find him.

Some of the other agents thought Dane left the island before we even knew we needed to look for him. And that could have been possible. He could have changed his name and gotten a fake passport and made his escape.

Tony asked me the other day if I thought Dane had really left the island. I wasn't sure how to answer the question. But the more I thought about it, the more I was sure the answer was no. He was still around. He was just waiting for something. Or someone.

In a way Dane was like Maggie—they hadn't known anything else. Dane had lost everything in that house. He had lost everything on this island. He didn't know any other life. Where would he go? If he had somewhere to go or thought he could leave, he would have done that by now. This wasn't about killing people and getting away with it. It was about getting information and then killing them when they had nothing else to give.

Kent Barnum and David Carter were rich men that had been rich probably all their lives. They weren't used to pain. Not experiencing it anyway. He probably didn't have to torture them as long. John Hargrove had a dungeon with children's Halloween costumes, and that probably really pissed him off.

Maggie Woods was a procurer of children. But she wasn't like the rest. She was used to pain. She had been in pain most of her life. She had been a prostitute since she was sixteen. In order for her to tell him what he wanted to know, he really had to hurt her. She wasn't going to give in easily.

If we just knew where he was, I could talk to him. If this had been revenge, and he wanted to kill the person responsible for what happened to his sister, we could tell him the man was already dead. He didn't kill him outright, but in a way, he was responsible for his murder.

The last time we talked with Love and she showed us how the victims were connected to the missing children, Ricky

Thompson's account information popped up next to Chelsea Wesley's missing poster.

He paid the company three days before Chelsea went missing. So the person who raped his sister was dead. And if this was just about revenge, if he was looking for the guy's name, then we could give it to him and stop everything. We just needed to figure out where he was.

After a few hours of running through everything in my head, I drifted off on the sofa. Soft knocking on the front door woke me up. I made my way to the door and opened it without checking the peephole.

"Figured you'd still be sleeping." Tony walked in and closed the door behind him.

"What time is it?" I yawned.

"A little after eight. I tried calling you a couple of times."

"My phone is in my room."

We stood in the foyer for a moment, and he finally shrugged. "You going to go get ready?"

I blinked. "Right. Clothes. I should put on clothes."

He nodded. "I think that would be best."

I ran to my bedroom, jumped in the shower, and got ready faster than I ever had in my life. A quick check of my phone revealed that Tony had called me twice and sent me five text messages.

I didn't remember when exactly I fell asleep, but I did feel more refreshed than I had in a while. I was glad for that much at least.

"Any news?" I called down as I hopped down the hallway on one foot, putting my shoe on the other.

"Love finally got into his computer."

I whooped and jumped so high that my shoe fell off my foot. Finally, someone had found something on Dane. Finally. Hopefully, this would tell us what he was up to. I scrambled to grab the errant shoe, snagged my badge, and followed Tony out to the car.

"What do you think they found?"

Tony shrugged. "Dane's not stupid. The only thing on left on his computer is what he wanted us to find."

He had a point. Dane had been three steps ahead of us from the very beginning. He probably knew we hadn't figured it out when we came to see him. He could tell from the questions we asked. But he might have figured we would get to him eventually, and so he left.

As soon as we stepped onto the floor of the IT department, Love's eyes lit up.

"Oh my god, finally!" The excitement in her voice was palpable.

"What did you find?" I asked.

She shrugged. "I called Tony as soon as I got in, but I haven't gone through anything yet. I don't know what's important and what's not. And I figured you both would want to be here for that."

She pointed to a large screen that the laptop was plugged into and set to work. "Honestly, I don't know if we'll find much on here. I don't think he's the type of person to leave a lot of evidence behind."

"It's got to be better than nothing though," I offered.

But Love wasn't paying attention. She already was squinting and looking closer. "Hmm…"

I inched closer to her chair. Tony followed suit.

"Well, looking at some of these programs, it looks like he was a hacker or something. Which makes sense for how heavily locked up this bad boy was. They aren't heavy-duty hacking programs, but if he needed to find something on someone or do in-depth searches on someone, these would do the trick."

She double-clicked on a program with a black magnifying glass icon. "Let me look at his last search." She clicked the drop box at the top of the program, but nothing happened. "Well, it looks like he cleared everything."

"Yeah, we figured he would do that," said Tony.

"Sorry," said Love. "I guess we were excited for nothing."

"It was worth a shot," I told her. Then I turned my attention to Tony. "If Dane is doing what we think he's doing, that means there is a child trafficking ring on the island. So maybe that's where we need to focus our attention."

"Find them and then maybe we'll find him."

I nodded. "There's no way he's finished. And ... well, he was clearly looking for information on who runs the organization. He wants to get to them. So if we can figure out who runs the organization ourselves, we can head him off."

Tony stuck his hands in his pockets. "Worth a shot. Let's talk to Detective Kalani. He might know something from when he worked in Vice."

§

"Dane Wesley?" Detective Kalani looked genuinely shocked by the whole thing. He stumbled back and fell into his chair. "You know, he used to call me a lot. Wondering if we ever found anything linking to his sister's abduction."

"Did he sound angry when you told him no?"

The detective looked at Tony and then at the ground. "I don't think so. He mostly just sounded sad. He always sounded sad, not angry. But there was nothing we could do. All of the leads had turned cold—not that we had any to begin with."

"We believe he's responsible, but we can't find him. So we figured we would try and figure out who he's looking for and then maybe we'll find him."

"Makes sense." He looked around for a moment. "What does that have to do with me?"

"Well ... we were wondering if you knew of any child trafficking rings in the area. Or any that run through Hawaii."

# CHAPTER TWENTY-EIGHT

ETECTIVE KALANI'S JAW CLENCHED. HE TOOK A DEEP breath and then sighed.

"If there was, for Chelsea to have been taken, they would have been on the island for a long time. Right under our noses." He tapped his knee with his forefinger. "I think I know someone you can talk to. Let me take you to our sex crimes division."

We followed the detective to the second floor. He led us through a series of hallways and past an interrogation room. It sounded like someone was being interrogated as we walked by.

"Hey, Mikey."

A man sitting at a desk engrossed in the stack of papers on his desk looked up. He smiled for a second when he saw Kalani.

But as soon as his eyes fell on us, his brows knitted together and his smile vanished.

He stood up. Mikey—or Detective Michael Nguyen, according to the nameplate on his desk—had dark hair and dark, almond-shaped eyes. He was tall, taller than Richards and Tony.

"What's up?" His voice was light and filled with apprehension.

"These are the two FBI agents that I was telling you about. They were wondering if there might be a sex trafficking ring on the island."

His right hand tightened into a fist. "There might be. Does the FBI want—"

I waved my hand dismissively. "We don't want to take over anyone's cases. We just want information. Anything you can tell us about the organization? We have a serial killer and think our suspect is going after the members."

"And you want to stop them?" he asked slowly. "You don't want to let nature take its course?"

I looked at Tony, but he didn't look at me. His eyes were fixed on Detective Nguyen.

"He's a serial killer," Tony repeated. "He's already got four bodies, at least, and we would like to get to him before he adds another body to his count. He doesn't get a pass because someone stole his sister." There was an edge to his voice.

We had talked about it at length. And while Tony understood what Dane was doing, he couldn't condone it.

He was right. But part of me still kind of agreed with Nguyen. And I needed to work on that. We still needed to catch him, no matter what. But my heart wasn't exactly breaking for his victims either.

Nguyen rubbed his nose and said, "Well, to tell you the truth, we do think there is one on the island. But we don't have any information other than that. It's a hunch really."

"What makes you think that?" I asked. It wasn't like they could just pull that idea out of thin air. There had to have been a case that aroused their suspicions.

He opened his mouth to say something and then stopped. He looked at Kalani for a moment.

"Can you take them into the conference room? I'll get my case files."

Kalani nodded, and we followed him to a room much like the one downstairs. A few minutes later, Detective Nguyen arrived with a stack of folders in his arms and set them on the table.

"It's strange really. I mean, it took a while for us to put it all together. I don't know why. The similarities were plainly obvious when looked at from the big picture. But on an individual level, none of the cases seem connected at all. That's what was throwing us off."

He gave us each five folders. All missing children.

"They take them and never leave a trace. And we never find their bodies."

"Are they from the same area?" asked Tony.

He shook his head. "From all over the island. And they take them at different times and places. One may disappear in their front yard, another may never make it home from school. All different ages, going up to seventeen, gone without a trace."

"How can they do that?" I asked.

"That's what made us think it was part of a ring. I mean, no one person could be in all these places. Someone was taking these children and shipping them somewhere. And if they were killing them, then where were their bodies?"

He had a point. None of the bodies of the missing children were ever found. Chelsea went missing fifteen years ago, and her body was never found. That didn't mean that she was still alive, but it was strange.

"So you believe there is an organization stealing children, but you don't know anything about the organization?" Tony flipped through one of the folders.

Nguyen nodded solemnly. "Sadly, no, we don't."

"Were any of these ever linked to Maggie Woods?"

"We thought they might be using prostitutes to find the children. Not so much to take them but to watch them. Recon, if you will. They would see a child that may look like someone the organization might want, and they watch them. Learn their habits and then relay what they found."

"What makes you say that?" asked Tony.

The detective sighed. "We did find a child or two."

"Like Bella Swanson?" I asked. She had been taken even though she said she ran away. She was found with Maggie Woods; only she never said what happened to her.

"Exactly. When we found them, they were working as prostitutes. They were adamant that they had run away. That no one had kidnapped them and that they didn't want to go home."

"Seriously?" Tony looked shocked.

"Benny Hardin and Celeste Villegas. They refused to say anything about what happened to them. Refused to name their kidnappers or even say they were kidnapped. They would have rather lived on the street than go home. They just kept saying they ran away and didn't want to go back with their parents. It was heartbreaking really. Especially when you looked at the parents. Their poor mothers."

"Could it have been a bad living situation?" I asked. Some kids did actually run away from home, to get away from their abusive parents. They would rather be homeless than go back. And some of those kids did end up working as prostitutes.

"We looked into it. Searched the homes, asked the neighbors. Interviewed anyone and everyone connected to the kids and their families, and we found no signs of abuse. They looked scared, and not of their parents."

"They were too afraid to talk," I mused. Whatever had happened to them must have been horrible. They must have been terrified.

"Yeah, and we thought if we gave them some time, some space that they would come around. Celeste and her family moved away from the island. I think Ohio or somewhere. Benny killed himself a year after we gave him back to his parents. He was only sixteen."

I clenched my jaw. I was starting to understand Dane's way of thinking, and that scared me a little. I would like to say that I wouldn't do the same thing, but now I wasn't so sure. It was wrong, but I understood what got him there.

What I didn't understand was, why now? What made him, after fifteen years, snap and decide he was going to go after the people responsible for the disappearance of his sister? That was what I didn't get. What set him off?

"But back to my point, with those two cases, Maggie Woods worked on the same corner as the kids. I don't know if they had the same pimp, but she was watching them. Now she could have been looking out for them, but I'm not sure. And they never said anything against her or brought her up at all really."

We hadn't really learned anything that we didn't already know.

I looked down at the files. "Can we borrow these?"

Nguyen traded a glance with Kalani, but he finally nodded after I reassured him that we weren't trying to take over his case. We weren't. Not really. Now, if that ended up happening in the course of this case, it couldn't be helped. I just wanted to see if we could find a link between the missing children and the mysterious company all these monsters sent their riches to.

Tony and I left the building in complete silence, both with an armful of folders. We placed them in the back seat before getting in the car.

That silence stretched in the car while we drove back to the field office.

"You okay?" asked Tony.

I shrugged. I wasn't sure how I felt. I still couldn't help but feel like I was failing my first case. We had a suspect, but we couldn't find him. How could he just disappear like that?

And the children. What about all the missing children? Where were they? Were they still on the island? Was he looking for them? Should we let him find them before we arrested him for murder?

Should we arrest him at all? My nails dug into the corner of my leather seat. We should arrest him. He killed people. Even though they were monsters. Their horrible actions didn't give him the right to murder them. To torture them. And while I understood why he was doing it, that didn't make it okay. We couldn't have people just getting away with murder. We had to bring him in. If we could even find him first.

I didn't think it would be easy to disappear on an island like this. But he had lived here most of his life. And he probably had this plan in the works from the beginning. As soon as we came to see him and asked questions about Chelsea, he probably knew then that we'd found Maggie's body. Then he knew it was time to go. It was a matter of timing really.

§

Love was practically bursting out of her seat when we got back.

"The local sex crimes division has these folders of missing children. They believe they were taken by a trafficking organization, but they don't have much more information than that," I told her. "We want to see if there's a link between these children and any of our favorite customers."

Love nodded. It didn't take long for her computer to ding. Her fingers moved across the keys so fast. I could never type that fast.

"Pattern holds for five out of the fifteen so far between David, Kent, and Ricky. If I had more data—more names from people in with the ring—then I could give you more information. Two days before Mina Tuttle was taken, Kent paid the company two hundred thousand."

All these men had too much money. They had money to spare.

"What is the twenty thousand for if you still have to pay extra to get the kind of child you want?" I wondered aloud.

That didn't make sense to me. It was like paying for a Netflix subscription and then having to pay extra for a particular movie you wanted to see.

Tony shrugged. "I was thinking about that the other day. That's a lot of money every month."

"They don't use it every month though." Several boxes scattered across the screen. "They paid the money every month, but they didn't use the services every month. Ricky used it sparingly. David used every other month, seems like. Kent had a problem. He was using it almost every month. And lately, sometimes even twice or three times a month."

"Three times a month!" I couldn't hide my shock. That was why he was moving clients' money. He was using the service so often, and his account couldn't cover the costs.

"Four hundred and fifty thousand, I think it was. The monthly fee was for, like, a membership fee. It allowed you access to their club, I guess. And then if you wanted something special, you had to pay for it."

That was insane to me. This entire case was crazy. Why was this my first case? Why couldn't it have been something simple, like, I don't know, money laundering or something?

A blaring, screeching klaxon sounded so loud it made me jump. My hand darted out and grabbed Tony's forearm. His arm tensed beneath my grip.

Eli ran out of his office. "Everybody, calm down. It's just an alert."

"Alert? Why is it so loud?" I yelled, my hands clamped over my ears.

Eli ran over to the computer next to Love and tapped a few keys, and then it stopped. "To get your attention."

I shook my head. My ears were still ringing. "It got that."

"It was getting ready to get shot," added Tony.

Love frowned. "Please don't shoot my computers. They would be a pain in the ass to replace."

Eli was busy clicking through windows and rapidly typing. "I put an alert for when Dane turned his phone back on. So we would get notified and the system would automatically track the location."

I looked over at Tony, but he was already grabbing his keys and barreling to the stairwell door.

"Send it to our phones. Storm, let's go!"

I darted after him, only pausing long enough to look back for one second. "Thanks, Eli."

# CHAPTER TWENTY-NINE

WHEN THE FBI LEFT HIS HOME THE FIRST TIME, Dane was excited. His body practically vibrated while he sat across from them. He hoped they hadn't seen it, his adulation at their presence in his home. And when they left, he knew they hadn't.

He wasn't sure they would get it. The clues he had left behind with the bodies. At first he thought he was being too abstract. That maybe they wouldn't be able to put the puzzle together. But they had. They had connected the dots and were looking into Chelsea's case. They weren't going to find anything though. That much he knew. There was nothing to find. No evidence, nothing.

The only way to find her, or find out what happened to her, would be to find the person who ran the organization. They had to keep records. How else would they be able to blackmail clients if they didn't keep a track record of what kid went where? They had to keep a ledger or something. If they were smart, it wouldn't be computerized.

And they were smart. The organization had been on the island for years and had gone unnoticed. Although no one was looking. Not really. But he was. He was looking for them. And for Chelsea. And one day she would be found, even if he wasn't the one to do it.

The way he had tortured Little Rose hadn't sat right with him. But he did his best to ignore it. Pushed the thought down until it was just a whisper in the back of his mind and nothing more.

It had taken him longer than he thought it would. She wasn't like the others. Her body was so used to pain that cutting off her finger wasn't going to make her do what he wanted. He'd almost admired her by the end of it. Almost.

§

"You're going to kill me after this, right?"

He nodded. He knew he was, and so did she. There was no point in denying it. He wasn't sure if the others knew or not before the end. Maybe they thought they could still talk their way out of it up until the very end, but not Little Rose. She wasn't delusional.

"Good. All this ain't really good for business."

"I'd imagine not."

"What are you going to do with what I tell you?"

"Kill them," he said matter-of-factly.

It was just that simple. He was going to kill all of them or go to jail or be killed himself. But he was going to try. He had to try. They had to die. To pay for what they had done. The lives they had ruined.

The lives she helped ruin.

"Good luck." She swallowed. A mixture of blood and saliva oozed from the corner of her mouth. "What do you want to know?"

"How does it work?"

Only after he had promised to kill her when they were done did she spill everything.

"We watch the children, I guess. They tell us what they're looking for, what someone wants, and then we look for that. We just walk around. They give us nice, respectable clothes to wear, of course. Can't walk into a nice neighborhood looking like a junkie. When we find... what they want, we let them know. Make note of their routine and then they go get them."

The Puzzler—or Dane—swallowed hard as bile threatened to bubble up his throat. How could she do that to children? She knew what they were going to do to them.

Sometimes when he looked at her in the hours they were together, he was so angry his vision blurred. Other times she looked like a sad, broken little child. He pitied her, but he hated her more.

"They give us a small percentage. Just enough for the drugs we want. And when you're so high, you can barely remember your own name, you'll do whatever a person asks. Especially if it means you could get more. I could forget with the drugs. I could do shit, get high, and then forget I had ever done it. But that only works when I'm high, so I have to stay that way. And doing what they want is the best way to do that."

"Why didn't you try to get out?"

This wasn't about her. It wasn't about her sad life story or her reasons for doing things. It was about the children that she had helped steal away from their families. And yet he was still curious. He still wanted to know why she couldn't just get away.

"And go where?" she croaked. "I have nowhere to go. I've never had anywhere to go. And that's still not a good excuse, but it is what it is, and we are where we are."

"Where do the kids go?"

She swallowed. Dane stuck his hand in his bag and pulled out a water bottle. He let her drink from it to moisten her throat.

When she was done, he walked back over to the chair in front of her and sat down.

"Some stay on the island. I'm not sure where. They never let us go there. But some of the guys that work for them *visit* us, and when men are happy or drunk or some combination of both, they talk. Some are kept here. Some are sent all over, one guy said. I don't know how true that is."

That would explain why none of the bodies of the children were ever found. They weren't on the island anymore. They were somewhere else. How could he find them? There had to be a ledger or something. They had to keep track of what kid went where.

"Who runs it?"

Silence stretched between them for a long moment.

"You are going to kill me, right?"

He nodded. It made sense to him why she would ask that. If she was going to rat on the organization, it would be better not to be around afterward. They couldn't come and kill you if you were already dead.

"Mark Gauthier," she said quietly.

After that, The Puzzler turned off the tape recorder in his pocket and set to work.

§

When the FBI left, so did he. The plan had already been in place; he was just waiting. Waiting to see if they would come. If they had gotten his clues or not. Now that he knew they had and would be coming back to get him, it was time to go. It was time to put the last piece of the puzzle in place.

He didn't have to run through the house deciding what to take with him. He already knew. His bag was already packed. He just had to tie up a few loose ends. For starters, he needed to wipe his computer. He didn't want them to be able to tell where he was going next.

Mark was a hard man to find. Given his profession, it made sense he would keep a low profile. He wasn't on any of the social media sites, and there was nothing written on him even though he owned a massive company.

It took a lot more digging, even for someone of his caliber, than he would have liked to admit, to find a picture of Mark. But eventually, he did. It had been uploaded to the company website for all of twenty-four hours and then removed almost immediately afterward. Someone must have talked him into it. And he probably fired that someone.

He was white with short black hair and a strong jaw with a dimpled chin. He screamed, "I have too much money." And he did. He was a billionaire several times over. Dane couldn't tell if that was because of his company or his organization that specialized in trafficked children.

Mark gave to a lot of charities too. And most of them dealt with children. Children who had been sexually abused. Children who were homeless. While he was doing his research, Dane wondered if some of those children that they paraded around charity functions looking for donations had been some of the ones trafficked by his organization.

He wondered if he knew their names. If it got him off, knowing he had done this to them. He was the reason they were there, and no one even knew it.

Once his computer was wiped and everything else was arranged the way he wanted them to find it, he left with one small bag. There was no point in overpacking or taking his passport or anything of meaning with him. He wasn't coming back.

He would either end the week dead or in jail. At this point, it didn't matter which.

While Mark Gauthier was a rich man who owned just about every expensive car brand, he still insisted on using car services.

Now that he had him, it didn't take long. Just a couple of days' worth of research to figure out what kind of car he liked. What time he left in the morning. When he returned home. His schedule was consistent. He was a creature of habit.

One morning Dane pulled in front of his building. He lived in a high rise on the top floor. He left the building at four every morning.

Dane was outside at three. When Mark came out, the black Lexus started and pulled into position. He immediately got into the back seat. He didn't ask the driver's name. Or if the company sent him. This was his routine, after all, and why should he change it? Why should he think something about that particular morning was different?

Why should he think that his driver was strange or out to get him? He had no reason to, so he didn't. He just slid into the back seat, closed the car door, and waited for the car to take off. His face was buried in his phone. He didn't notice the driver was new. The car was really new.

And the complimentary bottles of water were *tainted*. He took one sparkling water, opened it with one hand, and lifted it to his lips. It was a slow sip at first. And then he took three big gulps. Maybe his throat was dry. Maybe he was trying to wash something down. Maybe after a night of drinking, it was the first sip of water his body had had in over twelve hours and it was in desperate need. Whatever the reason, he drank half the bottle before he put the top back on. He set the bottle down and focused back on his phone.

And while focused on that, Dane focused on him from the rearview mirror.

Quick glances to the back of the car. He watched as Mark's eyelids started to droop. As his arms got heavy and he rested his hands on his lap instead of in front of his face.

His body leaned back in his seat. His head hit the headrest. His eyes closed.

And then the phone dropped to the floor.

When Mark made no attempt to pick the phone up, Dane knew Mark Gauthier was knocked out.

And now The Puzzler's real work could begin.

# CHAPTER THIRTY

M Y HEART RACED AS TONY SPED THROUGH EVERY stoplight on our way to the location. We weren't sure at first, but then decided against the sirens. We didn't want to spook him or alert him that we were coming.

Even though I thought he already knew we were coming. That was the whole point of turning on his phone. He wanted us to find him.

This whole thing was planned out, and we were always steps behind. He knew when we found Maggie's body, we would investigate Chelsea's disappearance. And that would lead us to him. And when he saw that we were following the clues he left, he went to fulfill the final act of his plan.

There was no doubt in my mind that we would be walking into a murder scene. I just couldn't figure out whether Dane would be there or not.

We traced the cell phone to an abandoned warehouse. One of the several old run-down buildings on this side of the island. The companies had moved out long ago, or shipping practices had improved, so what used to be thriving import businesses that needed hefty amounts of space had fallen apart practically overnight. All that was left now was the graffiti and trash strewn all over the dusty, crumbling building.

The parking lot was empty except for a car. One single black Lexus parked out front.

Police cars swarmed around the car. I jumped out before we even came to a complete stop. Tony barely had time to shift into park before he followed close behind. We got into formation: Tony and I toward the front, SWAT in front of us, and other officers and detectives behind us.

There was a loud boom, and the front door fell to the ground with a hard thud. A puff of dust particles rose into the air. We rushed into the building, guns drawn and everybody screaming.

"FBI!"

"Hands in the air!"

"Get down on the ground!"

Over and over and over again. I couldn't see behind the SWAT guys, so once we confirmed there was no active threat, I stepped out of position to get a better view of the room.

I wanted to see him. I wanted to see what he had done. Whom he had killed. The smell of blood hung heavy in the air. This time it was fresh. No decay.

Dane Wesley sat in a chair, fingers slick with blood. Across from him sat a man whom I didn't recognize. Not because I was new to the island or because I didn't know anyone, especially the local celebrities or the rich.

But because he didn't have a face.

The man's skull was almost entirely caved in. Around the chair were puddles of blood blending into one another. Body parts were strewn around the chair. Fingers. Two eyeballs with the connective tissue attached.

I moved closer. There was something on the ground that I couldn't make out. Once I got a little closer, I shuddered. It was his tongue. There was also an ear soaking in the blood pool. I had to force myself to look away. I tore my eyes away from the man without a head.

Dane eased out of the chair with his hands up. He got down on his knees and then lay on the ground.

He didn't say anything. Not a single word. Even when two officers yanked him to his feet, pulled his arms behind his back, and arrested him.

He never said anything.

Bile coated the back of my throat, and I swallowed hard. My stomach bubbled as I continued to stare at the body. Only then did I see the numbers etched into the victim's chest.

"What do those mean?" I croaked. My mouth was suddenly so dry. It hurt to speak, to swallow.

I stumbled back. I needed to get away from the body. Away from the blood and brain matter scattered across the floor.

But I still had to ask, "What do the numbers mean?"

Dane didn't say anything as they led him out. Not a word. He didn't even look at me. I looked back at the body as Tony pulled out his phone and started taking pictures.

"I'll send the pictures to Love and see if she can use some program to figure it out."

I nodded. Once Dane was in the back of a police car, crime scene techs descended on the warehouse in all their gear. Dr. Pittman wasn't far behind. As soon as she saw the body, her mouth fell a little.

"No offense, Agents, but I'll be *very* glad to not see you again for a while," she muttered as she walked toward the body. "Did you find the weapon?"

I pointed to the bat next to the metal chair Dane had been sitting in. She nodded. Dane must have tortured him for information and then beaten him to death with the bat.

I sighed. If this man was the last part of his plan, then why write something on his chest? What was the point? And if he wasn't part of his plan, then why turn the phone back on and wait for us? Why wait? Why sit there and get taken in without a fight?

"Let us know if you find anything of use on the scene," said Tony to one of the techs. "We need to go interview him and figure all this out."

I nodded and followed him out of the building. I gulped in the fresh air outside. The smell of blood still lingered in my nose.

I was eager to speak with Dane. I wanted to know how all the pieces fit together. What was his end goal? Did he even have one? Maybe the guy couldn't tell him anything else. Maybe he had exhausted all his resources, especially now that we were looking for him.

When we stepped onto our floor, it was silent. Kasey and Kai and all the other agents looked at us like we had just done something incredible. But we hadn't. Not really. All we did was wait for Dane to turn his phone back on. If he hadn't, we would still be looking for him. We hadn't done anything but what Dane let us do. He had left the clues like breadcrumbs. Not even to catch him or toy with us. He wanted us to pay attention. To know that people were stealing children from their homes. And if he hadn't done what he did, we wouldn't have known.

And I think that was what bothered me. Dane had to kill a bunch of rich people to get someone, anyone, to listen. This case, these killings, had been all over the news. Everyone was trying to figure out who the serial killer was and why they were doing this.

I tried not to listen to the news when they talked about the case. It wasn't like they could tell us anything new. They only knew what we told them, and it wasn't much because we didn't know anything. They were calling him The Puzzler, which I absolutely hated. That was supposed to be my nickname, not his.

Finally, I could see how all the pieces fit together. If he hadn't done what he did, we would never know about the organization, and all these monsters would have gone on and on hurting children. And to add to that, Alicia's and Laura's bodies would have gone unnoticed for a lot longer. Finding their killer wasn't part of his plan, but we were looking for him, and that led us to them.

I took off my gun and placed it in one of the small lockers across the interrogation room. I had never done an interrogation before. Well, not a real one. Not on a killer whom we just found inches away from a dead body. My hands shook as I locked the locker and shoved the key into my pocket.

"Take a deep breath," said Tony.

Blood rushed in my ears, and my heart pounded against my ribs. It felt terrifying and exhilarating all at the same time. I was about to interview a murderer. My first murderer. And he'd already waived his right to a lawyer.

Tony opened the door. Dane sat in a metal chair on the far side of the table by the wall. I sat across from him, and Tony sat next to me. He looked so cool. So calm. Like it was just another day. Like his victim's blood wasn't drying on his fingers and caked beneath his nails. Like there wasn't brain matter in his hair.

Like it was nothing.

I guess, to him, it was nothing. Just another day on the job. He had a few kills under his belt already. And I guess when you killed someone, especially someone you hated, that might make it easier.

"Nice to see you again," I said. It wasn't a cool line, but it was the only thing I could think of to say. "We've been looking for you everywhere."

He smiled. His shoulders shrugged a little. "Sorry. I had some business to finish."

"Yeah, we saw."

The corner of his mouth pulled up a little.

"Why?" I asked.

Dane sighed. It was loud and exaggerated. Like he didn't really want to tell us the full story.

"Do you want to tell us about the child trafficking ring?" I asked.

Something flashed in his eyes then. It wasn't anger or anything. His face was still relaxed. But his eyes... There was something in his eyes that I just couldn't place. Sadness, but something else. Something deeper.

"Guess I'll start from the beginning. Let me tell you a story."

Dane told us everything. As we'd suspected, he was a hacker, and whenever he worked with a client for the first time, he researched them. Looked into their financials and whom they did business with. And in this particular case, he found an encrypted file that even he couldn't break into.

"My curiosity was piqued, so I took another crack at it. And another. It took me a few days and some tricks I wasn't even sure would work, but eventually, I got in... And all I found was a list of numbers. Now that was unusual. It wasn't a sensitive company document or even financial information. Just a plain list of numbers."

"The account numbers from the Cayman Islands," I said.

Dane nodded. "You can imagine it didn't take me long to trace those and find names. That took me some more work too, but I wanted to make sure I had my leverage."

"How did you connect them to the missing children?" Tony asked.

He scoffed. "That part wasn't so hard. I've been watching out for this stuff ever since, ever since..." He blinked away the emotion that threatened to come into his voice and redoubled. "Once you know what to look for, once you figure out how the transactions come in and out... once you cross-reference the transactions with the digital trails, once you poke around in their hard drives, once you see the patterns—"

"Why didn't you go to the police with all this?" I demanded.

"Because they're stupid," he said simply. "And they don't care anyway. They wouldn't have done anything. They'd have just put *me* in jail for hacking. So I decided it was best to go and have some conversations in person."

I compressed my lips in a tight line. "What I couldn't figure out was, why now? What made you snap now?"

Dane shrugged. "Seemed as good a time as any. They needed to pay. Every last one of them needed to pay. Not just for Chelsea, but for every other family."

I chewed on my bottom lip. I wasn't sure how much we should tell him about what we found on our end of the investigation. Part of me, the agent part, felt like we owed him nothing. He was a criminal that murdered people and wasn't entitled to know any of the things we knew.

But part of me, I guess the human part, the sister part, wanted him to know. Wanted him to know everything so he could see what he did. What he had brought to the light.

I glanced at Tony, and he drew in a deep breath. "When we looked at the account numbers you left for us, we found out who paid for each child. There was a correlation. Did you know that?"

Dane's eyes went wide. He shook his head.

"Ricky Thompson paid the company over a hundred thousand dollars two days before Chelsea went missing," I told him.

Dane's bottom lip trembled, and his face dropped into a sheer mask of tearful rage. "I should have killed him myself. She was worth… She was worth so much more than that."

"She was. I'm sorry for your loss. But this isn't over, Dane." I placed my forearms on the table and leaned forward. "Who was the last guy?"

He stared at me coldly, all emotion suddenly gone. "Figure out my last puzzle piece, and I'll tell you everything you want to know."

We left the room.

*His last puzzle piece?*

We headed up to the IT department. Love was typing furiously.

"Did you figure out what the number meant?" asked Tony.

"Give me a moment," she answered. A few seconds later, she stopped typing. "There."

A screen flashed before us.

"Coordinates?"

Love looked at me. "Yeah, to another warehouse not far from where you guys found that body."

Tony pulled out his phone. "I'll roll a team out there. We still need to get answers out of Dane."

"What do you think it is?" asked Love.

"Another body," I said.

But who? Who else did he kill, and who was the body without a head? Why kill someone else and then lead us to a complete other crime scene?

"They'll let us know once they secure the area."

We waited, pacing back and forth intensely. I wanted to go with them. But if we did, we'd just have to come right back and interrogate Dane. It was better—more efficient for us—to stay in the field office.

After what felt like hours but was actually only twenty minutes, Tony got a call.

"Seriously?" His brows knitted together slowly. "Okay. Yeah, the hospital would be best."

*Hospital?*

He hung up the phone and shoved it back into his pocket, never breaking eye contact with me.

"There are children, fifteen to be exact, being kept in cages in the warehouse."

# CHAPTER THIRTY-ONE

"**W**ELL, WE FOUND THE CHILDREN," I SAID AS soon as I walked back into the room.

Dane smiled, but there was no happiness in it. Only emptiness and relief.

"Good. I'm glad you were able to get to them in time."

"You could have just told us from the beginning. Or better yet, before you went on a killing spree and ruined your whole life, you could have told us what you found."

"What life? When have I ever had a life since she was taken? When they took her, they took everything. They took everyone. Nothing was right after. Not even me. No, I like my way much better."

"Who is the man you killed?" I asked.

"You mean *was*, right?" He grinned, and in the harsh over-head light of the interrogation room, it looked manic. "Right. Mark Gauthier *was* the head of the organization. Or at least the chapter in Hawaii. From my understanding, there are chapters all over. Sometimes they trade children. Ship 'em off."

My stomach turned sour. I straightened in my chair.

"The *Cottage*—that's their little code word for whenever they have a child ready to ship out. Mark said they will say, 'We're taking them to the cottage.' If a child meets a client's cri-teria, they take them to a special place where they can meet the client. It's usually a one-and-done kind of thing."

"What does that mean?"

"Well, uh… he said that once the child is used, other cli-ents don't really like them anymore. They all want to be the first. So they either put them on the street and make them work for pimps they employ or they send them somewhere else."

My mouth hung open. So they used the children and dis-carded them. Why was I surprised?

"Some clients were into some *harsh* things that resulted in murder. The warehouse where you found the children—if you look behind it, you will find a mass grave."

My fingers tightened around the edge of my chair. How could they do that to people? To children? Use them and just throw them away?

I shook my head. Tears pricked my eyes. This was horrible. The worst thing I had ever heard in my life.

"Is there anything else you want us to know?" I asked quietly.

"Did you find my bag?"

I glanced back at Tony, who stood by the door. He nodded.

"In my bag, you will find everything that I know. Everything that I learned. And voice recordings of my interrogations. You'll have to excuse the screaming."

"Even Maggie Woods?"

He frowned then. The first glimpse of any emotion.

"No, there's no screaming on her tape. I tortured her, of course, but she was a trooper. She was used to pain. Her body could take it. It was only after I promised to kill her when I was done that she answered all my questions. The others weren't like that. They weren't used to pain. Could dish it out but couldn't take it. I barely had to touch them before they spilled their guts. The torture really was for me."

I chuckled. I didn't mean to; it just fell out of my mouth.

"We'll look over everything and show it to the DA. You are cooperating, so—"

Dane waved his hand dismissively. It was an awkward motion because his hands were still cuffed together.

"It doesn't matter what you tell the DA. I'll be dead before this ever goes to trial."

I opened my mouth to say something, but I couldn't figure out what to say. So we left him there while we walked back out to the hallway. He would be arraigned and hauled off to jail soon.

Tony sighed. "We'll need to follow up on all this, and it'll probably be a lot bigger, but... that's that," he said.

ASAC Davies was already waiting for us outside her door when we returned to the main floor. She looked up at us and waved us in.

"So tell me everything."

Tony and I recounted everything we found and learned from Dane. Every step we took and whom we talked to. It would be in our reports that she could read, but she wanted to hear it from us. When we were done, she leaned back in her chair.

"Not bad for your first case," she finally said.

I smiled despite myself. We had solved my first case. I was really an FBI agent now. I was both excited and sad at the same time.

"You think he knows anything else?"

Tony looked at me and then back to Davies. "We'll need to check on the files he compiled, but he doesn't seem like he has any reason to hold back. If he learned it during his *investigation,* then he told us."

She nodded slowly. "Okay. Good. We need to figure out who the head is. Obviously, he said Mark Gauthier was the head here, but there has to be someone over him. Someone over the whole thing. And that person is going to find someone to take Gauthier's place."

I inched to the edge of my seat. "You think so?"

I hadn't thought that far ahead. I just wanted to catch Dane and figure out what he was doing and why. I wanted to know what he knew. I wondered if that crossed his mind.

Did he know Mark Gauthier would be replaced and still did what he'd done anyway, just to bring the organization to our attention?

"I do. With these types of organizations, everyone is disposable. People's children mean nothing to them. Anyone and *everyone* can be replaced. There's probably someone already on a plane right now to take his spot. That's just how it is. If you want to kill a snake, you gotta cut off the head. And Mark Gauthier wasn't the head of anything, or he wouldn't have been so easy for Dane to find."

I was a little crestfallen, but she was right. Of course, he wasn't the head. Not really. If he had been, Dane would have had a hell of a time getting close to him. He told us during his lengthy story that he was Mark's driver. He laced the sparkling water that he kept in the back for guests and just waited for him to fall. That was too easy. He didn't even have any bodyguards or anything.

I wondered if Dane had noticed that. Did he notice how easy it was? I had to ask him. It had to be the last question I asked. Was this his plan all along? To get our attention so we could take over looking for the trafficking ring? And he could go off and die in prison?

"Dane said he wouldn't be alive by the time his trial came around," I said.

Davies looked at me. "Hate to say it, but he might be right. Men like these—organizations like these—kill all loose ends. And he knows too much. And they don't know what else he knows. I'll get him into protective custody."

Would that work? Would that keep him safe? I hoped so, but I wasn't sure. She seemed to think it was enough though, and who was I to argue with my boss?

"But really, good job in closing this case," she said. "And getting him to talk. It seemed like he wasn't going to tell us anything for a second there."

I smiled. I didn't know what else to say. Compliments were something that I had a hard time accepting. Especially for this case, I don't feel like we really did anything. I mean, we just followed the clues that Dane left for us. And we only found him because he wanted us to find him. If he had never turned on his phone, we would still be looking for him. Still waiting for him.

We would still be lost. But I didn't say anything out loud. I was eager to get back to Dane. To ask him if he knew that Mark would be replaced.

"Okay. Don't forget to do your reports before you go home. You know how they feel about that."

By *they*, did she mean her? I looked at Tony on the way out as we headed back to the interrogation room. The corner of his mouth was pulled into a slight smile. I think he was thinking the same thing.

I opened the door, and the room was empty. I felt like I couldn't breathe. Like invisible hands reached had inside my chest and were squeezing all the air out of my lungs.

He was gone. Where did he go?

I felt someone walk up behind me. I spun around, but it was just Baldwin. I let out a breath. She told us that they had taken Dane down to holding to wait for a transport van. The agent who had taken him thought we were done with him. And Dane had said he was done talking.

"We'll have him brought back in the morning so we can finish asking him questions."

I sighed. Something wasn't right. I could feel it. But he was just going to holding. He would be back tomorrow.

I closed the door before walking over to my desk. It took me a while to fill out my reports. Tony helped. It was my first time filling out reports on a case I actually worked on. When I closed the folder on my desk, Tony clapped.

"Now you are officially a special agent."

"Oh, so it's the paperwork that makes the difference?"

He laughed. "Yeah, and it only gets worse."

Kasey Swift was on her feet already, a wide smile on her face.

"Everybody, *pau hana* at the Shaka Lounge tonight to celebrate Special Agent Storm closing her first case and catching a serial killer. Everyone's invited—and the first round is on Tony!"

Everyone cheered and clapped.

Tony's mouth dropped open at her announcement, but he took it in good humor. "Drink something cheap," he called out. Everyone laughed.

§

I sat at the bar watching the TV screen on the wall.

"Congratulations," Eli slid into the seat next to me. He ordered two bourbons, one for him and one for me. The bartender placed our glasses in front of us, and we clinked them together.

"Cheers."

"Cheers."

Heat bloomed in my chest as I sipped the drink. Honestly, the liquor made me feel a little bit better about the case. I wasn't thinking about it now as much as when we first got to the bar. But now, with a couple drinks in me, I wasn't fixated on Dane anymore. I would see him in the morning and have more time to talk.

"You okay?" His voice brought me back to reality.

I nodded.

"Thinking about the case?"

I chewed on my bottom lip for a second, like I was trying to keep the words in my mouth. But in the end, they came tumbling out.

"I just feel like there's so much we don't know, and this is only the beginning. I feel like something bad is going to happen. And I feel like I didn't do anything to help solve this case. All we did was just follow every breadcrumb he left. We would never have even found him if he hadn't gone out of his way to show us where he was. So I'm wondering if I even did anything at all or if I was just in the right place at the right time." I slowly exhaled. It felt like a weight had been lifted off my shoulders, and I could finally breathe.

"You did though," replied Eli softly. "You're the one who put the pieces together. You are the one that got Dane to talk.

You are the one who asked Love if she could find a correlation between the victims and missing children. That was all you ... from what I hear. So you did solve this case. And as far as first cases go, you did a pretty damn good job, I think anyway."

I let out a silent laugh. "Thanks."

Kai waved him over for a round of pool, and he nodded to the taller man.

"Well, I'll see you around."

"See you," was all I could say.

He was right. I did do all those things. And I should have been proud. I should have been celebrating.

But instead, I was just worried.

# CHAPTER THIRTY-TWO

I WOKE UP EARLY. SO EARLY THAT I COULD ACTUALLY GO FOR the really good, extended run I had been craving for weeks. To explore the neighborhood. I jumped into my workout clothes and rushed out the door with my earbuds in and my keys in my jacket pocket.

The run was exhilarating. I felt the tension that had been building up in my body, especially my shoulders, just melt away the harder I pounded the pavement. I rounded the corner and passed by the house that had once been the scene of a murder-suicide. I wondered how the case worked out.

It wasn't really a case though. I mean, it was a murder-suicide. They didn't have to do a lot of work to find the killer. I passed the house and headed home.

The cool morning breeze whipped through my hair. When I got to my door, I had to pause for a moment while I caught my breath. I checked my watch and I still had an hour before Tony would pick me up.

That gave me enough time to actually make breakfast and take a nice shower, maybe even have a cup of coffee.

I took my shower first. When I got out of the shower, I took the time I was getting ready to call my mom back. She had called me last night, but I was so tired and drunk when I got in that I decided not to answer it.

"I called you last night."

"I know, I'm sorry. I got in late and didn't want to call you after midnight. Still trying to get used to the time difference."

She laughed. "Were you on a date?"

I combed my hair into a ponytail. I was happy she wasn't there to see me roll my eyes. I wasn't dating. It would probably be a while before I started dating anyone. Work was the focus. Building my career was the focus. The only focus, at least for right now. I had tried to explain that to her over and over, but she always acted like I never said anything. Like the conversations where I told her that I wasn't focused on finding someone never happened. So I stopped engaging and learned to change the subject.

"We were celebrating out at the bar. I closed my first case."

"Oh! Honey, congratulations. I'm so proud of you! I can't wait to tell your father."

I smiled. It was nice hearing her excitement. The first sign of genuine excitement either of them had shown about my job. It was good to hear.

I told her I loved her but that I had to get ready for work and then hung up. I got all my stuff together and then went downstairs to make breakfast. Nothing big, just eggs, bacon, and toast. I made enough for Tony just in case he wanted some when he came to pick me up me. I made enough coffee for him too.

As soon as I sat down, the doorbell rang.

"You're early." I closed the door behind him.

Tony nodded. "Yeah, I told them to bring Dane back so we could ask him a few questions. Figured you'd want to get there early."

I led him into the kitchen and fixed his plate. "I figured you might want breakfast."

We sat at the breakfast bar eating our breakfast and drinking our coffee. It was the first time since the case started that we could actually relax. At least for now.

Tony went outside while I put my shoes on and locked up my house. When I got into the car, he looked… not angry but annoyed. Or maybe it was angry. I hadn't been able to read his face yet.

"We have to make a stop." His voice was low and steady.

I nodded. It felt like right now wasn't the time to ask what was wrong. He was angry. Definitely angry. That was his angry face. I would remember it.

We pulled into the parking lot of the local jail, and my heart sank. We had no reason to be there, and yet there we were. Going through the security gate. Talking to the warden and then being led to a bathroom. I followed behind Tony. I didn't want to see it first.

*Him* first.

We stopped at one of the shower stalls. And there he was.

Dane Wesley. With his head twisted around so far his eyes were almost looking at his back.

Blood pooled on the floor around him.

Not only did he have his neck broken, but he had been stabbed fifteen times.

*Fifteen!*

I stumbled back. I had to get out of there. I rushed out of the room. Bile threatened to rise up my throat. I kept trying to push it down, but this time it just wouldn't work. I had to get outside. I needed fresh air.

The air inside of the jail was filled with sweat and fear and blood. His blood. He knew. Dane knew he was going to die. He knew they were going to come after him. He said it!

He said he wouldn't make it to trial. He told me. He knew. And he was right. They, whoever they were, found someone to kill him. Just like that. It was just that simple.

I ran outside. The fresh air in my lungs burned as I tried to take a deep breath. I stumbled my way to the car. When I reached it, I leaned on it for support. Dane was dead.

He was a murderer. And while he had his reasons, I shouldn't feel like this for him. I shouldn't feel sorry for him. I shouldn't feel sorry we couldn't protect him.

I mean, we did our job; we arrested him. We caught a murderer. We got him off the streets. His victims weren't exactly innocent, but still... He was a killer. And now he was dead. And I felt bad.

"I felt bad for a serial killer"—words I would never say out loud. But when I turned around and looked at Tony, I suspected the words were written all over my face.

"What happened?" I croaked.

Tony stuck his hands in his pockets. "The paperwork got mixed up. He wasn't supposed to be transported here in general population. He was supposed to be sent to isolation so no one could get to him. I checked the paperwork, and it's all wrong. It was changed, and that's why he was here."

"Someone did this on purpose. They changed it so he would be taken here, and then they could get to him."

Tony nodded.

"He was stabbed fifteen times."

"Yeah, that was what the warden said." Tony walked over to the driver's side of the car.

"You know it's been fifteen years since his sister disappeared."

He walked to the door and then stopped. His shoulders dropped. "I guess they remembered who she was."

"I wonder what she did to leave a lasting impression."

We got back in the car and headed to the field office. As soon as we walked into the building, Baldwin was waiting by the elevators for us.

Hattie Baldwin had the most sympathetic, kindest eyes I had ever seen. I don't think she felt sorry for Dane though. I think she felt sorry for me—or for us. The case was closed, but the suspect was dead. And I still had questions.

But someone changed the paperwork. So maybe the case really wasn't closed. And maybe that's why she felt sorry for me. Because my first case turned out to be bigger and more of a headache than anyone thought it would be.

Or maybe she felt sorry for me because she knew I wasn't going to be able to let it go.

251

We walked into ASAC Davies's office and closed the door.

She threw her hands up. "I'm not blaming anyone, but I would like to know what happened."

"So would we," said Tony. There was an edge to his voice that made it seem like he was just as irritated as I was. "I thought you were going to put in the paperwork to have him in protective custody."

"I did. I signed it. You can ask my secretary. But when I called down there, they said they didn't get it. It never got there."

I spun around and faced the door. There was a soft weeping sound coming from the other side.

"That's my secretary, Lynn." She placed her hands on her hips. "She's been crying all morning since we found out. She searched her desk for the paperwork even though she was sure she had turned it in. She feels responsible for that man's death." Her eyes softened. "Even though he killed a bunch of people, can you believe it?"

"Everybody deserves empathy," offered Tony.

Davies scoffed. "Tell that to the person responsible for this mix-up. Because if I find them, they will get a few things from me, and empathy ain't one of them." She took a deep breath.

She stopped pacing, walked over to her chair, and sat down.

"What do you think?" Her voice was so low I had to move closer to the desk to hear her.

"I think the only way any of this goes down is if there's a leak inside the department."

The hair on the back of my neck stood up. I stared at Tony, trying to make sense of his words. But Davies didn't look shocked by the allegation. She just nodded her head.

"Yeah, that's what I was thinking. That's the only way to ensure the paperwork for the right transfer doesn't get to where it needs to be. Two sets of transfer papers look suspicious. It would cause a problem. But one set, the wrong set, was nothing. Throw mine away, and slip in your own. That way it just looks like I forgot to do it."

"Is that going to cause problems for you?" I asked.

She shrugged. "Don't worry about me. They know I'm good at what I do. And one slipup doesn't change that. And Dane was a serial killer, lest we forget. It's not like he was some innocent teenager that we tried to pin a murder on. He came willingly. He confessed. His confessions were taped. No one will be in an uproar over this one. No, the *problem* is the leaker."

She glanced toward the door for a long moment. "But we need to talk about how we are going to handle this. If there is a leak in the department, then looking into *the Cottage* will be difficult."

"But we are, right?" I stepped forward until my hip touched the corner of her desk.

"Of course. But it's off-the-books until we know more about who's shredding up paperwork around here. We'll talk more about it later. But until then, business as usual. I think Baldwin has another case for you two."

I nodded. I wanted to finish what Dane had started. I wanted to finish what he'd died for. I wanted to take down the Cottage. Not just for Dane and his sister, but for all the children that we found alive. For the ones we found buried. For the ones we hadn't found yet.

And for the ones we never would.

# AUTHOR'S NOTE

Thank you so much for reading *Murder in Paradise*, the first installment in my brand-new series featuring FBI Agent Mia Storm!

If you haven't yet read my previous works, let me fill you in: I love to create cozy little towns nestled in picturesque landscapes. However, for this series, I wanted to push myself outside of my comfort zone and explore a real, bustling, modern paradise. Honolulu, Hawaii's gateway to the world, seemed like a perfect place to introduce Mia Storm and have it be the gateway to this series. Did I do this vibrant city justice? You tell me!

As a new author, I would be incredibly grateful if you could take a few moments to leave a review of Murder in Paradise. As a writer, I put my heart and soul into every word, and hearing from my readers is the ultimate reward. Your review and word of mouth will help me continue pursuing my passion for writing and bringing new stories to life.

And here's some exciting news: I'm already hard at work on the next book! So, you won't have to wait too long to join Mia on her next adventure.

If you liked this book, you'll love *The Lady in the Woods*.

Thank you again for your support, and I hope you continue to enjoy my books in the future!

Best regards,
Cara Kent


P.S. I will be the first one to tell you that I am not perfect, no matter how hard I try to be. And there is plenty that I am still learning about self-publishing. If you come across any typos or have any other issues with this book please don't hesitate to reach out to me at cara@carakent.com, I monitor and read every email personally, and I will do my very best to rectify any issues that I am made aware of.

Get the inside scoop on new releases and get a **FREE BOOK** by me! Visit *https://dl.bookfunnel.com/513mluk159* to claim your **FREE** copy!

Follow me on **Facebook** - *https://www.facebook.com/people/Cara-Kent/100088665803376/*

Follow me on **Instagram** - *https://www.instagram.com/cara.kent_books/*

# ALSO BY CARA KENT

### Glenville Mystery Thriller

*Prequel - The Bachelorette*
*Book One - The Lady in the Woods*
*Book Two - The Crash*
*Book Three - The House on the Lake*
*Book Four - The Bridesmaids*
*Book Five - The Lost Girl*

### Mia Storm FBI Mystery Thriller

*Book One - Murder in Paradise*
*Book Two - Washed Ashore*
*Book Three - Missing in Paradise*
*Book Four - Blood in the Water*

### An Addictive Psychological Thriller with Shocking Twists

*Book One - The Woman in the Cottage*
*Book Two - Mine*

Made in United States
Troutdale, OR
01/13/2024

16928674R00159